Eighth Square

G.R. (Jerry) Akin

All rights reserved. No part of this book may be used or reproduced in any manner whatsoever without written permission of the publisher, except in the case of brief quotations embodied in critical articles and reviews.

For information address:
>G.R.Akin Press
>Vtoler7301@gmail.com

ISBN: 13-978-1530825073
10-1530825075

This book is a work of fiction. Names, characters, businesses, organizations, places, and incidents either are the products of the author's imagination or are used fictitiously. Any resemblance to actual events, businesses, locales, or persons, living or dead, is entirely coincidental.

Printed in the United States

Cover Illustrations by Beth Boyce
We wish to acknowledge Elaine Chamberlain and Carol Sheridan for help with preparing the novel for publication, correcting grammar, and typing.

We also wish to thank the Florida Writers Association Manatee group for their help through critique sessions. We wish to thank Dona Lee and Al Musitano for plugging a few holes and formatting the novel for publication.

Dedication

The author of this novel, Jerry Aiken, passed away on September 1, 2015 after a short battle with cancer. He finished this book and worked on the editing with his critique group months before being diagnosed. He is missed by all those whose lives he touched. He was a strong advocate for the environment, loved animals, loved a nip of scotch neat—especially Johnny Blue, and he loved life. He enjoyed writing, playing chess, and chatting with friends and family. He hated rats!
This poem was written by his nephew to express his love. It expresses the grief of all those who lost this wonderful man.

Gerry,

I know that it could seem that I don't care
Or that I don't remember how you combed your hair.
Nothing could be farther from the truth.
Gerry, if nothing else you left your mark on me.

Every time I read a book,
or every time I do something impossibly cool,
Gerry, you left your mark on me.

Every time I stare into the night,
wondering what is right,
Every time I listen to jazz
While enjoying my favorite cigarette brand,
Gerry, you left your mark on me.

All of my imagination,
and my literary discrimination,

I wear it proudly like a brand,
Gerry, god dammit, you left your mark on me.

Through the times in my life
where I have struggled with what is right,
To the times of pure joy
Gerry, you left your mark on me.

I am sorry you're in so much pain,
I am sorry your hair is gone
I am sorry you might believe that my love for you is gone.
But Gerry, you need to know that you left your mark on me.

It's because you showed me how to listen and how to care.
Every time I impress someone with a thought or action
Know that your mark is often what creates that reaction.

Every time, I walk my dog
or remind myself to stop eating like a hog.
Gerry, for Christ Sakes you left your mark on me

I have held my friends hands as they departed this land
Never knowing how to comfort, I would often say
You are a part of me, slowly in their ear,
Hoping they could hear the silent promise I continue to hold dear.
Gerry, you have made your mark on me.

I am sorry I can't be near,
know that I hold this promise dear,
I will carry you inside me,

a mark on my skin,
constantly reminding myself
Of all the things you mean,
like the lessons I have learned or the places I have been
The way I "spoil" my dog,
the incredible passion for reading, my love of nature,
my definition of cool,
The fact that the only drink I can order is scotch neat,
These are all gifts you have given me.
I swear that anytime someone starts mentioning Roman architecture,
I shut up and listen now.
I scare people about bears in the woods,
and surprisingly I am ok with getting dentures so I can freak out kids in the mirror.
God Dammit I miss you.

Gerry, know that to eliminate you,
I would no longer be me.
And that's because Gerry,
You left your mark on me

Loving You Always,

Your nephew, Derek

Chapter One

    I woke to shades of light and dark. Translucent images of undefined shapes that spoke of life, smelled of emotions spent. The whirring of rotating blades came to me. A police helicopter? My eyes adjusted to the darkness and my mind to the memory of the evening. The whirring blades—only the ceiling fan. I was safe, the gun battle in the alley now a long ago memory.

    I gazed down at the top of her head, and spit out the last few strands of hair from a one shot evening. Not that it had been any part sacrificial, she was definitely a cutie and pleasing was her aim, but she seemed compelled to guarantee my presence by smothering me with her body. After what seemed like an eternity of her entanglement I couldn't take it anymore. Besides, everything smelled old now, time to move on.

    I threw her arms off me and rolled out from beneath her. Sat on the edge of the bed, head in hands, and sucked in great gulps of the darkness.

    Connie stirred. "Wha'sa matter?"

    "Nothing, I just had to get up."

    "Give me minute. So asleep." She wrapped her arms around my neck, massaging my back with her breasts.

    "Stop it, Connie."

She ran her mouth up and down the side of my neck, blowing kisses on it. She reeked of staleness. I pulled her arms off me rougher than intended.

"For Christ sake, stop it! Hear me? Stop it!"

"You hurt my arms, Rik," she said, talking like a baby. "Lie back down, make better."

I sucked in some air. "Sweet Jesus. I'm not in the mood for a pale imitation of "Cat On A Hot Tin Roof."

"What?"

I gathered my clothes, got off the bed and started dressing, my back to her.

"Where you going?"

"To the john."

"Why you dressing?"

"I'm bashful."

"NO!" she screamed. "You're leaving. "NO!" she screamed again. "You can't leave. Please, Rik, you hafta stay. Please, please, PLEASE!"

I escaped the bedroom into the darkness of the living room, let my eyes adjust and headed for the door. The light came on. I turned. Connie leaned against the bedroom door frame.

"YOU GOTTA STAY!"

She'd thrown on a blouse, unbuttoned. If she was trying to appear sexy or alluring, it failed. Instead, she appeared hurt, pathetic, childlike. I almost felt guilty. When I didn't respond, she began waving her hands around like crazed doves. She clutched at her blouse, her eyes widening, wild looking

She rushed up to me, grabbing the lapels of my sport coat as if that would make me stay. Getting hold of me seemed to calm her. She looked up at me, her eyes showing she was still confused, unable to grasp what was happening.

"I don't understand. What did I do? You hafta stay. YOU HAVE TO STAY! I love you, Rik."

She pronounced the words I love you, as if they were magical, contained the power to change everything. She took her hands off my coat, wrapping her arms around me, squeezing as hard as she could, laying her head on my chest.

With some effort, I broke the stranglehold and held her hands in mine. Not knowing what else to say, I tried to appease her. "Listen, I'll call you." I let go of her and quickly headed for the living room door.

She called after me. "Tomorrow? The restaurant? I'll see you there, right?"

I didn't bother turning around. "Yeh. Sure. Fine." Walked out the door, over to the elevator and punched the down button. "Rik!"

God, the broad's like getting fresh gum stuck to the bottom of your shoe. I turned. She was holding the door open giving me another shot of the only thing that interested me about her. Her face drawn, vague of understanding.

"Tomorrow! I have to know I'll see you tomorrow!"

Her eyes, deeply haunted, desperate, on the edge of deranged. I felt a light movement of goose bumps. "Soon, I promise, soon."

The elevator doors opened. I smiled as tenderly as I could, turned from her and got into the elevator. The doors took forever to close. Outside the building, I heavily exhaled and then sucked in fresh summer air.

I couldn't clear the sight of Connie's eyes from my mind. They mirrored the inner workings of a tormented and twisted soul. A light chill surfaced against the warmth of the summer night, settling on the back of my neck. I turned up the collar of my sport coat against it and headed for my car. I checked my watch, four-thirty in the morning. You're one insatiable piece of tail, Connie.

The hairs on the back of my neck bristled, I turned. Connie stood at her window, the palms of her hands pressed against the pane. Her body convulsing as she sobbed uncontrollably. She pressed her face against the window and emitted a scream loud enough to be heard on the street.

"Good God," I said to no one and anyone. "What did I get myself into?"

Chapter Two

I was happy to see my car. I'd hesitated leaving Baby unprotected parked on the street, but Connie insisted I come up to her place and I hadn't intended on staying long.

Connie lived in an area being refurbished with the hope of bringing white suburbanites back to the city, with rent tags high enough to keep it white. I puzzled over how she afforded living here on a waitress income, but she hadn't asked for a contribution, so more power to her.

I don't consider myself obsessed with possessions, but everyone is allowed to have one fetish, and mine is Baby. She's a forest green, 1968 AMX with tan leather seats accenting her beauty.

My grandfather collected muscle cars, storing them in six garage stalls on his mansion grounds. He gave me Baby as a gift for returning from Iraq alive and in one piece. It took some work, as her manufacturer, American Motors, had long ago folded. But the magic fingers of a mechanic friend of mine put her back on the road. It didn't matter that my grandfather drove her first; she was my fantasy virgin, sweet, clean, and anxious to please only me.

She's built like a woman is supposed to be. With a sleek chassis that says ride me, and a hot engine that purrs in passionate desire to my urgings without making demands afterwards. She handles curves like a sure-footed cat, and a V-8 engine equipped with carter four–barrels produces three hundred and fifteen horsepower at 4600 rpm, leaving the modern day Detroit tinker toys panting behind her, as she purrs in ecstasy on the straightaways.

Connie continued pounding her fists against the window, crying and screaming at the same time. A chill up my spine caused me to shiver. I turned away from her.

Jesus, Rik, Go. Now!

Normally, I would check Baby from end to end, making sure nothing had been disturbed or damaged. Right now, all I wanted was to be long gone from here. I'd check her in the morning. From old habit, I patted her as one would a cherished pet, opened the door and got inside. I took in the scent of fine leather, ran my hand down the passenger seat and turned on the engine. The quiet arousing of her motor brought a feeling of calm over me. I smiled.

"Good morning, Baby. Let's get the hell out of here."

Chapter Three

The man's nostrils filled with the acid, sick odor of sweat. He rubbed the palms of his hands against his nude body, but the skin didn't absorb sweat.

The excitement was over now. All that remained was an emptiness, a sorrow. Such a shame, it had been good tonight. He'd picked this one up on North Clark, New Town. Eager he'd been, showed promise. But, in the end showed no appreciation for his power to bestow pain, had even begged him to stop. Only his Sam understood, appreciated that the fulfillment of love can only come when there is pain. His precious Sam, why had he left?

He'd worked so hard to please, was dry now, thirsty now. The bottle of beer was warm, but that was okay. He was too spent to walk to the kitchen for a cold one. The bottle slipped through his hands. He swore. Why wouldn't his hands dry?

His pale, gray eyes gazed upon the lifeless body. Such a waste, this death. So lovely he was, not like his Sam, but still lovely. He cradled the young man in his arms, carried him to the bathroom and bathed him. Those that corrupted his Sam, stole him away, they would pay. With sweet thoughts of revenge, his hands dried.

****

O'Halloran pressed his fist underneath his sternum and tried to belch. Damn chili was wedged somewhere just above his stomach. He'd passed on greasy eggs for health reasons. Now he had gas and sharp pain in his chest cavities. Cholesterol build-up had to be healthier than this.

He'd stopped at the all-night spoon out of the boredom and loneliness from the inactivity on his beat. His stop satisfied neither one. He'd been the only customer and the cook was too busy cleaning crud off the grill to pay any attention. Christ, cops didn't walk beats anymore. But, the directive came from the mayor's office. A goodwill mission. He wanted cops visible on the streets, to make the taxpayers feel safe, see their dollars at work. He'd been assigned the 12 p.m. to 8 a.m. shift.

It wasn't all that bad until around 2 a.m. and then the beat became ghost city. Hell, anyone dumb enough to walk the streets alone after 2 a.m. deserved to be mugged. Everything by then was locked and dark, nothing to protect. Any eatery still open had a squad car parked in front. He wondered whatever happened to the glamour being a cop was supposed to bring.

He stepped off the curb and did the automatic check of the alley, as he had two hours ago. The street lights only reached halfway down. He's never felt any need to walk further in. Nothing ever happened in this neighborhood. A smelly derelict sleeping one off wasn't his idea of a bust. He doubted he'd even find that. A week on this beat and the most he'd done was help a drunk home.

He was about to move on when the noise of metal landing on metal broke the stillness. The sound seemed to come from McGruder's Meat Market. Just out of sight of the street lights, someone was throwing something into the garbage bin. No big deal, but it was a little late in the day for someone to decide to deposit kitchen trash.

He walked down the part of the alley lit by the street lamp and stopped. The only way to leave the alley was the same way O'Halloran had entered. If the noise was nothing, then why hadn't the person making it let their presence be known? He pulled out his flashlight, the beam not strong enough to reach the bin.

"If anybody's down there, you need to show yourself—hands raised."

He waited, nothing. No person, no sound. That scared the shit out of him.

"Last chance," he called. No response. *Shit, I have to go in.* He hesitated. Why? *Because that's what I'm paid to do.*

The walls closed in, no place to turn, only one direction to run. Blackness penetrated by the beam from the flashlight, leaving shadows, the hidden unknown. Was there movement over there, a figure, over there, crouched in a corner?

He reached down and popped the safety strap on his holster. Rested his hand on top of the pistol and walked further into the darkness of the alley.

"Whoever is in here, come out into the open. Now! Don't make me find you."

Air too heavy to breathe, held the musty odor of dampness. He felt the walls closing in, confining him, the smell of things rotting—dead things. He reached the area where darkness hid anything that did not move.

"You have one last chance, come out."

He proceeded slowly, scanning the alley with his flashlight showing turned over garbage cans, misplaced trash. Three, no four doorways, he flashed each one, empty. Was there movement over there? Silence, he held his breath listened, nothing.

No one was in this alley but himself. How? He flashed the doorways again, the dark corners. Nothing, no one, just a feeling, a feeling something wasn't right.

A sudden sound coming from the bin caused him to reach for his gun, spin on his heels sharply. He let out a nervous laugh as a stray dog scraping for food at a small opening under the bin took off for parts unknown. He froze as the beam from his flashlight caught bare, human feet sticking out of the far end of the bin.

A body, oh blessed Jesus, a body!

A real body. He was a rookie, too new for a real, dead body. He tried to move toward the container but his limbs were paralyzed. All except the hand holding the flashlight, which shook violently.

"Come-on, come-on, you're a trained professional."

His throat burned as his mouth filled with chili gas. With great effort he forced himself to touch the feet. They were still warm. Police training took over, the person might still be alive. With deliberate movement he raised the lid, rats scurried over the rim of the container, and the lid clanged shut.

He sucked in air, raised the lid again and froze in horrific fascination at the sight inside. No need to feel for a sign of life, the victim's eyes told him he was viewing his first corpse. A face twisted in pain and terror. He wanted to turn away from it all, but was held by the tentacles of fascination at the dark grotto of the grotesque. The body was nude, a male, young. Above the odor of meat remains came the smell of scented soap. The corpse's arm had been placed so that his hand rested on his stomach. Something was enclosed in the young man's hand. O'Halloran brought the light down on the hand.

"Oh, God. Heavenly Jesus and Mary Mother of God," he screamed.

With sudden swiftness all the gas and cavity pain left O'Halloran's body as the contents of his stomach spattered chili over the side of the dumpster.

Chapter Four

The phone startled me awake from a restless sleep. By the time I could bring all body parts together the phone quit ringing. I checked the time, nine-thirty. Shit, might as well get up.

I brewed some coffee, washed my face, poured a cup, went to the den, turned on the computer, and stared at the screen.

Supposedly I make my living as a writer. At least, that's what I pass myself off as. Lately I'd done neither one, make a living or writing. For the last few years a CEO by the name of Lou Baron provided me a road to easy money editing quarterly business organization speeches and monthly trade magazine articles. I've attempted no other writing since, and it showed. To make things worse, Mr. Baron hadn't contacted me in six months.

At the moment, my first attempt back at legitimacy, a high-tech article on computer usage in modern medicine, had me bogged down. An idea picked up by a computer salesman I'd met. I placed fingers back on the keyboard. No words appeared on the computer screen. I breathed in deeply and remembered what an asshole the salesman had been.

"Damn your computer shit!" I screamed. "You're a bigger asshole than I remember."

It really wasn't rocket science stuff. Basically no more than putting research into your own words, except I was unable to find the words.

A voice startled me. "Got coffee?"

I looked up at a steely, light-brown colored face. A set of dark, cold eyes stared at me. Anger fumed at his silent presence. "How the hell can you walk and not make any noise?"

"You got carpeting in the hallway. It's hard to make noise walking on carpeting," his smile iced the room. "You got coffee?"

"Don't you know how to make coffee?"

"Why should I, I drink yours." He headed for the kitchen.

By the time I made it to the kitchen, Jim had his coffee and had secured a seat in the booth. I poured a cup and joined him. I come packaged on the tall side and brawny. Jim monopolizes an entire side of a booth. At six-four he has three inches on me and about the same in shoulder and chest width. His arms are long and heavily muscled; hands large and strong. As he's demonstrated more than once, he possesses an extremely light step and reflexes with animal-like efficiency.

"You're hard to look at this morning," Jim said. "That little waitress of yours hurt you?"

A scar runs from the bridge of his nose to the middle of his left cheek, taking away from a handsome face, leaving the impression of street hardness. It reddens when he angers, adding a nastiness that can be menacing to strangers and friends alike.

He'd spent time on assault and battery charges against a fellow worker who made the mistake of telling him he was nothing more than the company's token nigger. So, if the scar reddens, I make sure to leave him alone. He's also not only the best friend I have, but at the moment the only one I can find.

"Tried." I drank some coffee, shook my head. "Talk about freaky." I couldn't contain a shudder. "She makes love like the next day she's sentenced to die."

I'd discovered early you had to learn Jim's ways, respect them, much like a stray dog. He is friendly and trusting to the familiar, cautious and tense with new people or new situations. He's also the custodian of my building and uses his passkey to come and go into my apartment at will.

Jim laughed. "So, you goin' backs for mo' tonight?"

"Not funny. Something's not right in her head, and I don't want to find out what it is."

Jim stared hard enough to make me uncomfortable. "What?"

"I want to be an uncle," he answered.

I choked on my coffee. "Great," I replied. "But why are you looking at me?"

"Cause you the only family I got. You and Margo."

"Margo? You telling me you want Margo and me to make you an uncle?"

Jim smiled and nodded.

Forget left field, that came from out of the ballpark. "You're nuts, or something this morning. Margo's a child."

"You don't look at her like she no child."

"She's easy to look at, that has nothing to do with anything."

"Margo nineteen. Lots of men looking."

I just stared at Jim, when I couldn't hold it anymore I burst out laughing.

Jim scowled. "She do you right. No more Connie girls. She do you right, and you know it. So do her right." Jim's face hardened again. "You know I'm right."

"I know you're nuts." I worked on a fresh cup of coffee.

"I be dead serious 'bout this."

I just nodded. The conversation had moved to the ridiculous side.

"We family, you, me and Margo. I want to be an uncle. Don't mess up my family, do what's right."

When I turned to face Jim, he was gone. No footsteps, no door closing. Here, then gone. A ghost. The man is a ghost…

The phone rang. "Yeah?"

A light sob, then a deep-throated voice whispered, "Sam." A muffled sob. "My precious Sam."

"What? Wrong number."

"Tick, tick. Beware, your time is ticking away. Soon vengeance will be mine. Tick, tick. Sweet vengeance will be mine." The line went dead.

Summer time in Chicago. Ding-dong season with the kids out of school. Still, strange message for a crank call. Christ, first Connie, then Jim, now ding-dongs.

"Shit," I said aloud, "and it's too early for a drink."

Chapter Five

The four of us stood by the grave.

"….And so I ask you not to grieve for the body lying in this coffin. For it is not Joe, Joe is alive, happy, living with his maker, Our Lord. He has found his permanent peace."

Contrary to what the Preach said, Joe was indeed dead. Jim found him Monday morning lying face down on the garage floor. Car door open like he had stumbled out looking for help. Heart attack on a guy that young, makes you think. Not about a whole lot, but being at his funeral sure starts your day off differently.

Of course the broken neck he'd sustained hadn't helped his tenure on earth either. Which, as far as I was concerned, was neither here nor there. He was dead and I was standing in stifling heat listening to a Reverend who could say more about a dead guy he'd never met. We had Renaldo, and his goal to be Good Samaritan of the century, to thank for that.

No one else from the condo had the time, or interest to show up. So Jim, Bobby McCabe, Renaldo and me made up the funeral procession. Margo was noticeable by her absence. 'Good old Joe,' supposedly took it upon himself to attempt to deflower her, Renaldo's sister, our condo princess. Not surprisingly, Renaldo felt Joe didn't deserve the honor of her presence.

"…I didn't know Joe that well," the Reverend said.

You didn't know him at all, you phony. None of us did. Joe was a strange cat. He was just tolerated, and that was the best and/or the worst you could say about him.

I pulled out a paper towel and mopped at the sweat on my face and neck. I looked at the men gathered around the grave. None particularly liked Joe, and he tried to rape Margo. So what the hell are any of us doing here? Renaldo coughed, and I remembered why. Renaldo can be a pain in the ass at times.

The gravesite was only a few feet from the roadway and Bobby's Cadillac. Renaldo, as organizer of the affair and chief saint, designated himself to the front seat. Jim squeezed into the back, I took the open door. For no particular reason, I turned for one last look at Joe's grave.

A man stood there. I hadn't noticed him in the vicinity during the funeral. He was small in stature, almost delicate-looking. Dressed in a dark blue suit and matching fedora, a red rose in his hand. He looked down into the grave and released the rose. Then he stared directly at me, eyes intense. I decided to find out why. Bobby honked for me to get into the car. I turned, motioned for Bobby to wait. When I looked back at the grave the man was gone, no sight of him in the area.

"Anybody see that guy standing at Joe's grave," I asked.

Bobby and Renaldo shook their heads no. Jim looked past me at the grave.

"Who?"

"He's not there now, just disappeared into nowhere," I answered.

"Hard to see him then," Jim replied showing no further interest.

I decided there was no reason for me to have any either. I loosened the tie and imagined the refreshment of a cold beer going down my pipes.

Chapter Six

A neighborhood without a corner bar always appeared unhealthy to me. Sterile environments totally void of character. Not one of those plastic new bars, but an old-fashioned, man's corner bar. One with a steady brass rail to rest your foot on, and beer nuts served with foamy headed steins of beer to wash them down.

Luckily my neighborhood had a corner bar. McCabe's was a couple of blocks down from the condo and the favorite watering hole. It was one of the last turn-of-the–century taverns left in Chicago, owned by a ruddy-faced, real live Irishman, Bobby McCabe.

Bobby parked his car in front of the place. Free beer and a corned beef sandwich, ensured the police didn't notice the no-parking zone. He let us in, locked the door and nodded toward a table. He returned from behind the bar with four cold drafts. We drank in welcomed silence, all of us too withered to talk. The silence seemed appropriate for Joe and a wasted day.

"Considering, we did okay," Renaldo had to hear himself talk. "It turned out nicer than I thought it would."

All grunted in agreement.

"Maybe a little wordy."

So are wannabe politicians. "It was swell," I said. "I'm sure Joe is thrilled."

Renaldo pulled his shoulders back, chin slightly jutted out in that, "holier-than-thou," repose. I found it quite tolerable of myself to allow Renaldo a place in my life as a friend—considering he most often was an ass. The fact Margo resided with him across the hall from me more than likely helped my tolerance.

Bobby returned with refills, sat down, and pushed himself away from the table to give his ample belly more room, then turned to Renaldo. "How's that race of yours for Alderman going?"

Renaldo beamed. It got the conversation off funerals, but I'd heard every blow-by-blow detail last week as a dinner guest, which also got me hooked into writing a political speech. I tuned out as Renaldo took over the discussion again.

A knock at the door put a lid on Renaldo's mouth. Bobby ignored it. The knocker was persistent. Bobby sighed, probably his most vocal expression against the ignorance of mankind. At least what he allows us to observe. It is a magnificent sigh. Starting at the bottom of his abundant belly and echoing upward as its cohesive anger forced it to escape through clenched teeth. A McCabe sigh elicits notice, and usually quiet and guilty bearing from his patrons.

He glanced at the glass panel in the door and spread a grin bringing a boyish dimple to his cheek. He rose in a smallish manner of the Nero Wolfe style and answered the knock. I didn't have to look. McCabe smiled like that for only one person. Margo entered. She ranged on the petite side, but her equipment was superb. If her jeans were any tighter her circulation would have been cut off.

There were tears in the pant legs giving a glimpse of tanned thigh and knee. The white tee-shirt advertising the "Rolling Stones," was too small for her, exposing a magnificent sensual belly button resting in a flat stomach. I watched with amusement as Renaldo's nostrils flared.

Her smile held a special kind of radiance. She refused a drink from Bobby, but laid a kiss on his waiting cheek. There was a light blush of pleasure that ran from his forehead to mid-dome where it stopped at the growth of remaining hair. She caught Renaldo's disconcerting glare and it unnerved her. The smile disappeared. She headed immediately for Jim. I had no idea what had changed between Margo and her brother, but I did know I didn't like it. Renaldo had always been stern, domineering of her, but recently she seemed to appear disquieted around him, fearful.

Jim opened an arm to her and she walked into its protective strength. I know Margo relied on Jim as friend and protector, but I'd never been certain what Margo meant to Jim, except more and more, he was turning into mother hen.

She focused on me, I gazed over at smoldering dark eyes, large and luminous, the beautifully modeled features of a Spanish beauty. She smiled, the special one that said something only for me. Renaldo's eyes never left us. Something of an obsession I was growing more than tired of. I soaked in her beauty and returned her smile. Her eyes danced with flirtatious messages.

Renaldo barked something in Spanish at her. When angered, he appears downright ominous. From the look in Margo's eyes it grabbed her the way a whipping stick elicits fear of punishment in a wrong-doing boy. Enough was enough. Margo might be Renaldo's sister, but she was my girl, if I wanted her to be. I decided it was time to protect what was mine.

Margo broke away from Jim before I could put his two cents in. Long, raven black hair, flipped with a head toss, covered her small shoulders. Hands went to hips, legs slightly spread. It was a defiant gesture on her part, a total ball-teaser for the guy looking at it. It's worth being the recipient of it, along with the tongue lashing that usually follows if she's in a string bikini.

"I wasn't aware I had to wear a dress to cook dinner for you!" Her eyes flamed. "If you can break from your beer, it is waiting for you." Her chin jutted out in defiance.

Good girl. I wanted to applaud, but smiled and gave a reassuring wink instead. Jim was watching me.

"Thank you, I will be there shortly." I couldn't see Renaldo's eyes, but whatever they said visibly shook Margo. The pose was still there, but the fire in her eyes had dissipated. Renaldo looked her up and down, slowly and deliberately. Any semblance of bravado no longer existed with Margo, her head bowed. "Is my sister a la puta?"

Her eyes widened with disbelief. She fought back tears welling in her eyes. I figured Renaldo was enjoying himself way too much. I'd had more than enough. Jim placed a hand on my arm, his eyes saying to stay out of it, even though his right hand was formed into a fist.

"I think you got your message across, Renaldo," I said.

He returned a thin smile that had all the warmth of predatory friendliness. I wasn't Margo, and didn't wince. I motioned for Margo to come to me. Renaldo barked something else in Spanish to her. She didn't move, nodded at Renaldo, head bowed.

"And not Wells Street, the back way," he ordered her.

Renaldo took a long drink of beer, unable to make eye contact with any of us. His anger seemed to have receded, mine hadn't. He looked up, a different man now, sadness infusing his face.

"I want to apologize to everyone. That display should have been private, not for your eyes." He was still having trouble making eye contact. "You have no idea the honor that awaits Margo, and not too far in the distant future."

"Maybe making you a eunuch?" I asked.

Jim shot me a "shut-up" glance.

Renaldo pretended not to hear. "Margo is a beautiful girl, we all agree. It is my job to protect her from street slime. Dressing like that does not make my job any easier, and advertises her as a willing whore." He paused, looked down at his hands, then cleared his throat and sighed.

I had to admit he was good.

"Margo deserves much better than that. She has to be nurtured for what awaits her. Protected from those who just want to use her." He glanced over at me.

As far as I was concerned, we were being played, a practice session in politics.

"I better go, dinner's waiting. Don't want to make Margo mad." He smiled like he'd been funny. "Again, please accept my apology."

Bobby and Jim were gracious. He hadn't sold me.

Chapter Seven

Only three of us left now. A rather deadpan group to be toasting Joe farewell, I thought. Jim was looking at me like I was dribbling beer on my shirt.

"You fault Renaldo yelling at Margo. You make her flaunt in front of everybody," Jim said.

"You directing that at me?" I asked.

"Why I be directing it at Bobby?"

"Yes, and I also dressed her. Shit. How long does Renaldo intend on keeping her a little girl? If he would give her some space, he might be surprised to find she's perfectly capable of earning respect without his help."

Jim didn't answer, just glared at me. When it was about to get to the uncomfortable side, he spoke. "Maybe he 'fraid to, cause the type of 'spect his friend across the hall tries to give her."

"It's been a trying day for all of us," Bobby intervened. "Let's put it in perspective with a shot of Irish whiskey."

Jim declined. "Like you, Bobby, I gots to work to live." He scowled at me.

I smiled. "That's why they call it freelance writing. Gives you freedom. Get it?"

Jim thanked Bobby for the beers, avoided looking at me and left.

Bobby patted his stomach, leaned back in his chair and stretched. "You realize Joe went out without music, even a voice raised in song?"

The thought hadn't occurred to me.

"No matter what kind of person you are, a man should depart this world hearing music and laughter."

I nodded, although I saw no importance to what a man heard or didn't when he departed. Bobby went for two more beers. "Cigar?" I declined

"Don't know what you're missing." He flipped one at me. "Havana. Give one to Captain Mac." He brought back two stouts and his bottle of poteen. I hid a cringe from Bobby. He poured two shots of his Irish moonshine and passed a stout to me.

I looked over at him. "You going to re-open?"

Bobby spun the shot of poteen between his forefinger and thumb. "Guess it kinda depends on a lot of depending."

We sat in silence, neither of us making the move to consume either the stout or poteen. Bobby worked his cigar over, and lit it. The sweet aroma from fine tobacco leaves filled the room. He seemed to be contemplating something deeper than a song for Joe.

"Quite a scene between Miss Margo and Renaldo. Seen brothers heavy jealous over watching their sisters, but never the extreme shown by Renaldo."

"Obsessed, and the older she gets, the more obsessed. Lately, it's become something close to religious fanaticism."

Bobby shook his head. "That ain't good. For either party." Bobby looked at me and nodded.

"Why not?" I answered.

The shots remained unattended as we consumed the stout, sort of an Irish pagan ritual. A peace offering, as it were, to soothe the shocked nerves of your insides so the onslaught of the more potent poteen wouldn't send your nervous system into a paranoid frenzy.

I hated stout, especially warm, but never had the heart to tell Bobby. This was special, what we were doing, drinking his poteen. Something Bobby shared with the very few. We downed the first shot in one gulp. No use teasing the stomach with what was about to invade it. I would have loved a glass of water, but you didn't dilute Bobby's godly whiskey in any way or the other. So, I talked to take my mind off the territorial battle the stout and whiskey were waging in my stomach.

"At the moment life kind of sucks for Margo," I said. "Renaldo's on her ass and lately Jim's turned into a pretty good mother hen too. She used to run to me when Renaldo became too much, but I think Jim's put a leash on her. Think 'ol Jim's' decided my only respect for the lady languishes between her legs."

Bobby grinned. "Not a bad place to languish."

I had to belch something awful, but that was ill-mannered when drinking stout and poteen with Bobby.

He set-up two more stouts. "Guess you never really know people, though. Never figured Joe as a rapist."

I nodded. "More so, that the thought even occurred to him." Bobby concentrated on me. "I can tell you it wasn't the female gender that turned him on."

Bobby nodded as he enjoyed a moment with his cigar. "I had him read that way."

"Yeah, he'd go out with me and Jim. Hit on the girls, try to be one of the boys. Never took any home though." I stopped, sipped at the stout. "Probably the reason Renaldo let him go out with Margo. She couldn't be much safer."

Bobby put his cigar down. "Can't figure why Renaldo didn't shoot Joe or something. Way he is about his sister, instead of worrying about burying him."

I took a sip of stout. "Way I hear it, Jim got to him first."

"Well, well now," Bobby responded. He picked up the shot glass and capped off about one–quarter of the poteen. I followed his example. "So, she told mother hen. Well, well now. Jim can be an awesome presence. Man, know Jim mad at him over misbehaving with Ms. Margo, could put a heavy duty on one's heart."

"Very," I agreed.

"Make one want to be where Jim ain't."

"Joe is now."

Bobby nodded, seemed to ponder. "Course, the broken neck, didn't help with Joe's situation either. Cops talk to you?"

That caught me by surprise. "No, I wasn't around. You?"

"Yeah, they couldn't figure the neck angle. Wanted to know if somebody didn't like him." He stopped, stared at me. "Jim the only one talk to Joe?"

I concentrated on Bobby. "What you getting at?"

Bobby shrugged. "You know Jim better than anyone."

"What?" I gave a disbelieving stare. "You telling me that even crossed your mind?"

He shrugged again. "Falling out of a car don't seem the way to break a neck." He gazed down at the table top. "Wish I could think it the way it got broken though, I like Jim."

I chugged my poteen. "Jim can be many things, some not very nice. But he's no murderer. Joe would have been scared shitless, and Jim might have been mad enough to smack him around some, but work on his neck, no way."

Bobby agreed. We worked on our stout. "Always figured you and Margo would be a thing by now," he said.

"I'm not ready to be a thing."

"You telling me you wouldn't like that cuddled up next to you? Lord knows she'd like to be."

"The problem being, that would be one permanent, binding cuddle. And that's not on my list of life's necessities right now."

He gave me a fatherly, concerned stare. "She just might get you back on track."

"My track is just fine, thank you. I know where I'm headed. Just taking my time getting there, so I'm prepared properly when I do."

"Yeah, time. Funny thing about time. Soon enough seems like it ran away and there ain't any left anymore." He nodded at the shot glass.

I shook my head. "You know anything about computers?"

"Don't even know how to spell the word."

"Wish I didn't. Have to go, earn a living."

Bobby observed me for a second or two. "Don't come back later. Ain't gonna re-open. Be sad not to take advantage of being dressed up and all. Think I'll find me a place serves big porterhouse steaks. And if luck's around, grab me a woman to share one with me." He smiled a reflective thought. "And a glass or two of wine. French wine."

"Yeah, wine and a woman is good," I said. "Especially if she's mellow like your wine and prime like your steak."

"Yeah, prime is good, but right now I'd be happy with aged."

Chapter Eight

I walked out of Bobby's into the stifling humidity of the day. First, the heat hit me and then the poteen boiled over and fried my brain. I turned onto Wells Street but found the foot traffic a bit heavy for my weaving stride to meander through. I retreated the back way home, down Wieland, a residential street, quiet, dinner time.

Except I didn't recall the sidewalk being so crooked. It's hard to walk straight on a crooked sidewalk. A broken neck? Something wasn't right. Especially pointing to Jim. Yeah one hell of a temper. But he didn't have to get his message across breaking Joe's neck. The possibility he did sure gave Bobby cause to wonder. He went straight to Jim, no one else, Jim.

The poteen began working its way through my pores. I leaned against a tree seeking out its shade. Don't worry old buddy Jim, I've got your back. I shook my head and laughed. Christ, Jim, just don't get pissed at me if I don't make you an uncle—shit, that's not funny.

I left the shade of the tree, the short hairs on the back of my neck ruffled. Someone was watching me. Not that I'd noticed anyone, just felt it, knew it. I turned and stared behind me, at the trees, the buildings, no shadows, no bodies, no one. Probably some mother showing her son what he would turn into if he didn't study.

No proof of anyone, but I'd heard the light footsteps since I'd left McCabe's. I stopped walking. Whoever, stopped. I waited. No one tried catching up to me. I turned. Nothing there, no one, no shadows, but the feeling someone was watching, following me, was too strong to dismiss. Why should someone follow me?

Bobby claims his Irish poteen is ambrosial, and therefore had none of the side effects felt from mortal booze. It was time to convince him that wasn't true when consumed by a Scot. It plays with their heads causing things that weren't there to appear real.

I approached my condo and crossed over to Wells Street. Wearing a blue fedora, a man stood across the street under the corner street light, intently watching me— the man from the funeral? I stared back, the man didn't flinch. "Hey, who the hell are you, asshole?" The man continued to stare, but braced himself to run.

Still somewhat controlled by the poteen, I wasn't at prime best for a chase. But I chanced it. Stumbling, as I crossed the street without falling.

By the time I reached the corner, the man was nowhere in sight. At least twenty places accessible to get lost in. I steadied myself against the street lamp. "Come back here, damn you! Who the hell are you? Come back here, now!" I continued to yell until I realized people were gawking and avoiding walking anywhere near me.

I was close to sober by the time the elevator made it to my floor. Margo stood across the hall from me, a small Walgreen's bag in her left hand, her right resting on the doorknob, giving the appearance of a posed mannequin. She didn't appear to hear my arrival. An earth-toned kimono hung down to her ankles and concealed the suppleness of her body.

The dress was a bit of a shock, I'd become accustomed to seeing her in much less. Bikinis so skimpy I wondered if the girl understood apparel meant cloth. Curve hugging jeans, tee-shirts straining over her breasts. The kimono looked good on her. She looked all of fifteen bringing back memories of the bright- eyed innocent I'd met four years ago. The hall ceiling light reflected through her dress, reviving pictures of the contours of her body, emblazoned on my mind.

"Rik!" She took a breath, gained control and smiled. It was sad, embarrassing, but it still had the ability to break or mend a man's heart. I wondered why my mind didn't respond. She tugged at her dress.

"Renaldo bought it for me. I didn't want you to see me in this."

"Why? You look lovely."

"No, I don't." She fought back tears.

One escaped, I brushed it off her cheek. "You always look lovely to me, Margo. The sight of you has warmed an otherwise cold and drab day."

She crossed her arms over her chest and stuck her chin out in defiance. "It's summer time and still sunny out."

"Yes, but my heart was cold and drab."

She laughed. "You're drunk," she reported.

"No," I replied. "I'm just not sober."

She smiled. It was that special one meant just for me and my blood heated.

She let the bag drop and without a word walked up to me, stood on tiptoe, and brushed my lips with hers, leaving a tingling sensation across my mouth. She ran her fingertips down my wrist. The move was clearly calculated and effective. I took in the scent of cologne in her hair, the spiciness of her skin. Her sexual strength was overpowering.

Her smoldering dark eyes flashed with suggestive fire, I placed my hands on her shoulders. The warmth of her skin penetrated the thin cloth of the kimono, causing my hands to ache for the feel of her body. I fought the desire to let them slide down to the small of her back and pull her to me.

And do what, Rik? Start something here in the hall you can't finish? Or, let the heat of the moment, the mind dulled by drink, allow you to take her into your condo, from where she'll never leave?

The sound of Renaldo's voice answered both questions. "Margo, is that you?"

I let go of her and she quickly picked up the Walgreen bag as the door opened. Her face was flushed and she remained, back to the door, until it returned to its natural color.

"Yeah, so Bobby's looking forward to a night out," I said. "Hi, Renaldo, what's happening?"

He didn't answer, smiled instead. It's a politician's smile, hard to read its sincerity.

"I need that prescription now, Margo."

She turned, with head bowed, tried to hurry past him. She wasn't fast enough to escape his scowl.

"Sorry, did I interrupt anything," he asked.

"Just conversation, Renaldo."

His eyes appeared focused on nothing in particular. He inhaled and slowly began to concentrate on my face. "Yes, you and Margo do spend quite a bit of time talking to each other." The smile appeared again. "Sorry I interfered."

I decided not to accept his apology, it belonged to Margo. "Are you, Renaldo, really sorry that it bothers you when I talk to Margo?"

His smile disappeared, a palpable look of disbelief appeared. Renaldo knows how to play emotions in front of an audience. "We are friends, you, Margo and me, are we not? Why should you talking to Margo bother me?"

"That's what I'm asking you. Why, all of a sudden, do you treat Margo like she's committed some unpardonable sin every time she comes near me?"

"Treat Margo badly?" He gave a look of disbelief again. "I worship Margo." He shook his head. "I think you're overreacting, my friend. Perhaps it's due to the alcohol you've consumed." The smile reappeared.

"Supposedly, I've been drinking holy water. So, if there's a problem here, why don't we just plain get it out,"

At first I thought Renaldo was trying to avoid eye contact until I realized he was off somewhere, immersed in his own thoughts. I let the silence stretch while I studied him.

"You are lucky, my friend," Renaldo said. "You have no understanding of the complexities of being both a brother and father to Margo. She is a treasure, a gift. You suffer none of the responsibilities of protecting her." He paused. "Margo is very important to me."

A strange look came into his eyes. Whatever it said didn't play in this world, like something had control of him.

He came back. "Important to me in ways impossible for you to comprehend at this time." The practiced smile returned. "So, it is necessary we remain friends. Most necessary." He did his best to stare into my eyes. "Don't destroy that friendship. I have a gifted power…"

He didn't finish. Turned and entered his place, closing the door on any more discussion. Renaldo was growing weirder by the day, though I seemed to be the only one who noticed.

Chapter Nine

Margo pulled at the kimono, so grotesque, making her look ugly like the thing itself. A punishment by Renaldo for not dressing in the manner he approved. And a punishment it had been. Rik had seen her in it.

The night was emptier than any of the nights before, the minutes longer. The darkness that had moved inside her after Jim found Joe, weighed like the refusal of absolution. She needed understanding, but Rik had walked away, left her with Renaldo.

Poor Joe, he'd only been a tool, an innocent, a lie, a reason to make Rik angry and jealous. To make Rik take her, protect her, love her. Not once had Joe reached for her, even though she'd teased him unmercifully to do so. Not once had he showed any desire for her, only fear and confusion.

It was she who forced her blouse open, ripping it, not Joe. She, who caused the bruise on her arm hitting the car door as she left in frustrated anger. Frightened, so frightened he'd looked. It was just supposed to be a white lie, told to Jim, because Rik wasn't home, so Jim would tell Rik. Just a little white lie, Joe wasn't supposed to die. A lie meant for Rik, who was rightfully hers, who would never belong to anyone else.

The pounding that started in her head after she learned Joe was dead, returned. She grasped her head, her screams lost in the vast emptiness of Renaldo's condo. "God, Jim, please tell me it was an accident. He fell out of his car and broke his neck. Please, please tell me you didn't kill him!"

Margo sat on the edge of her bed. Renaldo had eaten, bestowed his brotherly, good-girl kiss on her, and then sent her on errands while he worked on his speech, staying long enough to make sure she returned promptly before he left to go over campaign plans with his manager. They used to meet at the condo, until Renaldo caught him eyeing Margo, and he was forbidden to ever come back.

She ran her hands over her ugly dress, looking at herself in the Cheval mirror and fought back tears of loneliness. She walked to the mirror, placed her hands on the dress and pulled it tight around her body. This is what Rik should have seen, then he would have taken her away from Renaldo, taken her to his condo and made love to her. She unzipped the dress and let it fall from her shoulders, eyed the reflection of herself in thong bikini panties and French bra. She'd put them on in defiance of Renaldo.

She'd been blessed. Knew she was pretty, maybe even exotic looking. Something she couldn't help but be aware of, just as she was aware of the way men looked at her. It pleased her, the way men noticed her, but she also felt sorry for them. She was spoken for by Rik, who would soon take her away from the life Renaldo had forced on her. Her body full of promise, ecstasy for any man. Certainly, she was more than enough to keep Rik satisfied.

She lay on the bed and pulled the body pillow against her, wrapped her legs around it, closed her eyes and rubbed herself against it. Opening her eyes to a room filled only with dreams, barred from the reality she deserved, barred from Rik.

"Damn you! Damn you to hell, Rik Burns! You are mine, mine! No other will ever have you!"

She curled into a fetal position, no longer able to control the tears, sobbing into the pillow. She got up and viewed herself in the mirror again.

"Why the others, when this is waiting for you?" She smiled and jutted her chin out. "Listen to me, Rik Burns, listen. With each tick of the clock the time comes nearer when you will be mine. Listen and beware, you will be mine— or no one else will have you.

****

I entered my apartment and kicked off my loafers, letting the thick piled carpeting massage the bottom of my feet. I never tired of my place, a cozy cave. Muted white walls, light gray carpeting, splashes of color here and there. Contemporary comfortable I call it. I walked the semi-circle walkway that encased the living room and ended up at the bar.

The last place you need to be. My stomach agreed, though I seldom listened to it. This time it was doing some heavy talking. I sat on the bar stool and contemplated Margo and me. How far would I have let it go, if Renaldo hadn't interfered? She was doing a good job of manipulating bedroom ideas.

Christ, are you that easy? Hell, face it, when it comes to beautiful women, easy is your tough side.

I listened to my stomach and left the bar for the kitchen. The freezer side of the refrigerator contained several items, only they were all wrapped in aluminum foil and unlabeled. Bleak was the first description that came to my mind on the refrigerator side. A partially used bag of Dunkin Donuts coffee beans, a wedge of green cheese, and milk I didn't dare test. Three eggs in the egg keeper, I couldn't remember how old, but the shells were still white.

I took them out, cracked them open into a bowl. Milk was out of the question so I blended them with brandy. The blend came across uninteresting, so I added some garlic salt, dried onion flakes, what I could find still good from a green pepper and a dash of Tabasco. With nothing else available to drink I washed them down with a beer. I should have had just the beer. I left the kitchen with my stomach in a really nasty mood.

Curled up on the couch in the living room, I played flip the TV stations. Finding nothing worth watching, I could hear a drink telling me to wash away the taste of dinner. I poured a healthy slug of scotch and allowed a local jazz station to pick the selection of music. After the poteen, the scotch went down easy. I fixed another. The mellow tones of the Duke and his orchestra told the story of a Satin Doll. I could still catch the traces of Margo's cologne.

"I'm fifteen," she stated, I remembered. She was filled with wonderment then, that first summer she introduced herself to me at the pool. Eagerly awaiting to claim all the promises she was certain life held for her when she reached womanhood. We spent the summer that year meeting at the pool.

I sighed at the remembrance of those happy days. She began to room in some of the empty spaces of my life and I found myself waiting for her presence each day. A nymph, normally only alive in men's dreams, she filled my days, as her counterparts were unable to fill my nights.

It seemed only after Renaldo demanded she sacrifice her dreams so he could achieve his that a hint of sadness found her eyes, her smile withering at times. That a young girl's crush turned into a woman's obsession.

Up to now, I'd escaped the opportunities to show her the error in choosing me. And there had been many. The white on white bed linens I'd purchased to act as a contrast to that long raven colored hair, still waited for her in the linen closet.

Still, she remains a rose among weeds and perhaps I wish her to stay that way. I laughed. A man can learn to tolerate the pain of a knee in the balls if it happens every day. Something that beautiful, that close—what a martyred life I lead. The sacrifices you make for friendship and virginity. The bitter taste of truth entered my mouth forcing me to make a fresh drink.

I sank, slowly at first, then faster, until I was totally immersed, drowning in a glass of scotch. When I realized I was making no effort not to drown, I forced myself awake. A bleary reflection of someone was staring at me from the mirrored back wall of the bar. I raised my glass in a toast to myself. "Here's to another day of productive writing and a night of fellowship with those who care."

"So much glee in my life, I should really spread it around. Maybe do something for mankind, like donate my liver. Right now it should be swollen enough to take care of two people."

That definitely needed a second opinion. My reflection wasn't very sociable. I had no one to drink with. The silence of my existence became deafening. I made it up the four steps to the master bedroom, found the bed and passed out.

Chapter Ten

Clanging—lots of clanging— jolted me awake. I sat upright, pain cascaded through my head. Everything was hazy, unfocused, my mind surrounded by fog. The clanging stopped—thank you. Started again— the building's on fire. I stumbled out of bed, knocking the phone off the night stand. The clanging stopped. I cursed Verizon for convincing me I needed a phone by my bed. The phone rang, I picked up the receiver.

"Jesus, what?" My tongue thick, I doubted it got all the way around the words to push them out. More than likely it sounded like a croak. Which, as sick as I felt, I might not be far from doing.

"Have you thought about dying lately?" The voice asked.

Two seconds ago.

"If not, do. You are mine. You cannot escape from being mine to kill."

My mind was still too immersed in fog to make any meaningful reply.

"Feed my need with your blood. Drench my hate with your spilled blood until we are one forever, through your death."

"Who the fuck is this?"

"The wanton boy who stole the fly, shall feel the spider's ire," the voice said.

Whoever it was hung up. I slammed the receiver into the phone cradle, looked at the clock—7:40 A.M. Doesn't this asshole sleep? The fruitcake had a strange voice, effeminate, yet smoky masculine. One crank call is aggravation, two, from the same person, is more than aggravating, though exactly what that more is, was too much for my hangover to define. I made it to the kitchen, reheated yesterday's coffee in the microwave, and downed two aspirin.

The hangover hurt something awful. The phone rang, I refused to answer it. I couldn't grasp the fascination with cell phones, now I was losing any interest in owning a landline. Ten rings, no message, a pause and it rang again. I gave in on the seventh ring and answered it.

"You up?" Jim asked.

"No."

"You get my message?"

"No."

"Then play you damn message machine." He hung up.

Maybe Bobby's poteen ate away the part of my brain that handles lucidity, and everything, like phone calls, are now twisted out of the realm of normalcy, or understanding. The blinking light did signal recorded messages. I pushed the play button. Tiffany, my good time girl's suggestive voice, asked if my sperm sack had dried up. I laughed. My head wished I hadn't. Tiff brought the morning back to reality.

She'd make good company. She had a propensity for hidden away ethnic coffee houses no taste buds would desire to find. And films nobody ever heard of, or would ever want to. And she is able to make you enjoy every minute spent in both with her.

It's possible people might even consider us lovers—if I didn't pay her to have sex with me, at a much more moderate fee compared to what her real clients forked over. But it kept any illusion about our relationship at a proper distance. I smiled. Either business was slow, or she wanted to break routine and sweat with pleasure for a change. I made a mental note to call her. The second call was from Captain Mac.

"It's I love to be a cop time," he said. "A smorgasbord of felonies on the streets, depicting the rather raw slices of life. Maybe even a taste of a serial killer. Case load sucks, see you in nether time. Forget me showing up for chess tonight."

I'd forgotten we were due for chess. Jim wouldn't be pleased, he was a game ahead. Speaking of which, he was the next caller. For a phone normally unemployed, it had a busy day. Jim sounded formidable and basically unpleasant.

"Don't forget promise to Margo 'bout tomorrow. 9:40 A.M. good for me. We'll have time for breakfast. Be on time less you dead. Then leave Baby's keys handy so I gots transportation."

Margo? Last time I'd made a promise to anyone, I'd ended up in Iraq. At least now I had a day to find an excuse for not doing whatever I couldn't remember promising to do. I headed for the bedroom and gathered fresh clothes to slip into after the shower.

Jim was waiting for me in the kitchen booth. "This yesterday's coffee. You taking a break from writing?"

I didn't answer.

"How you gonna take care of Ms. Margo, you no write?"

I just shook my head and sighed.

"You what now, twenty-seven, twenty-eight? Should be established by now. Need established to take care of Margo. This condo must take most you money."

"None of your business. But, my money is fine. Only took half what I inherited, plus I still have stocks and bonds."

"That ain't no security. No income, no money soon." Jim consumed some of yesterday's coffee and made a face. "Didn't hear no phone call back confirming you promise."

I stared at him. "Maybe because I wasn't sure what I was confirming."

Jim let out a disgusted sigh. "Helping Margo decorate the school gym for Renaldo's speech."

"I don't remember anything about a gym."

"Figured you wouldn't, so's I promised yesterday for you."

It was my turn to sigh. "I'm having a little difficulty seeing how that can be held as a direct promise from me."

"I'm not," Jim replied.

"Sorry, not sure I can make it."

"You plans on bein' dead?"

"The phone call this morning makes it a possibility."

"It be a definite, you not my place by 9:30 A.M.. What phone call?"

"The one that got me up. How long this thing with Margo going to take?"

"Whats you care. You freelance, 'member? Here, this be in your magazine rack."

45

Jim handed me a large manila envelope, I judged it to be twenty by twenty-four inches. In capital letters, hand written with magic marker, was my name. I stared at it. Jim stared at me.

"Ain't got all day, open it."

It was one of those notices the city puts on telephone posts in alleys to notify residents rat poison has been distributed in the vicinity so they won't be shocked when their pet dies. The notice was copied after the international picture motif for the benefit of those dwellers who can't read, and the civil service employees who can't write. A picture of a venomous looking rat exposing long, sharp incisors, enclosed in a red circle with a red line joining the circumference of the circle, signifying a short life expectancy for the creature from the city's poison.

Accompanying the poster, a message scrawled underneath the circle, was meticulously written in magic marker. Whoever wrote it had been diligent, taking their time to be extremely neat. As though it lay embossed on the cardboard I could feel the hate seething from the author.

> **"Blood is the metaphor of life, don't you see?"**
>
> **"You spilled my love's blood—**
>
> **now it is time to spill yours.**
>
> **You are never safe from me.**
>
> **I am everywhere you are.**
>
> **My vengeance can strike at any time,**

even in your safest haven.

Live with the morals of a rat—

die like one."

"Jesus, what the…"

Jim grabbed the poster from me. This shit wasn't funny anymore, although Jim laughed.

"Oh, looky, a love letter. Who husband you pissed-off now?"

I slammed my fist on the table top. "Damn it, enough is enough. This is getting very old."

Jim shrugged. "Look like someone don't like you. I tell you, time and time, Margo. Margo, and there be no more love notes, sees ya tomorrow morning." He left.

I heated coffee and re-read the rat notice. A fairly intelligent retard, whoever wrote this. So, my next question, why not just throw it away? Because of the reference to blood—different metaphors, but all leading to the same end—the spilling of mine—which should be a so-what, unless I'm accepting the phone calls were meant for me, and not a wrong number. What kind of a person does shit like this, and more importantly, 'Die like a rat,' okay, sure, but, does he know how much I hate rats?

I bent the notice in half and tossed it at the trash can. It sprawled over the top of the can. I couldn't take my eyes off it. "What safe haven? Who the hell are you?"

In the guest bedroom, I pulled down a shoe box off the top shelf of the empty closet, and returned with it to the kitchen booth. I opened it and stared at the Glock Gen4 automatic pistol. Hesitant, I finally removed the gun, but unable to control the shaking of my hand, laid the gun on the table top, "Damn you! Get hold of yourself. It's over, can't change anything, it's over."

Captain Mac returned the gun to me after I quit the police force. "Hold it, become friends with it again," he said. "It will be your best friend when you return to the force."

That was two years ago, I hadn't touched it since. When my hand came under control, I broke the pistol down, pulled out the kit, and cleaned it. Reassembled it, slammed the fifteen bullet magazine into the handle and put it back into its holster. I tentatively made it to the den and deposited the gun into the middle drawer of the desk. I scooted down into the chair resting my head on its back, and took in deep breaths.

"Okay asshole. You want to play? Let's play."

Chapter Eleven

Morning came without even a vague sign of a hangover. Outside of a badly needed shower and brushing my teeth, I felt like I could bravely face the day. I stopped at the den and verified that placing the gun in the desk drawer was not a boozed-up dream. I stared, but didn't touch it, though reason told me to put it back on the closet shelf. The desk phone rang.

How many phones does one guy need? Especially when that guy hates them.

"Oh Rose, beautiful rose, you have been defiled by wrongly loved and then defied. The poison of deceit he laid in your crimson bed of joy—chastened your luster, so you would wither and soon die."

There was pause. Not sure of the expected reaction, I laughed.

A deep sob, answered his laugh. "Do you find enjoyment in desecrating that which is beautiful? Why my Sam? My beautiful rose?"

"Okay, head job, enough is enough, bugger off and disappear."

"Don't make the mistake of not taking me seriously. It's your blood that will spill."

One thing was for certain, this was one sick asshole. "Listen, whoever you are, I don't know a Sam. Especially one who thinks he's a rose. Understand?" I started to hang up but, was stopped by a wrenching sob. I could almost hear the tears fall.

"The rhapsody that was our relationship, the love and caring shared, is unfathomable to you. You took its purity and debased it with your lust. You destroyed my Sam, took my love away from me."

I'd had enough. "Listen, Lollipop, nobody said life was fair. He did, however, mention I'm better in bed than you." I slammed the receiver into the cradle. The last thing on my agenda this morning was listening to deranged laments over lost loves. I took a shower.

After completion of the rest of the morning rituals, I made it to the bedroom. The phone rang again. I didn't answer it, finished dressing and went to the kitchen for coffee. The phone rang.

Shit, this is one determined asshole. Might as well answer it, and let him talk to the kitchen booth.

"You have caused your death knell."

Death knell? Cute, but lost your nuts would have been more effective.

Another pause—this time for effect.

"Roses are red, Violets are blue, Cherish your moments alive, because bang, bang motherfucker, there's a bullet waiting for you."

A bone-chilling laugh and a click.

I stared at the phone. "Who the hell is this guy?" I asked it. Whoever, he was delivering a cold warning. His emotion authentic, the voice emasculated, above the mere sadistic pleasure of a phone sickie. He definitely wants me… to be afraid of him. Wants me dead—won't be happy until I am.

The only remaining uncertainty is why am I the recipient? Outside of Joe being a closet queen, I can't think of a soul I knew who was gay, and Joe is Joe, not a Sam. And without saying, I certainly didn't sleep with him. I don't play in la-la-land, and try as I may, I can't think of anyone past or present by the name of Sam.

I poured a cup of coffee and absently sipped at it. Shook my head, and finished my coffee. Who the hell are you? The man dressed all in blue at the funeral threw a red rose into Joe's grave. But I don't know him, and he certainly doesn't know me—although his stare seemed to concentrate on me. Plus, I'm pretty sure that was him waiting for me across the street from my condo today.

This is what? Three phone calls? That's a lot of determination. I don't know who you are 'Blue Boy' but if you keep it up, you're going to leave me with only one choice. I walked to the balcony outside the kitchen and looked over the view it gave me of Chicago. "Keep it up and it seems the only way to stop the calls, is to kill you."

I was five minutes late in picking up Jim, too late to find an excuse, even if I had one. The phone rang as I reached the door. I left, the ringing, darkening my mood as sound continued to play in my mind.

Chapter Twelve

Jim leaned against his apartment door. His face showed the rigors of a sleepless night. I smiled, Jim grunted and headed for the elevator. Dressed in tan slacks, tan slip-ons, highly polished, and tan and black shirt depicting jungle foliage. I wore Levi's, a black tee-shirt with White Sox logo, and worn Nike's.

"You late."

I addressed him up and down. "Unlike you, I thought I'd spruce up a bit. We posing for some Catholic magazine or working?"

"We workin'. Jus' figure you do more of the work." He shook his head and sighed. "Don't hurt none, you take time to look good for Ms. Margo."

He somehow stretched his frame prone into Baby, closed his eyes and kept himself and his thoughts private on the way to Gus's. Jim doesn't show the morning-after effects of consuming stumble broth. Whatever was bothering him was mental not chemical, and heavy enough to take a physical toll and bruise his psyche. I didn't ask, when ready, he'd spill.

The sun glistened off the fresh spray of asphalt oil laid down by the city. Their version of street repair. Translucent stones in the sidewalks sparkled in what early immigrants thought were diamonds. I put sunglasses on. I once thought life would be better than diamonds.

A parking spot was available close to Gus's, I grabbed it, and looked over at Jim. He didn't open his eyes or move.

"We're here, breakfast if you still want."

"I didn't think you stopped for a piss."

Untangling his long legs from beneath Baby's dash, was a fairly formidable task. He clipped a kneecap pretty good in the process. He glared at me. "You car a dumbass."

He climbed out of Baby, took a step toward Gus's and stopped. I heard a culpable sigh. Jim turned around, patted Baby and apologized. I didn't let him see my grin.

It was the kind of day that slips into Chicago on rare occasions. The sun shone brightly from a hazeless sky, giving the illusion of a sparkling clean city, with pure air to be breathed in deeply. The kind of day that hints something good may be waiting to enter your life.

The day had yet to speak to Jim. "We going in or what?"

He took the incentive and walked into Gus's where he found a stool and slumped, shoulders and arms spread on the counter. I found one next to him, spotted Gladys down at the other end wiping the counter, and motioned for coffees.

Gus's is a spoon hidden on Illinois Street. It exists for the most part on clientele that would feel a tad unwanted in the eateries housed in the high rent district. Jim and I stumbled on to the place after a loft party in Printers Row section of town had lasted into sunrise. The food is good, the waitresses friendly, and it's the site of the infamous Thursday night card games, where judges and local politicians can satisfy their gambling habits—unnoticed..

"Don't mess up here, I just wiped it," Gladys ordered us. She stepped back and eyed Jim. "You dress up for your funeral? I've seen better looking mugs on corpses."

Jim didn't acknowledge her. I ordered for both, Jim stared at his cup.

"Who 'They'? Who give them the right to judge what you do right or wrong?" Jim asked.

"To judge concerning what?"

"Right or wrong. Just cause 'They' don't approve it, be wrong?"

Cigarette smoke drifted into his face. He coughed and brushed it away. "They think they so hot shit, they be able to judge?"

"Just what did you do?"

Jim looked at the smoker. The smoker gauged his half smoked cigarette and reluctantly put it out. A narrow little man, with nicotine stained teeth, nervous, quick movements, and a bald dome. He sat with shoulders hunched like he was waiting for another load of shit from life. Jim just might have been a load too much. His forehead wrinkled and his hand shook slightly as he reached for the coffee he was nursing.

Jim concentrated on the back wall keeping his thoughts silent. "See, I not sure it was wrong. 'They' say it was wrong. If that be true, then I scared I be a bad person."

"Did you feel wrong when you did it?"

He pondered. "No. Only afterward, maybe so.'

"Would you do it again?"

His answer took a while. "Samey, same happen, think so." He brought his fist down on the counter hard enough to draw the attention of the other diners. "That the question you see?"

"Not sure I do."

"Then maybe I not ask you the answer. Who gave anyone the right to be my conscience?" He turned to me. "Who? Who the hell?"

I shrugged. "Don't know. Churches mostly I guess."

"Then fuck 'em."

"I think you can only do that if you don't enjoy it," I replied. "Although I did know a preacher's daughter once."

The smoker lit another one. Jim turned and stared down at him while he continued to talk to me. "Prison had rules, but no one play God if you right or wrong."

The smoker caught the word prison and came to full alert. He fidgeted for a moment under Jim's stare then laid two bucks on the counter, put out his smoke and left. Jim looked at the pack of cigarettes and lighter the guy left behind.

"I feel more better 'bout being me, now," he said. "Making a man see the error of his ways good for one's soul."

I gazed at him. "Yes, sanctity becomes you."

Jim spread a grin, laughed, and worked on his eggs.

I inhaled the feta cheese omelet. "You getting any crank calls lately?"

"Phone don't ring period. Why?"

"Because I've received three."

"You waitress say she don't love you and you can't believe it." He thought that was funny and laughed.

"These aren't funny."

"What they want?"

"My life."

Jim nodded. "Ain't doin' you much good. Might as well gives it to them."

"And I think I was followed home from McCabe's."

"Why someone follow you?"

"I have no idea, but I'm pretty sure he was waiting for me across the street from the condo."

Jim tilted his head to the left, shook it lightly, then turned and stared at my face. "What I think, Bobby's poteen screwed you head. Renaldo say you pretty wasted."

"Did he also say he thought I was trying to molest Margo in the hall?"

Jim's scar reddened. "Probably read you mind." He finished his eggs and announced it was time to go. Outside he took in the blue sky. "Know you problem, Rik?"

I acknowledged I didn't.

"You has no soul. Beautiful day like this and you no notice it." He took in a deep breath. "Something good come to a man day like this."

He was right. And I was looking at her. And the day couldn't compare with her. She was, I thought, one of the most breathtaking creatures I'd ever encountered. She was kneeling by her bike, examining its front wheel. The cropped tee-shirt she wore gaped at the front and I couldn't stop myself from stealing a glance.

"Problem?" I asked.

She shook her head. "Flat tire, wheel looks pretty bent out of shape."

Nothing I was looking at did. "You okay?"

She looked up at me. Her eyes were fantastic. Doe eyes, soft as a spring shower.

"Why shouldn't I be?"

"I noticed you fell. You have a smudge on your face and thigh."

She apparently wasn't vain enough to rub the smudge off her face. "You're very observant."

"It's a talent."

"I bet."

I watched as she ran her hands up her thighs and straightened her jean shorts. She was around five foot-nine, slits in the shorts, accented long, shapely legs. A rich feminine exterior, athletically tuned, deeply tanned. She brought her lips to a pout and fluffed her hair. Thick, luxurious auburn-colored hair cascaded around her shoulders in a way that was once faultlessly coifed and yet suggestively erotic. Jim rammed a shoulder into me as he passed by.

"Christ, let me look at the bike!" It came off with no inflection of sympathy, sounding like the order it was rather than an offer of aid.

If she hadn't noticed Jim before, she did now, and he startled her. She directed her attention to him, her eyes narrowing as she examined him. She backed away, stepping out of her sandal. She retrieved it, arched her foot and slipped it back on.

I couldn't take my eyes off her. She was a fantasy, belonging to those dreams lodged in the subway of your mind. The ones you've nourished since puberty, when all girls were pure and magical and you believed life and love were truly enchanting. The type of female forbidden to ever happen in the life of an average, mortal male, but just had in mine.

"Strange place for woman to ride a bike," Jim said.

Her eyes narrowed again, though she appeared frightened of Jim she held her candor. "Not if it's on your way home," she said. "That okay with you?"

"Not my problem lady, time is. We late."

My brain seemed incapable of sorting out the pictures I was sending it of her, and forming speech at the same time. I went over and picked up the bike. "Hell, she can't go anywhere with this."

"I was doing just fine by myself, you two can go anywhere with my blessings." She was on the hot side now, it looked good on her.

I had the bike in Baby. At least far enough it wouldn't fall out. It shouldn't have fit at all. I thanked the bike gods. "I'm Rik, that's Jim." I waited, she didn't offer her name. "I'll be happy to give you a lift home."

Jim avoided her and glared at me, the scar bright red. "You really a piece of work. Pretty face and you forget you promise to Margo."

Her facial features showed she really wanted no part of either of us. She gave me a deep study, quickly looked at Jim and just as quickly looked away.

"Thanks, but I think you better be on time for wherever you're going."

I opened Baby's door for her. She was obvious in her reluctance to get in. Jim was glaring at us. More at me than the girl, but there was no way she could know that, his face hard, eyes threatening, and the crimson scar frightening. Jim moved toward us.

"Stay away from me," she ordered him and got into Baby.

"I'll be right back. Promise Jim."

"If not, best for you, be dead."

Chapter Thirteen

I noticed she sat as close to the passenger door as the bucket seat would allow, and hadn't fastened her seat belt. The rear tire of her bike protruded between us. She held her hand on it like it was a shield.

"My name is Rik Burns." I tried my cherub smile. Terribly successful when I was a kid, it apparently had lost some of its charm with age. She didn't respond. We drove in silence for a block. She had her head turned, looking out the side window. There was nothing for her to see, unless vacant lots and dirty old buildings caught her fancy.

"I would appreciate it if you would pull over and let me out," she said.

"If that's what you wish." I noticed the twin towers, the only building in the area fine enough to house someone as classy as she. "However, if you live in the Marina Towers, I can have you home by the time I let you out and get your bike out of Baby."

She looked briefly at me, and then gave the road ahead her concentration. "Laura," she said softly.

Her deep tan highlighted the skin and hair that glistened from expensive oils. She was well kept. Hopefully out of her own pocket and not some man's.

"Does your friend make an effort at being so frightening, or does it just come natural with him?"

"My apologies. It's a gift. Actually he's the exact opposite of what you saw today if you get to know him."

"No thanks, I'd rather not."

The twin towers of Marina City came into view too soon. I turned into the entrance way, circled the inner court and parked at her building.

"Thank you," she said, getting out of the car before I could play gentleman.

I removed her bike from Baby. "Where do I take it?"

"The lobby's fine." She opened the door so I could enter the building.

"I'll carry it up to your condo for you."

She tilted her head and smiled. It changed everything about her, once again I saw the girl in the subway of my mind. "Thanks, but that's not necessary."

She took the bike from me and waited for the elevator. "Everything happened so fast, your friend…" She lowered her eyes. "I was frightened at first. Thanks for the ride. And being so nice."

I gave my best smile. "I would have been frightened also."

She laughed. It was all throaty and came out like honey. "You don't strike me as someone who frightens easily."

"All part of playing the macho male, I'm not as tough as I look. What are you doing today?"

My question seemed to catch her off guard. She stared into my face, her eyes defensive. "Something very boring."

"Then maybe I can help you un-bore it."

She studied me. "Your friend is right, you do forget promises made."

Think, Rik. "Actually it's not my promise. Jim made it for me." I could tell that didn't fly. "Then how about tomorrow?" She didn't answer. "Noon good?"

She smiled. It was to herself and not very promising. "If I said yes are you sure you wouldn't forget?"

"Was that a yes?"

The elevator doors opened. She turned to enter. "No, just a question. But thanks for the lift."

"Are you living with someone?"

That brought a flare to the nostrils and a spark to the eyes. She pushed a hip out and placed a hand on it. It wasn't Margo's ball teaser, but pleasant to the sight.

"That is none of your damn business." The elevator doors closed, leaving her in the lobby with me. She pushed the up button again.

"I'll take that as a no. Then why can't we have lunch?"

She turned her back to me and faced the elevator doors. "Are you always this obnoxious?"

"It has something to do with the eighties honesty bit between man and woman. I've conquered the macho John Wayne bit, but I'm still working on the sensitive, unisex thing."

The elevator doors opened and she leaned against one, stopping them from closing. She laughed, a little too sarcastically, to make me comfortable. "Did you find playing John Wayne successful with women?"

"Apparently, not today. But this unisex thing isn't great either." I focused on her eyes. "I even have adult clothes to wear, if you'll have lunch with me tomorrow?"

She entered the elevator, turned and faced me. There was no evidence on her face, but her eyes said she'd been smiling. I received what I considered a long pondering stare. "I work for Giordanian Imports room 385, the Merchandize Mart. Lunch time is usually quiet. If there are no customers, we can talk, and I'll decide if I want to get to know you better. Monday's are best."

I couldn't contain my smile. "Monday then."

"Sure a pretty face won't make you forget?" The doors to the elevator closed and she was gone.

"Thank you, God."

It really was a beautiful day. A cop was writing me a parking ticket. He finished and looked over at me.

"Hope she was worth this."

"Every cent, thank you."

Chapter Fourteen

Jim borrowed a brick wall belonging to a print shop next to Gus's to lean on as he read a copy of the Chicago Sun-Times newspaper. He looked over at me, discarded the paper into a trash can and climbed into Baby.

"No news is good news?" I asked.

"Nothing I dint already sees on TV. Except Captain Mac giving info on a body they pulled out of a garbage bin."

"This have anything to do with a serial killer Mac mentioned to me?"

"Paper say nothing 'bout any serial freak." Jim looked over at me. "You ever read a paper or watch TV news?"

"No reason to. Why or what people do to themselves, or to others, is no concern to me."

Jim shook his head and checked the time. "Couldn't knock missies shorts off with you bullshit?"

"Time will tell."

Jim directed me west, turned away and stared out the side window, his jaw muscles rotating.

"We got a problem?"

"Yeah, sure do." He turned his attention to me. "Next time you disappoint Ms. Margo over some bitch, don't make me a part of it. You got that?"

Still high over my good fortune I let Jim's churlish muttering fly out the window. "I take it you know where we're going?"

"To make you labor for Margo's affections."

I glanced over at Jim. "Then what's with your clothes?"

"This be a Catholic-owned building we be at."

"Really? This a new rule with the 'holies,' you have to dress up to do work in their building?"

"Don't know. But, this be Margo's thing, and I don't have to look like a janitor." He shot me a look. "Or, a bum."

I let the wind talk to Jim for a while.

"You know how you imagine the perfect girl in your mind." I asked, "until she becomes real. Only she remains in your mind, because you can't find her. Well, mine just walked into my life today."

Jim turned, looked incredulously at me. "What that shit?" He continued to stare. "Know what I think. Think you ain't got no mind no more. A broad from you mind. Christ!" A stone cold stare. "Margo be real. This new chickie just some dream—and a bad dream."

When we reached Racine Avenue and started south, I realized we were headed for the Lower West Side, a great place to leave Baby. Might as well just save some kid the trouble and give Baby's keys to him. We turned west on 18th Street into the heart of the Pilsen area.

Eighteenth Street played a part in my childhood. My Grandfather decided it was time I saw life other than through my Grandmother's sheltered eyes. He would take me to Harrison Park for the Bohemian celebrations. The Street seemed magical to me then. A lively and colorful street, where children played, and everyone seemed to hang out to gossip, drink, and eat. Immigrant businessmen sold their wares, girls flirted, and grandmas and grandpas sat on stoops and watched the activity. For a long time my nightly dreams were filled with blond, blue-eyed, big bosomed girls.

It was still a lively street. Girls still flirted, immigrant businessmen sold their wares, and grandpas sat on stoops and watched. The only difference was now punk gangbangers roamed the street and shot each other over turf rights, while the Mexican community that was now Pilsen drew its blinds and pretended not to hear or see.

We turned south on Troop St. down blocks lined with two-story brick homes set about a body width apart, resting almost on the edge of elevated sidewalks. Once proud edifices, filled with the laughter of people who asked for no more than an honest day's work and peace. Now the buildings were old and neglected, cowering in their hidden secrets about the tenants who now possessed them.

We parked in front of a brick, two-level school belonging to a St. somebody and got out of Baby. Something very large and grotesque approached us. It walked like a human, but I wouldn't have been surprised if it proved not to be. Jim looked small next to him. A swarthy, pockmarked face supported a nose broken too many times to repair. Hair slicked back and greasy, shoulders that could hold refrigerators, and the swollen knuckles of boxer hands.

He showed yellow teeth when he smiled, except for the front two which were gold. He looked at Jim and me. "Car yours?"

I nodded. He walked past us where he squatted cross legged in front of Baby and kept his eyes glued on her.

"Baby safe now," Jim said.

"Yeah, I guess. What happens when nature calls?"

"He trained not to have to go."

"I looked back at him. "Maybe that's why he's so big."

Watch you tongue in building," Jim said. "Nuns humble something or other."

"Yeah, I forgot you're sanctified now."

We walked down the hall to the gym, dark eyes suspiciously sizing up whether we represented the law. The Spanish flavor of the participants definitely put Jim and me in the minority, except for the nuns. The Church had found it expedient to place Irish and Polish teaching nuns in the school to tell their Spanish pupils how to conduct their lives.

Margo, attired in jeans and a loose fitting washed-out gray pullover, hair done in braids, gave the appearance of a sweet and innocent seventeen year-old for the nuns. The jeans though, were unable to hide the curvature of her buns pronouncing she was all woman. I received my special smile.

It all turned out to be fun. We hung paper streamers and posters with Renaldo's face on them and his 'you can believe in me' smile. The prune faced nun supervised and watched me as I watched Margo, scolding any time I scraped chair legs on her precious parquet floor.

It was over. Margo, nuns or not, embraced me with a very warm and enticing hug. I allowed myself to enjoy it. Jim apparently decided I didn't have the right, grabbing me by the shoulder and pulling me away. .

"Tomorrow night, Margo," Jim said.

Outside 'Tiny' still protected Baby. He got up without a creak of cartilage and headed for the school, not waiting for a thank-you.

"Think Renaldo do good with his speech?"

"I rewrote most of it, he should knock their socks off. You obligate me to attend?"

"That be up to you."

"Yeah, I figured you would."

"We four also goin' out for dinner after. You Margo's date."

I took my eyes off the road and fastened on Jim. "Say what!"

"She be waiting six o'clock."

I pulled Baby over to the curb, screeching her to a sudden halt. "Who the hell made you my date mother and forgot to tell me.?"

Jim shook his head. "Sad, she be all excited you taking her out." His stare said I wasn't worth looking at. "Don't bother nothing. I'll tell her you don't have no time for her."

My anger pulsated, I grasped the steering wheel to control the shaking of my hands. "Did it ever occur to you that if I knew about dinner, I would have asked Margo myself?"

"Sure you would. You don't care bout nothing but you."

I didn't respond, took in deep breaths trying to control the anger.

"You a shithead," Jim said.

"Okay, now you're going to listen. Margo thinks I'm her date. I'm not. How much do you think I'm going to hurt her when I don't ask her out again?"

"You a shithead. You think you not hurting her now? Think you not leading her on?" He stopped, glared at me, scar bright red. "You lust her body. Don't like no man around her, 'cept you. She know that, wait for you to commit, but you don't. Why? Don't know." He paused. "Cept you a shithead. "You 'fraid to commit to anything. I be you best friend. You don't let me in. Captain Mac half raised you. You don't let him in. You don't even let life in.

"And look, you no got one." He stopped, looked out the side window. "Get me home, away from you."

I put Baby in gear and drove in silence.

Jim started in again. "You all dicked-up over some chickie from you mind. You a shithead. Margo real, you let her in and she give you life, a reason to live and love."

I slowed Baby down. "I'll be her date." I pointed at Jim. "But one mention from you, Margo and I are your family and you want to be an uncle, and I'm gone. Got that!"

Jim leaned back and smiled.

I wanted a beer, but not with Jim and not at Bobby's. I dropped Jim off at the front of the condo and parked Baby in the garage. Got out of Baby, stretched, and from habit glanced around the garage. Lonely place, can't remember ever seeing anybody down here the same time I am. But then, it's a garage, not Grand Central Station.

I headed for the elevator, stopped. Someone or something shared the garage with me. I looked it over. No one, nothing, silence, empty, except for cars, nothing but solitude. "Hello?" I laughed to myself. Probably just scared the hell out of some building resident. Except, I couldn't see one. The elevator doors opened, I scanned the garage one more time. Nothing. But I couldn't kick the feeling someone was sharing the garage with me.

Chapter Fifteen

I sat at my condo bar working on a beer. Jim had demolished my high over Laura, but the beer wasn't doing anything to revive it. Maybe Jim was right about life, and I didn't have one. I needed more than the loneliness this bar offered. I hadn't been out west of Chicago to the suburbs in years. I grabbed my keys and headed for the door. Maybe that's where I needed to be. Maybe somewhere out in suburbia I'd find a flashing neon sign exclaiming, 'Here's Life'.

The elevator doors opened onto the garage. The lighted elevator an oasis against the opaqueness I entered into. A shadowy spaciousness, this garage, heavy with the permeated musty odor of cool dampness, the cars lifeless, victims of a post-mortem, a nice perk, but all the warmth of a morgue.

I headed for Baby. There it was again. I hadn't paid any attention to it the first time I heard it. Hadn't noticed anyone down there with me—big garage. But, again the muted sound of footsteps. Behind me, somewhere. I stopped, turned, no one. Silence, total, heavy, only shadows greeted me—some, maybe dancing a little, one in particular was someone hiding?

I moved toward it, nothing moved. Closer, no one ran, just a shadow. I waited, silence. I reached Baby and patted her. "Your old man is starting to succumb to the credence of things that go bump in the night."

I climbed into Baby, closed the door, and from habit slowly moved my hand down the soft leather of the passenger seat, stopping abruptly when it touched something warm and furry. Something weaved its way up through my fingers—a long, coarse-skinned something, coming to rest on the top of my hand.

My right hand instinctively shot up protecting my face, left cupped my crotch. Rat—a big rat—I felt cold sweat on my skin—frozen in my seat, braced for attack, waiting for the feel of teeth, for the feel of skin ripping. The rat didn't move, except for its tail, which slowly un-curled and straightened. I heard a light gasp—its or mine?

Tried to take deep breaths, tried to gain control, the large knot in the middle of my stomach constricting my breathing—disgusting, diseased filled rat—God, I hate rats. What was one doing in Baby?

Okay, move slowly, get out of Baby. Can't do that to Baby, I can't leave a rat in her. I can't stay. Afraid to move anyway, might antagonize it.

Its mouth opened, my hand reached for the door handle, its eyes glazed over. I wasn't an expert on glazed eyes, especially those belonging to rats. I continued with cold sweats. High school biology class on rat diseases and long needles flashed in my memory. The rat remained stationary. "Christ, be a man!" I opened the car door, looked at the rat. "You better not be playing dead." Bolted out of Baby slamming the door behind me, can't trust rats, don't move, please, be dead.

I walked in front of Baby, leaned on her hood and stared at the rat. It didn't move. My mind flashed back to when I was a lad of seven wandering through the mysteries of an abandoned riverfront warehouse, only to walk into a darkened room lit by a single ray of sunlight, and finding myself challenged by river rats the size of cats.

It didn't matter that Grandfather found me and placed himself between me and the rats. That Captain Mac fired his revolver and scared them away. I could smell their stench, hear them hissing under my bed for weeks. And my nightly dreams found me in some darkened room cornered by large, heinous rats. God, I hated rats, feared them more.

The one in Baby looked very dead. Still it was a rat, can't trust rats. My nausea subsided, constrictions resided, nerves calmed to a rat-a-tat beat. It was contaminating Baby, had to get it out.

I walked over to the steel drum Jim used for refuse left by the less considerate tenants. It was about half full. The Chicago section of yesterday's Tribune newspaper lay on top. The lead article concerned ward politics in the city. That seemed an appropriate coffin for a rat. I rolled up the paper, went back to Baby, prodded the rat. Ugly, fucking thing, prodded it again. Don't move. Please don't move.

It didn't. It was long past caring. Apparently too close to death to do anything about my touching it. I'd just disturbed the only dignity allowed its kind—taking its last breath in peace.

Still, dead or not, I couldn't touch it. After several attempts I got the paper underneath it, lifted it out of the car without having to touch it. One for Rik. Took it to the drum, dropped it in, spread the paper over the rat. Didn't touch it. Two for Rik.

I walked over to Baby, patted her. "I know, I should clean your seat. But, it touched me, Baby, I have rat all over my hands. Tomorrow, I promise. Today it's me."

I rushed to the elevator and pushed my floor button. Scrubbed my hands, again and again, took a shower, hot and cold, and still felt infected. Went to my bar, had a shot of scotch, then refilled the shot glass and opened a bottle of Heineken's beer. The beer went down cold and cleansing. At least the insides were sterilized.

A rat. A big rat. What was it doing in Baby? That it had such exquisite taste to pick Baby to die in, lacked a bit in feasibility. But, someone putting one there didn't make much sense either. Unless I'm dealing with a completely deranged psycho. The message on the rat notice. "Live with the morals of a rat.

Die like one."

The footsteps belonged to somebody. To a somebody carrying a rat with them? What kind of weirdo carries a rat with them?

Nothing had any meaning, and I had no answers to give anything any meaning. All that was certain, my life had been filled with too much weird the last few days, and I couldn't explain why. I couldn't help wondering though, who it was that could.

Chapter Sixteen

Sitting at my bar wasn't doing anything to clear my mind of rats, so I left for McCabe's. Bobby's was filled with college kids celebrating mid-terms being over. I cruised with a young lady with long legs and a super leather mini to show them off, who liked to dance barefoot. She loved talking to writers being an English major herself.

We lasted together until she talked me onto the dance floor where she thought booty dancing was the only way to dance to Sinatra's "I've Got You Under My Skin." So I tried my thing and she did her thing, which left my thing feeling old, so I left.

Storm clouds had moved in, bringing an early darkness to the summer sky and my apartment. I opened a beer, poured a shot of scotch, sat on one bar stool while I propped my feet on another, and let the tranquil sound of rain drops mellow me out. I drank to young minds and barefooted teenyboppers.

The short hairs on the back of my neck bristled. I spun the bar stool around and let go a right jab. It was blocked. I was grabbed under the armpit and tossed to the floor. We both stared wide-eyed at each other for a moment. A ghost, the man was like a frigging ghost.

"You light bill too heavy to cover? The dark making you jumpy?" Jim asked.

I took in a long breath and returned to the stool and the beer. "You ever consider knocking? Then I go to the door and ask, 'who's there'? And you say Jim, then I let you in. See how civilized that is?"

"I saves you the trouble. Use my passkey and just come in."

"Then can you make a little noise when you walk?"

"You have carpeting. It hard make noise on carpeting. What with the dark, and you nerves?" He settled onto a barstool.

"I was enjoying some solitude, and you disturbed it."

Jim looked around the bar and shook his head. "Mind I disturb it some more and sit?"

"I suppose now you want a beer?"

"Nice you offer."

I got him one. "What are you doing here, Jim?"

Jim stared at me like I'd gone senile. "It be the third Thursday of the month. I always be here third Thursdays."

Jim, Captain Mac, and I have a standing round robin chess match on the third Thursday of the month. It's a twenty dollar ante, the winner of the first match plays the one who sat out until one player wins the majority of the games. No one wins, the pot doubles. Jim set the first game up.

"Shit!" I went into silence mode, Jim stared. "Mac can't come. I forgot to tell you."

I received a deep sigh and a look that asked if I'd suddenly gone simple. "Had I know, I be somewhere can afford lights."

"Sorry, I forgot.'

"Swell," Jim said. "You had dinner?"

"Have a beer nut."

Jim played with the beer bottle and looked at me over the top of it. "Here, "he said. "'Fore I get you forget disease."

He slid an envelope down the bar top. It was a slightly oversized envelope, tan and official looking, stamped special delivery. My name and address were typed on it, but there was no accompanying return address.

"Mailman couldn't get you interest, so I took it."

I laid it down on the bar top.

Jim looked at it, then at me.

"To dark in here to read it," I answered his stare.

Jim rattled his beer on top of the bar and stared at my face. "This gonna be you action for a Thursday night, or maybe since I be here we can play some chess."

I shrugged. "Chess sounds boring tonight."

Jim looked around again and shrugged. "Yeah, I 'fraid might put a damper on the wild time you having by suggesting it." He continued rattling his bottle and started drumming his fingers on top of the bar.

I turned to him. "You going to keep that up?"

"Good beat ain't it? You like, I tap my feet to it. You know we Blacks and rhythm."

"Yeah, but I've seen you dance, and in your case you don't have any."

"You just say that 'cause you ain't got no quarters to throw at my feet." I became the recipient of a deep sigh. "Can't handle the excitement here. Think I take my beer where I can see what I'm drinking."

"Can I follow?"

"You asking me for a date?"

"Don't tell anyone, you're black, the neighbors might talk."

Jim finished his beer. "That right. Maybe best we go in different cars. You got somewhere in mind?"

"Don't care, any place but here."

Jim ate some nuts. "Could be a long night. Best I eat some repast."

"Let me go upstairs and change."

"Mind I lighten the place a bit while I wait?"

"Jim," I yelled. "How big a hassle would it be for someone to sneak in and out of the building without being seen?"

I didn't get a response.

"You hear me?"

"I hear you. Why you want to know something like that?"

I made it back to the bar. Jim stared at me.

"Call it writer's research."

Jim was still questioning me with his eyes. "Then axt Captain Mac, I didn't serve no time for burglary."

"But, you know the building better than anyone. How could they get in? I'm talking amateur here. What's his best shot?"

Jim's eyes showed a lot of white, they usually did when he was agitated. He drummed his fingers harder on the bar top. "Ain't none. A pro knows a dozen ways but no better for him." He chewed on some beer nuts, his eyes narrowed as he looked at me questionably.

"Come on. Tenant buzzes him in by mistake?"

Jim sighed. "Unlikely, shit going on the streets these days." He shook his head.

"The garage door?"

Jim gazed through the French doors in the living room. A slice of blue sky appeared between the high rises. "Forget it, man have to be invisible so no one sees him, and an Olympic track star."

"That's not what I wanted to hear."

"Don't care," Jim answered. "You ain't researching nothing. That bottle be the only researching you doing. What this 'bout?"

It was my turn to delay answering. "You won't like it."

Jim replied with a long, hard stare, and waited.

I took a breath. "I found a rat in Baby."

Jim's reaction was what I'd expected, where Jim had grown up rats shared living quarters. Rodents knew better than to try and inhabit his building. Jim's eyes narrowed and his jaw muscles worked a heavy beat. He threw some beer nuts in his mouth and took his anger out on them.

"No rats in my building!" He didn't give me a chance to respond. "You saying there be? Then you bullshit. No rats, never been, never be."

"What I said, I saw one in Baby. I heard footsteps, I think someone put it in her."

Jim fastened his eyes on my face, then mumbled something about my ancestry. "Why someone do that?"

"I don't know, maybe...."

"Footsteps? You hear footsteps." His scar reddened and his stare became penetrating. It was effective on someone who didn't know him, but he was working it on the wrong guy. "Last time you go crazy, it be gunshots and screams you hear."

I could have become angry, but held cool. "Get it straight, I'm not crazy. A rat died in Baby tonight. I heard footsteps, someone put a rat in Baby—if you don't like that scenario, then you like a rat found in Baby to die better?"

Jim's face grew cold, the only color hate, the only emotion menacing. "What I don't like, is you. You sit here mind screwed from drink" He eyed the shot glass. "And talking imaginary rats. Where you put it?"

"Under some papers in your trash can."

He got himself a beer. "This not right, Rik. And what not is you." He turned and looked me up and down, his eyes saying all he saw was something pathetic. "Don't go sucking booze on me again and hearing things don't exist in the garage, you hear?" He continued eyeing me up and down.

"There was a rat in Baby. I don't like it any more than you do, but it was there. Come, I'll show you."

Jim sucked on his beer. "I tell you straight, you best not be shitting me."

I led the way to the trash can. Waited until Jim stood beside me, and then removed the newspaper I'd laid over the rat.

Jim didn't say anything, he didn't have to, his eyes said it all.

"Jesus, it was dead. I knew for certain, otherwise I wouldn't have touched it." I started to pull more trash out of the can. "I put it in here, Jim, I swear, it's in here somewhere. I took it out of Baby, put it into here. I did, I did, Jim."

Jim was headed toward the elevator. "I gonna leave. You stay, play with you rat. Don't even think 'bout coming near me, hear?"

Chapter Seventeen

Jim took the stairs out of the garage, I took the elevator. No longer hungry, I went to my condo and sat at the bar. What was going on? The damn dead rat sure as hell didn't climb out of the steel drum. Which meant someone took it. Why would someone take a dead rat? My only answer was a growing headache. The bottle of scotch didn't look like it had any answers either. My very important looking letter caught my eye. I took it to the kitchen.

I heated a cup of coffee in the microwave and settled into the booth. The phone rang. Not expecting a call, I hesitated, took a sip of coffee, then answered it with a guarded, "Hello?"

"Do you think I'm mad, insane? I don't feel you're taking me seriously." The slightly effeminate, yet raspy, male sounding voice of the gay came through the receiver.

Wonderful, just what I needed to make the day perfect, a growing headache, a cold cup of coffee and fruitcake. "I wouldn't want you to marry my sister, if I had one."

"If I am mad, then love is nothing but madness. A madness you stole from me. So, I have no choice but to steal from you, in your case, your life. Only with your death will beauty, love, and understanding once more be mine."

"I agree, for the both of us. So, let's meet, you name the place, and we'll play draw your gun when ready."

A muffled giggle at my response. "Now what fun would that be? I prefer a game of chess. I win, you lose. You lose your life." This time the laugh was deep and hearty. "The game will be fair, but you will have a slight disadvantage. You will be playing virtually blind.

"The game is actually a metaphor for 'you better find me.' Soon, you need to find me. Which will not be easy, since you won't be able to see my move except in your mind—thus—blind chess. So, you better practice your skills, memorize the chess board, practice, practice. Your life hangs in the balance."

I was going to tell him to stick his phone up his ass, but decided he'd probably enjoy doing it. "Okay, listen asshole. One more time, I don't know your Sam. Do you hear, do you understand?" I started to hang up the phone but was stopped before I could remove the receiver from my ear.

Like a distant train whistle, it started—a low, soulful wail. It built in crescendo until it became a scream. A wretched, tortured scream. The hairs on my arm bristled, goose bumps rose.

"My Sam!" he yelled. "My beautiful Sam, my Sam you took away, and you say you don't know, can't remember?" The scream came again.

This guy was a walking, talking psycho, and he wanted my ass? A cold shiver traveled down my spine. "Listen, I don't know a Sam, yours or anybody else's. You have the wrong person. Can you understand that?"

I waited, nothing. For what seemed an eternity, nothing. I would have been happy with a wail. All I got was controlled breathing.

"I poisoned the rat. The one you found in your car." Laughter, like nails against a blackboard followed. "I couldn't see from where I was hiding. Did it bite you before it died? Shame, painful things those long needles." More laughter.

"You are one sick asshole." I decided to play with him. "I don't think so, you lie, no way you can get into the garage."

Laughter. "I am everywhere, anywhere. As far as you and your life are concerned, you have no safe haven. If you haven't realized that by now, then start, Rik Burns."

I felt like he'd just delivered a chopshot to my windpipe. He'd never called me by name before. He had written it on the rat notice, but never called me by name. These were not some sicko random phone calls; the notes and the phone calls came from the same guy. He now not only had my full attention, he had me fighting for air.

"I followed you home from your favorite bar the other night. At times close enough to kill you. Were you aware? Of course you weren't. Believe in me."

I sat like a mute not wanting to hear what I was hearing.

"It's just begun. Believe in me. Remember all the worse happenings in your life. All of them. And know they are the best of times in your life. From now on, you see nothing. Days will be black, filled with gut-wrenching terror." That weird laughter again. "Beware, the Black Queen will soon make her move. It's just begun. Believe."

I held the phone long after he'd hung up. I believed. Didn't want to, but I believed. But, who is this guy, and more confusing, why me? And who the hell is this Sam? Jesus—I had heard footsteps in the garage. That left me knowing it was true, and him knowing. And no one else. I needed to make someone believe. But, who?

So many questions rattling inside the confines of my head, but there were nothing but empty spaces where answers should lie. Some unconscious portion of my mind stated I knew who the gay caller was—that I had heard the voice before—and knew who it belonged to.

I picked up my very important looking letter. The envelope had some heft to it. I stared at it, then decided the contents might take my mind off things. I opened it. The envelope was lined inside to keep moisture out. I pulled out a sheet of plain white, unbonded paper. There was no letterhead on it, just addressed to me. The message, was double-spaced typing. While the spelling of the words was flawless, the message appeared to have been typed rapidly, with no attention given to form, or punctuation.

Chapter Eighteen

"A day of vengeance….
(mine, my day of vengeance)
So that He May avenge
Himself of His adversaries…
(And humanoid rats)
The sword shall devour…
It shall be satiated and made drunk
With your blood.
As well shall be the justice of all
Who are blessed! And I am!
Vengeance shall be mine.
My cause is just
And I shall triumph over your EVIL!
I will watch your sins cleansed
with the flow of your BLOOD!"

    I stared at the message. The part about a drunken sword dislodged memories. Grandmother would corner grandfather and me on Sundays when we often missed church for a White Sox ball game. Jeremiah: the prophecy against Egypt. It had been her favorite. Probably because she felt we both needed roasting, if not cleansing.

    "See, your lectures weren't wasted," I said as I looked upward as if God and grandmother were both looking down, giving their approval.

Your mind's turned to jelly, Rik. Maybe the left side has melted and covered the right side of your brain. Ergo, I can no longer function as a writer. My first reaction was to rip the letter to shreds, but I couldn't stop myself from re-reading it. I didn't find it particularly frightening, but someone definitely wanted to let me know they hated my guts. It would be interesting to see if Jim thought the letter was as crazy as my rat.

I laid the letter on the table and wiped my sweaty hands on my jeans. Large beads came to rest on the crisscrossing lines on my palms. More heavy sweating of the hands, more bead-sized sweat balls. I stared at my hands, and became familiar with each and every pore as they opened to emit the beads of sweat.

I looked into those pores and into the insides of my hands. I marveled at the magnificence of the muscles, the pulsating blood vessels, and gazed into the workings of millions of cells. I could see inside my hands. Funny, I began laughing, deep, uproarious, laughter. All so funny, uncontrollable, side-splitting laughter, laughter that turned to high-pitched screams from the voices of those being killed in the alley.

Bang, bang, rat-a-tat-tat, boom, boom. Explosions of colors as bullets left their weapons—violent reds, sun brilliant oranges.

BOOM.

All you can hear is your heartbeat, and you're afraid they can hear it too.

****

A tip received by the police where the Pachukos gang headquarters, and its leader, can be found. Four undercover cops ordered to check it out, brutally killed. A letter to the Chicago Tribune newspaper from the gang letting the police force know, fuck-off, we are bigger, more powerful than the City itself.

Street cops, swat teams, patrol officers, traffic cops, anyone wearing a police uniform, except for women, emerged on the Pachukos. The headquarters existed in an area fast becoming abandoned around a decaying industrial center on south Halsted Street. The Pachukos claimed residence in an apartment building on a side street that cornered half a block.

My partner and I were directed down an alley in back of the building. The Pachukos were already firing on the police when we arrived. Lines of police cars riddled with bullet holes greeted us. I counted three cops down. We ended up at the end of the alley, our back windows shot out. The Pachukos fire power far exceeded that of the police.

My partner, Max, was a good cop, a bit of a hot head, with little patience, each of which got him into trouble sometimes. He decided hiding behind a car wasn't going to get the job done. He rose to get off some rounds, an automatic rifle ripped through his throat nearly taking off his head. No use yelling policeman down, medics couldn't get to us, and Max no longer cared.

I duck-walked to the front of the squad car, bullets weren't paying any particular attention over there. I could scan the area. Hidden behind steel drums and large cardboard boxes, I spotted someone shooting with an automatic pistol at the police. Late afternoon turned into the dark of evening providing me some cover.

I was almost to the shooter when I stepped on something announcing my presence. The gun turned toward me, I let off three rapid fired shots. The gun fell from the shooters hands and the body crashed against a box dumping him into the alley.

Police helicopters arrived on the scene, spotlights lighting up the building and the alley. I look down at the man I just killed. A boy, twelve years old, if that, lay in the alley. A boy I just shot—brown, dead eyes, looking up at me. A boy, his chest shattered by the bullets from my automatic. The whole alley is red and orange, lit up like the Fourth of July. I walk upright down the alley, it doesn't matter if I can be seen, they can't kill me—for I am already dead.

****

White, white is all I see, then a little gray with splashes of color, blues and reds and yellows. Walls? I realize I'm on the floor, hunched up against a wall, in a corner. My body curled up and I am holding my knees to my chest. I am coated with sweat and shaking, shedding the tears of a child, while the passions demanding manhood scream at me to stop.

My body is trying to come together, like the pieces of a suit. It has been traveling in time, to escape something evil that controlled it. Where am I? On a floor. Hiding in a corner.

I've forced myself to escape from an evil place. From death, but not mine. Yet there is fear. Cold, I am afraid, where am I?"

My shaking subsides, I come to a sitting position. Must leave the corner, to where? I try to stand, my legs won't hold me. I sit back down, mind muddled. I rest my head on crossed arms, what has happened to me? Cold, it deepens to winter, won't brush away. Fear. Of what? The wind comes, darkness, screaming voices of hate speak to me from corners. Profound fear creeps though me, I recognize it. Fear of myself.

I crawl from the corner, realize I am home, something, someone has played with my mind. How? I crawl to the kitchen booth, able to raise myself so I can knock the wall phone from its cradle. I dial Captain Mac. "Please Mac, be there. Please, be there."

Chapter Nineteen

"MacCloud here. Talk."

He spoke with his usual great economy of emotion. Hard, maybe cold to most people, but his words covered me like the protective warmth of a blanket on a frigid night.

"Mac, I think...think, somebody just tried to kill me."

"Rik? Rik, what the hell? You want to say that again?"

It wasn't all that easy the first time. My tongue thick, mouth dry, nothing came out.

"Never mind, where you calling from?"

"Home."

"And where did you almost get killed?" he asked.

"Here."

A prolonged silence. "And someone was in your apartment and tried to kill you?"

"No, I was reading a letter, and the next thing I knew, I was in a corner."

I endured some more silence. "I'm having a little trouble following you, Rik."

"It was all pretty scary. Maybe that's what he wanted, to scare me, let , know he could...maybe that's it."

"I'm on my way."

Mac must have flown here. He gave me a short once-over. All cops age before their time, are over the hill by forty. Bitter. Mac was fifty-nine and couldn't hide it tonight. Whatever weighed him down, its effect showed on him and his clothes. His shirt collar was open for comfort to his thick neck, and the black knit tie wandered several directions down the front of his white shirt. His gray sharkskin suit showed wrinkles in places that aren't supposed to wrinkle, and rested uncomfortably on his large-boned frame.

He headed for the bar, I followed. He gave a short grunt as he settled onto a bar stool. He looked at my drink. "You shouldn't have that. I'll take it." He leaned back and rotated his shoulders, ran his fingers through his thick salt and pepper colored hair. He removed a stub of a cigar from the left side of his mouth, started to put it in his breast pocket, eyed it and deposited it in the ashtray, pulled out a new one. He didn't smoke them, chewed them to death.

He turned his face to mine. The cartilage had been broken so many times the bridge of his nose went both east and west. His eyes concentrated on mine. "Talk to me, what happened here?"

I averted his stare. "It's all pretty weird."

"Most things are if you take the time to try and make sense out of them. Just tell me why you think you were dead."

I fumbled for words. Mac continued to stare at me. Pale, even with an afternoon growth of beard, he looked pale. I wondered when he last saw the sun. "I was reading a letter…and—and…the next thing I know, I'm curled up in a corner in the kitchen as if I'd been drugged or poisoned."

"How many drinks have you had?"

"None, you drank it."

"Good. What'ja have food wise."

"Nothing."

"Good dietary habits. Probably best. Easier for them to pump your stomach."

"Say what?"

"Let's go, only way to find out what's in you. Where's this letter?"

Mac became part of my life when I turned seven. He and grandfather belonged to the same Scottish society. Both took a liking to each other and he literally became a family member. My grandparents gave me a home after my parents were killed in a car accident, along with an education and what they hoped was some culture. Mac gave me a taste of street life in Chicago. Taught me how and when to fight, the proper use of firearms, and how to drive stick shift with a beer in one hand.

We reached the kitchen booth, I reached for the letter, Mac grabbed my hand. He pulled tweezers out of his coat pocket, picked up the letter, read it twice. "You been fooling around with some preacher's daughter?" He followed the tweezers act with the envelope. "It's lined for moisture protection. Interesting."

He took some heavy chews on the cigar. The letter and envelope seemed to interest him more than me. Mac was a lean, tough street cop when my grandparents were alive. Now a precinct captain, but still a hard-nosed street cop at heart. His face, like the rest of his body, had grown fleshier, softer, from too many years behind a desk and making scotch whiskey his best friend. His jade eyes were the only remotely predatory thing that remained. They roamed beneath bushy eyebrows and peered out through weighted eyelids. Mac was older now, softer on the outside, but harder on the inside. It was your mistake if you didn't read his eyes.

"Special delivery. Mailman give it to you?"

I shook my head. "He couldn't raise me, gave it to Jim."

Mac looked off into space. "But he knew to give it to Jim? Interesting. Let's go. You can talk on the way over."

The car was unmarked. Smelled like cop. I started from the beginning.

"A city rat termination notice saying you should die like a rat? Jesus." Mac exclaimed. "You still have it?"

"Did, on top of the garbage can. Saved it to show you." I looked away from him. "Somebody stole it, along with my garbage."

Mac stared at me in disbelief. "Somebody steals your garbage?"

"Not usually, but then who steals dead rats?"

Mac ran his hand over the afternoon stubble. Took a long look at my face finding something I didn't know was there. "People poison rats." He focused on me. "Who wants to poison you? Think."

"Don't know, but he could be serious." I told him about the dead rat in Baby.

His eyes grew wide. "A rat? Christ, you must have shit! What did you do."

I told him about my less than manly reaction. He laughed.

"I'm certain he was in the garage watching."

"The rat guy? You see him?"

"No, just felt his presence. Then figured it was just my imagination."

"What changed your mind?"

"He called me, confessed to it. After Jim couldn't find the rat, I decided he was definitely there and took it."

"You told Jim about the rat?"

I nodded. "Had to tell someone."

We came to a stop light. Mac ran his fingers through his hair. "This guy tell you how he got into the garage?"

"Just said he's everywhere. Anywhere in my life."

Mac sighed. I began to feel his weariness. He rubbed the bridge of his nose. "And, what does Jim think?"

I took a breath. "He doesn't believe me. Thinks I'm flipping out again."

"Are you?"

I stared into his jades. He smiled. "Just a question, son. That's what I do."

"I need you to believe me, Mac. Stop him."

"Who?"

"Shit."

"Exactly. From now on it's just you and me. No Jim, no anybody but me."

"Why?"

"Because I said so."

Chapter Twenty

Mac made me play patient in the hospital and picked me up mid-morning. We sat at Gus's while he feasted on chili and a cheeseburger. My insides burned like hell, bile filled my mouth, and the smell of Mac's food churned my stomach. The vanilla shake mellowed the nausea fighting to erupt. Gratefully we left Gus's and headed for home.

"Your life may be in danger, Rik. But I don't think necessarily in the immediate future."

"Why?"

"Because whoever this guy is, he wants to play with you. You had nothing in your stomach, poison or otherwise. The blood sample showed some heavy concentration of LSD. You took an acid trip to the badlands."

Mac studied me.

"I did some what, with what?" "LSD? I don't use the shit."

Mac nodded. "I know. You picked it up from the letter. It was coated with the stuff. It entered through the pores in your skin and mailed you to the place you fear most—the past."

"LSD through my skin? Whoa, sorry, but that's stuff that plays in a horror movie,"

Mac picked up on my disbelief. "That's why the inside of the envelope was lined. Stopped the mailman from getting stoned." The thought of a stoned mailman trying to deliver mail must have tickled his funny bone. He let out an uncontrollable laugh. Choked it back and laughed again. He seemed removed, chewed the hell out of his cigar. "I did a lot of thinking, this phone guy, so far, is acting very much like a stalker"

That surprised me. "I thought nuts only chased after celebrities."

"That kind is the most infamous. Yours can be the most dangerous."

"I'm not sure I understand. Why would someone want to stalk me?"

He removed his cigar, made a face and threw it out the car window. "You claim this guy is gay? He shook his head. "Your grandfather came from the Highlands of Scotland, toughest man I ever knew. Nothing life could throw at him brought him down. He was so proud of being a man." He shook his head again. "Mixed up with a gay. Rik, Rik. What would he have thought?"

I glared at him. "That's not funny." Mac seemed to think it was, he let out a belly laugh.

"I hate to bruise your ego, but if he is gay, I don't think he desires you. Though his drive is similar to sexual anticipation. His very need for existence is to obtain total control of your mind," he continued. "He won't kill you until he has achieved the ultimate orgasm."

If what happened to me yesterday didn't arouse him to an orgasmic state, then he was walking around with a hard-on. My body and mind had been completely controlled by someone so aware of what was happening to me, he didn't have to be in the room to see it.

"Now think, the more obsessed a person is, the more dangerous. Anyone out there overly obsessed with you?"

"Don't think so. Connie maybe was."

"Connie?"

"A girl who thought because I screwed her a couple of times, I loved her." Mac let a short chuckle escape, then shook his head. "How strange of her. Women can be stalkers too."

"Not this one."

"Now listen. You ain't seen nothing yet," Mac added. "His goal is to make your life so miserable that you will give in to his obsession."

"Won't happen," I said.

"You say that now. There's a crux here that raises a big problem. Usually there's a bond between the stalker and his victim. He's gay, you're not. So where's the bond?" He looked at me.

"It's your stalker, if you don't know, how am I supposed to?"

Mac fixed his eyes on me. "You'll be wishing he was mine soon enough. I can only figure he blames you for whatever happened to this Sam. What we have here is a reverse angle to the usual. If you have him, he wants him back. If you hurt him, he wants revenge. He's going to harass your ass until he gets either one."

"But…"

"But," he interrupted. "You claim you don't know this Sam."

"I do more than claim. I don't. Period."

Mac nodded. "Whether you remember or not, at some point you had to meet him. He's convinced you have, and, it just might be he knows you have." Mac chewed on his cigar. "Even though you don't think so. So, for health purposes, I'd give this Sam person some heavy thought."

He faded away. When he returned, I realized he was giving me as close to a fatherly stare as his eyes could fathom. "Whether these freaks are dangerous depends on the depth of their obsession. Sometimes a threatening letter is just that, a letter."

I smiled. "I'll be careful."

"Better be. I've dealt with too many of these freaks. If he's doing the stalker thing, then he's going to learn everything he can about you. Get into your head, make your habits his, try and take total access of your life, and if possible, your property. Make you feel there's no safety anywhere. He'll drive you to the edge."

"Sounds a little like paranoia, but I'm listening, Mac, I won't let him."

He nodded. "I'm counting on that. That's why everything here is between us. People talk. They just might be talking to the wrong person."

I wasn't sure I completely accepted his scenario. I talk to friends, none of whom had anything to do with my situation, or, with anyone who might cause my situation. But, I nodded I understood and got out of the car.

"Don't go macho Marine on me. Don't get in over your head. Call, and I mean call."

I nodded again. Mac knew me too well. He was afraid I'd let my temper get the best of me and go after the guy on my lonesome. Unfortunately, he was right.

"Want me to walk up to the condo with you?"

If the sincerity of his question hadn't been so damn comforting, I might have laughed. "This is my home, he's not going to get into my home."

"Yeah, home, everybody's safe haven. At least that's the way it's supposed to be. See ya. And I mean call."

I'd needed Mac beside me today. The voices I'd heard after the fight in the alley were history, a then, not now. What I was hearing now was real. Yet, I could feel a dominating power leading me to a return to, 'then.' I needed Mac's strength to stop me.

A single rose waited for me at my door. It was withered; the petals faded of color. A note hung below the flower. I took it into the condo.

> My beautiful rose.
> Withered because of you.
> Faded of life because of you
> Your blood will flow for your sins.

"Damn you to hell!" I grabbed the rose and tore it apart. A thorn penetrated deep into my thumb. I watched blood run down and flow across the palm of my hand.

The phone rang.

Chapter Twenty-One

Jim, seated in the kitchen booth, was waiting for me when I got home.. "No coffee, here, at you place, needs coffee," he yelled at me.

I joined him in the booth. "Just got home from the hospital. I'm okay—thank you very much."

"I'se know. Mac here sniffin' you place. Makes me lets him in. Axts me about some letter, I 'posed to gives you." Jim paused, penetrated me with his stare. "He don't say much more, but gives me looks like I'se might be guilty of somethin'." He watched me make coffee. "You have any idea whats I'se be guilty of?"

I shook my head. "He didn't say anything to me." I filled two cups and brought him one.

He sucked in a heavy breath and just as heavily let it escape. "It be you rat, you know? But guess you don't feel no necessary to help me find it?"

I studied Jim's face trying to read the mood he'd brought with him. "Hard for me to do. I wasn't here. Besides you know I can't handle rats."

Jim concentrated on his coffee. "You comes from white linen. Wheres I'se from, rats share you bed. Don't mean I makes friends with them." He took a couple sips of coffee.

"But being the janitor, it mean it be my job to get rid of white man's rats, right?"

I looked into his eyes. They didn't say anything I wanted to hear. "That's bullshit and you know it! But, you're right, I should have been here. I couldn't, but should have."

He headed for the balcony. I joined him. He was paying particular attention to a small, snow white cloud visible from the balcony. "I thinks what he say it be bullshit, but when my good buddy, Rik call me, say he seen a rat, it got to be true. Cause my good buddy, Rik, he wouldn't lie to 'ol Jim." He drank from his coffee. "Buts guess what? Ol' Jim don't find no rat." He began to grind his teeth.

I didn't like the way this was leading. "Bullshit, Jim!"

"So's I'se check the stairs, the whole garage, every corner. Shit, the whole damn building! 'Cause I wants to believe my good buddy, Rik. How many rats in garage, Rik? One, two, how many?"

Now I definitely didn't like it. "Make your point, Jim."

He looked at me as if surprised he'd discovered someone else other than himself sharing the balcony. He finished his coffee, gave a leer of a smile and let go of the cup watching as it shattered on the sidewalk below. It didn't take much to realize I was the cup.

"No rat, Rik. No rat hair. No rat shit. No rat. Negative number rats anywhere."

I grabbed his shoulder. "Damn it, I didn't imagine a rat. It was in Baby! Got that Jim? In Baby!" I focused on Jim's eyes. "I'll be damned! You don't believe me."

Jim looked at me and we locked eyes. He lowered his look to my hand. I removed it from his shoulder. He gave me one of his condescending smiles, his chest rising and falling in short, heavy, intakes of air through flared nostrils, his scar, crimson.

"I'se hopes Mac gives you talk and same advice. Get help, Rik!" He looked like he was fighting back the urge to grab and shake me. "Christ, you scarier now than when you start sucking dope from that Nam creep, and seeing people's heads in the garage. Floatin' head of a boy screaming you made him dead." He stopped, his eyes burning through me. "You 'member? Scare the shit out of Margo and Renaldo. "'Member those days, after that alley shoot out? 'Member how scary bad you was. Made this building bad, scary shit, then."

He left. I stared at Jim's cloud. It didn't do anything for me.

Chapter Twenty-Two

Chicago has two seasons. You either freeze, or bake well-done. Today was stay in the house with air conditioning. Only 9:30 in the morning, I was left to face a whole day of contemplating what tonight held, without the aid of drink.

The rat notice was not to be found in my garbage can. Nothing was. It had been emptied. Something I hadn't done, and was the major cause of my headache. Who the hell would break into someone's place and steal their garbage?

At five o'clock I picked-up Jim. He was all bubbly over Margo, him and me spending a night together. I was less thrilled.

Gaudy Mexicali ambiance, decorated the restaurant, the food "across the border 'hot-and spicy'. Jim and I put aside our differences so Margo could have a good time. We celebrated being a threesome again with Margaritas. To my surprise, I was having fun. It was like the old days before Margo became obsessed with making me her permanent partner and Jim wanting to be an uncle. The time came and we delivered Renaldo at St. somebody's school for his initiation into political campaigning.

Jim and I stayed in the background while Renaldo and Margo mingled with well-wishers and husbands, forced to be there by wives. On cue Renaldo would pull Margo by his side and introduce her, which gave the male audience reason to smile, and probably ensure their vote.

"Somebody got into my apartment and stole my garbage," I informed Jim. "I had something important in it."

"That sure to ruin a day—havin' you garbage stole." Jim kept staring at me, his face lacking in expression. "You keep 'portant stuff in you garbage?"

"It wasn't important when I put it in there. He called me and confessed."

"He who?" His stare hardened. "You saying this mysterious rat-carrying 'Phantom Of The Garage' give you a call?"

"That's why I needed my garbage. The rat notice was in it, which is proof the rat man exists, and he wants to kill me."

Jim shook his head, questioned me with his eyes. "It be gone. Garbage picked up. You not home yesterday, garbage smelled, I took it for you."

"My garbage didn't smell. Damn it, Jim, I needed my garbage."

Jim shook his head. "Don't say much 'bout you cleanliness, you no smell it." He moved his eyes up and down my face as if some message was engraved on it he couldn't decipher.

"Now, it be a rat man wants to kill you. Rats and footsteps." Jim watched Renaldo work the crowd. When he faced me again, his eyes showed only pity. "Tell me you be suckin' booze this morning. Cause not, you startin' to scare me."

Some man gave a brief introduction, reminding the audience of Renaldo's service to the community, and asked them to imagine what would be accomplished by him once he represented them in City Hall. Jim and I joined Margo in the front row so we could beam encouragement to Renaldo during his speech. And I had to admit I was more than interested in how he would deliver what I'd written.

Renaldo approached the podium exuding the confidence of a leader, and almost looking like one. He gave eye contact to the audience and smiled. My idea. We'd practiced the Cary Grant smile for sucking in the women, the Mortimer Snerd smile of Jimmy Carter for capturing the across the board vote. But, somehow it made him look more simple than it had on Jimmy, so we dropped it.

He started: "Once, a great nation existed, inhabited by great people, a society so advanced and wealthy, it truly amazed the visitors who came upon it. Visitors who came to this nation in the guise of friendship, only to destroy it in the name of their god."

He paused, eyeing the crowd, letting his words settle.

"Visitors," he continued "so jealous and fearful they were of these great people, they subjugated them to servant status in their own land, ripped away their pride and crushed the fabric of their society with the tyranny of their church. The nation they destroyed was that of the Aztecs—our fathers."

Another pause, a penetrating stare, a drink of water.

"We, as ancestors of these great people, the Aztecs, are treated no differently in this new city we adopted, called Chicago, than our fathers were treated in their own land."

Jim turned and shot me a questioning stare. I was on the edge of my seat. Where the hell did that come from? At his request, I'd dropped a line or two about the pride of the Aztec people, and how his constituents should renew that pride again. But, so far nothing else in his speech contained anything I'd written.

Renaldo's face was stern looking, his eyes demanding complete attention to his words. "The people of this city try to subjugate us to the rank of second rate citizens. Servants to their ideology of what our role as citizens of this County and City should be."

He let that soak in. His facial features softened and he smiled warmly, looked over the crowd fatherly. "I look to the day when once again you hold your head high, walk in this City with as much pride as our ancestors, the Aztecs, did in their land." He gave eye contact and smiled. "As your elected official, I will make that happen."

The smile disappeared and his eyes showed an intensity that was piercing. "This is my message to you. Pride once more! Freedom to hold your head high once more! The quality of life equal to those who try to subjugate you!" He looked directly at row after row of the Hispanic audience. "Not tomorrow, maybe not in a year, but soon. With your vote, with your belief in me, it will happen." The smile again. Unhappily, I possess neither that eloquence of diction, that poetry of imagination, nor that brilliance of metaphor…"

Finally, something I wrote for him. Borrowed from a speech by General Douglas MacArthur. It was supposed to be my wham, bang ending, except Renaldo went off ad-lib again.

"The unbelievers, the political hypocrites, every bigot will tell you what I speak is just words and not to believe in me. But, try as they may, they cannot stop me, they cannot stop you. Our time has come to be free, our right to the American dream will be ours to grab."

He drank some water, his voice boomed.

"The voices have been heard. The power divined to me. I am your voice, believe in me. Follow me. Vote for me. Thank you."

Jim grabbed my shoulder. "What that Aztec shit? You write somethin' make him look stupid?"

I shrugged. "Have to ask Renaldo. None of his speech was mine."

Jim didn't. I didn't. We patted him on the back and gushed over his performance. Still, I wondered why he obligated me to write a speech he didn't use. I constrained the impelling urgency to ask who these voices belonged to, and just who his divined power was. If I wanted to flirt with paranoia, it wouldn't be hard for me to accept that my gay stalker composed his speech.

Jim proposed we all go out for a celebratory drink. Renaldo declined the offer, claiming he and Margo had an early morning and it would be best if he took her home. When I didn't insist Margo was coming with us, her smile disappeared and with a bowed head she followed Renaldo, but not before I was the recipient of scorching eyes that burned with her total disgust of me, and spoke of something close to hate.

Jim left with Renaldo. I drove home alone.

Chapter Twenty-Three

Renaldo was pleased with himself, the speech had gone well. It was too soon to speak of his destiny, but a little knowledge of his divine power didn't hurt. And they had believed, followed his every word. You could tell by their eyes. The eyes always told the truth. Except for those of Rik and Margo's.

He'd almost laughed at the expression on Rik's face when the speech he'd composed hadn't been followed word for word. But the power blessed on him, Renaldo, had to be known so all who heard would believe. Especially Rik, it was most important Rik believed.

For Margo's sake, he would be forgiven for not following the speech. He needed Rik near, even though he despised him. Needed to know where he was in order to be able to keep him away from Margo. Would have to tolerate his sardonic wit, suffer Margo's affection for him. But, only for a little longer, until the powers came to him, bowed to him, and he controlled them. Only then would he eliminate Rik from their lives forever.

Margo went directly to bed; that was good. He didn't have the time or the mood to put up with her pouting over being chastised for wanting to go out with Rik. Tonight had been the first step, the beginning of his destiny—his to taste, to savor alone.

He swore softly, the bicarbonate took longer than usual. He belched out the last of the gas left over from dinner. His distaste for Mexican food equaled the loathing for those who made it their daily fare—the ones he would soon represent.

Once he'd cared for these lowly people. When he was naïve, just turned lawyer and shunned lucrative offers from firms so he could take his practice to the Pilsen area. In hopes his counsel would motivate them, make them achieve. But, he found them too weak, lacking the substance needed to achieve status in this country. People, who instead hid behind their archaic culture, blaming all but themselves for lack of equality.

That was before the messengers of ancient voices heralded his birthright and opened the heavens to the glories that awaited him.

He studied the reflection of his face. The left side showed his best features, but there were really no imperfections for a camera to pick up. A handsome face, strong in appearance, noble bearing, as it should be. Hereditarily perfect for the heir apparent of Ahura-Montezuma.

He, a man destined to avenge the betrayal of his ancestral parentage by the very Catholic Church he'd been born into. To reign supreme in all the glory and power that once was the Aztec nation. Renaldo, King of the Americas. He smiled, and then laughed with joy. Until the time arrived, he was forced to keep a kindred relationship with his Mexican constituency. Use them as his stepping stones, and most of all, keep their "hot pants" whores away from him.

These Hispanic women, all so willing to spread their legs for him, sap his strength with their sexual desires. Did they think that he, a descendant of gods, would mate with them, allow his children to be born of common stock?

Everything was on schedule, moving as it should be. His future now satisfactorily under his control—all except for the sudden rebellion by Margo against his restraints and counsel. He could no longer believe her eyes, for they lied. Rik had seen to that. Rik had molded her, laid the seeds of desire and lust, and he wouldn't allow that, had to keep her protected, the ultimate virgin, for she was his collateral, his sacrificial virgin, his pawn for the scriptures that would be his history.

For a man with the power and connections would come to lead him to his destiny. Then he would place his sister, the only thing he loved in life, the only woman he desired, wanted, on the sacrificial alter for this man to do with as he pleased.

But, she was slipping away from him. He'd searched her room, discovered the flimsy underwear, the bikini swimsuits, filthy apparel for Rik. If she were not a virgin, the gods would not be pleased with her sacrifice and his destiny would be denied.

His time, his destiny waited. Too close to let Rik destroy it all. He had no choice, he could no longer trust either one, Rik needed to be destroyed before he defiled Margo. Tighter reigns needed to be placed on Margo to stop the corruption of her mind and soul before vengeance became his just due.

Physically he was no match for him, but there were other ways to equate the game, other pains more excruciating than corporal punishment. He knew how to play Rik's mind, destroy him mentally. Disgrace him in front of Margo.

The thought of destroying Rik sexually aroused him. The power, he felt the power growing within him.

He checked his watch and smiled.

Chapter Twenty-Four

Thursday through Friday aped eternity, she'd stated Monday, but I fought taking a chance on an earlier day. Saturday and Sunday seconds ticked away like minutes. Monday finally arrived. I rose at eight, went to my den, found my briefcase, and dusted it off. Now, all I had to find was something to put in it. Notes are good, they look like research. I picked out the ones that didn't have doodles drawn on them. Next, I put in two medical magazines I'd actually read, followed by a yellow writing pad, pen and pencils. Reluctantly, I laid four pages of typed manuscript on top with the hope Laura wouldn't want to read them.

After showering and shaving, I wasted time to go through my closet trying to find something impressive but not overstated to wear. I gave up, totally uncertain of my choice, and left.

Architecturally, the Merchandise Mart is one of the ugliest buildings in Chicago. A huge box for containment of hundreds of offices and showrooms, it comes from a period of architecture that has no justification that would belong to any period of architecture. The colonnaded hallways and arched ceilings offering the only resemblance to designing something of class and an obvious apology by the architects to the public for the outside appearance of the building.

There are three entrances, all leading to the center of the building and what looks like a garage for elevators. I found mine and impatiently waited for it to be of service to me. If you pick the wrong one all you do is ride up and down to the top of the building. The overabundance of self-confidence I had this morning of being able to 'wow' Laura, was quickly dissipating as actuality loomed.

I fidgeted with my tie. A last minute decision deciding jeans, loafers, dress shirt, and sport coat looked a little too collegiate. I wasn't sure now if the tie was a bad idea, and discarded it.

My elevator finally arrived at Laura's floor and after numerous wrong turns, I located her place of employment. It was a windowed showroom, affording you a view of the merchandise inside. Large, gold letters, announced the name—Giordanian Imports. I entered, and stepped on what I assumed was a Persian rug. I found myself alone. The merchandise adorning the room was a little too ornate for my taste. Dark wood furniture inlaid with brass and silver, heavy cloth drapery samples fighting a never-ending battle with dust, four to six foot high, hand-carved statues of some kind of animals with wings, dancing Buddha's and Eastern gods, highly polished. Fancy-dancy love seats, that looked too expensive and too small to make love on. All told, for people who liked this stuff, I guess it was impressive.

The lady who stepped out from behind velvet curtains hiding a back room, sure as hell was.

Laura presented a totally different picture from the number I'd met at Gus's. Her hair was tied back severely, exposing a long, graceful neck. Her attire looked costly and conservative in a lightweight, pin-striped suit. Nice outfit, but I'd been hoping to see some leg.

Apparently, she felt her beauty interfered with her role in the business world. The business suit an attempt at hiding her sensuality. I could imagine the difficulty in keeping a male customer's attention on the wares in the showroom rather than on her. In my opinion the suit failed. It would take a whole lot more to hide her femininity from male scrutiny.

She gave me her pleasant business smile. Her eyes showed no recognition as she assessed my clothing, but remained non-committal. I guess a cut of a man's clothes no longer tells you who might be walking around with a cool million in their pockets. I doubted mine hinted at that possibility. Even the animals and Eastern gods seemed to be eyeing me suspiciously.

She walked toward me, her smile still official. "May I be of assistance to you?"

I felt like saying, Yeah, I want to get into your pants, and see how her Eastern gods handled that kind of business.

She stopped, tilted her head slightly, and gave me more of a discerning stare. "Rik?"

"Hi." That always works when you can't think of anything else to say.

Her smile spread and the doe eyes lit up. What an amazing face.

"I didn't recognize you at first. What a nice surprise."

"It's Monday," I said.

That didn't seem to register with her any more than mild confusion over why I'd informed her of the fact in the first place. "Yes it is," she said.

"Ah,…you clean up good."

That only accomplished to add to her confusion. "Pardon?"

"You look good in clothes."

She smiled, her eyes laughed at some private thought, or, at me, and then she laughed lightly. "Thank you, I guess."

"I mean you look different from Thursday."

"Yes, clothes do present an image."

Obviously mine failed. We stood looking at each other, caught in the air-hanging moment between us. She probably had difficulty keeping up with my dazzling conversation. So far, I liked the fantasy of this date far more than the reality of it.

"I was doing research on a magazine article that I was writing before I got here."

That bit of information seemed to impress her about as much as stepping on dog dung. I think I heard one of the gods giggling. Jim was right. What made me think I could play ball in her league. Time to tuck tail and leave.

She raised her hand to her mouth. "Oh, no. I'm so sorry, Rik. I invited you to come here today. Lawrence left me with so much to do…and…and, I let you stand here, embarrassed." She gave me a sad little smile. "Please forgive me."

I gazed into her doe eyes and forgave her every transgression she could have possibly committed in life. "Looks like I picked the right time to visit."

"Yes, Lawrence, er...Mr. Giordanian is away on a buying trip, so the appointment schedule is light." She inhaled deeply. It did interesting things to the front of her blouse. "He used to take me, but now he feels I'm needed in the office. Sometimes I do miss the travel."

I bet he took you with him. Feeling pangs of jealousy over a man I hadn't met, nor had the right to dislike. "Then I owe him one. Can you leave your treasures long enough to allow me to buy lunch?"

She looked apologetic. "Sorry, I'm needed here. In case of calls, that sort of thing." She brightened. "But, I did bring a lunch. I eat light, but I brought enough for two."

She waited. "Okay?" She touched my arm. "I would really enjoy some company."

All the carved animals couldn't drag me away.

She disappeared into the back room. I noticed a small writing desk, reminding me of grandmother's French Victorian piece. A brass plate supported Laura's name, and the title 'Assistant' underneath it. She returned, and on a small table with ornate legs and a faded red velvet cloth, she busied herself setting white, gold-rimmed plates on it. Salad and appetizer sizes, two for each, and brass-plated knives and forks. Out of plastic containers, she portioned food on each plate, accompanied by two Evian waters, and glasses.

"Caesar salad," she said. On the other plates, several finger sandwiches of some unannounced variety were displayed. She motioned for me to sit. "I always bring more than I can eat, in case Lawrence can't get away for lunch."

Laura sat, crisscrossing her legs until she was comfortable. Her thighs smoothed out the material of her pant leg and I tried not to act like a school boy. She took a bite of her salad, I tried one of the sandwiches. Some sort of spicy mayonnaise spread, but what rested on the spread, I had no idea.

"Good?" she asked, with an impish smile.

"Um," I lied.

She laughed. "Sorry, not exactly man's fare. Cucumber sandwiches."

"Oh, sure. We had them at the last poker game."

"Yes, they go great with beer and cigars," she laughed again, it's all throaty and infectious. She reached over and touched my hand, quickly withdrawing her fingers. The brief encounter changed the mood at the table and once again we experienced silence.

I tried to get the mood back. "Just what does an assistant do?"

"A variety of duties, but mostly making sure the customer is satisfied and happy."

I wonder how much it would cost to become a customer. "Do you like our merchandise?"

I hang on saying yes, but I don't like any of it and have no knowledge of who would want an Eastern god. "Not really, sorry."

Her eyes say things when they smile, and I make a mental note to become an expert on the language they speak. She tilted her head and ran an exquisite manicured nail over her lips. "You speak honestly. It's a nice change."

I've never been accused of that before. Ask her out, asshole. "Do you get lied to often?"

She answered with a slight shrug. "In life, only recently it seems. But then, I guess life can be a lie."

I wonder who he is, and what the broken promise was. "It can contain its falsehoods."

"So, you're a writer? I've never met a writer before."

I assured her she still hadn't. "Magazine articles, while I complete my great American novel," I lied.

"Does your briefcase contain some of your writing?"

I felt my brow knit into a tight frown. "Nothing interesting. Dry, factual stuff for a medical magazine."

She did a great job of feigning disappointment. Her eyes became warm pools, I wanted to swim in them. She manipulated a little girl's pout. I surrendered the briefcase, as I imagine men before me have surrendered much more.

She returned to the hidden room and brought back two cups of coffee. Time slowed, I burned my tongue on the coffee and have no idea what to do with my hands. I found the Eastern god who laughed at me and stuck my tongue out at him.

She stopped just as she was opening the briefcase. "Oh, Rik, I'm sorry. Time flies. I'm afraid lunch is over and I'm expecting a client. Unfortunately, there's no time to read."

I sighed silently, disappointed my time was over. Relieved she wouldn't be reading the papers. Ask her out, asshole.

"That gives me a reason to come back. Perhaps we can do this again?" God, you're feeble.

Her eyes appeared to be trying to tell me something, but I hadn't learned their language yet. "That would be nice, except Lawrence isn't always out of town."

"Perhaps then, we can make it dinner instead." I took a deep breath, held it.

She smiled. I'm certain it's compassion for my ineptitude. "You mean the kind where we pretend we're adults and get dressed up and you pick me up at my place?"

I laughed. I didn't intend to, but that happens when you've regressed back to feeling sixteen. "Tonight okay?"

"How about Wednesday?"

"Seven?"

"Seven-thirty. Apartment 1636.. Don't forget. And now leave." She reminded me of my briefcase, put two fingers to her lips, kissed them, placed them on my lips and pushed me out the door. "Don't forget. Causal, movie and pizza?"

I head down the hall, I think toward the elevators, but I didn't really care. I have a date with Laura. Not a barfly, not a waitress, but with unattainable Laura. I had no idea how I got it, unless babbling idiots turn her on. "

"Hot shit!" I exclaimed to anyone who might be listening.

Chapter Twenty-Five

I arrived home at the same time the phone rang.

"I need to know something kid," Mac said. "Have you told anybody about this LSD thing?"

"Not yet."

"Then make it never."

"Why?'

"Because I want it that way. You know, I know, that's it. Anything new?"

"I have a date."

"I ain't your mother." He hung up.

The phone rang again.

"I could lie down like a tired child

And weep away the life of care

Which I have borne and yet must bear,

Till death, like sleep, might steal on me."

"Did I win something and got you as my prize?" I asked.

He continued,

"If not for you,

I could beckon death,

And end my tormented soul.

Cease the beat of my tortured heart.

You owe me.

I have to live until you die.

Thank me, Rik. Thank me for your still being alive. I killed all the others, because I wanted to. But, I care for you, Rik. Soon though, death will call. Tick, tick."

He hung up.

The phone rang again, I let it. It stopped, but only for a moment, then rang again.

"Sorry to disturb you again, but I forgot something. I know you were on the way to your bar." He laughed. "It's driving you crazy, how I know what you're doing every minute of your day, isn't it? I am the spider, the collector in my web of your habits, all your frailties, and even the few moral strengths you possess. But, best of all, I know your mind." He sighed. "But, as much as you enjoy talking to me, I must run." He paused. "Beware of whispers and echoes of things to come." He was gone.

What the hell was that? So he knew my frailties, so did a lot of people, except possibly the one person who needed to—me. But, how was he able to be so exact on the timing of his calls? An icy shiver traveled through my spine. I went to the bar and poured some brandy, consumed a sip. Brandy warms the gadgets that fine tune the thinking apparatus. I didn't like the fine tuning.

Jim said that my life consisted of bits and pieces. The rest I concealed behind brick walls allowing no one to see the whole, which would be fine, Jim added, except my bits and pieces weren't worth a whole lot to look at. Some of my closest friends had pried some of the bricks loose, but the most private parts still lay hidden. So, how could an outsider know what only my close friends knew? I didn't like where this was heading. Besides, I should be celebrating. I headed for McCabe's to bore Bobby with my good fortune.

Bobby's was quiet. Frank Sinatra's voice emanated from the jukebox and filled the room. He was asking some chick to come fly with him. Bobby's selection of Sinatra recordings gave customers good reason to come here. The people sitting at the bar were in a good mood; new jokes were being passed around. I told Bobby about Laura. Two beers turned into five before I pushed myself away from the bar.

I headed home down Wells. A clear moon lit the sky and showed an abundance of stars. An unusual abandonment of people on Wells Street greeted me. The Monday evening inactivity caused my footsteps to echo against the outside walls of closed and empty businesses. Security lights from inside the stores cast shadows on the sidewalk.

The hairs on the back of my neck ruffled. Something didn't fit. A shadow moved, and then disappeared. I slowed my pace and waited. Again the shadow appeared, and just as quickly disappeared. I spun around, saw nothing. I listened to the silence of the street, searched for shadows that didn't belong. Nothing. I was the sole occupant of the street. Succumbing, I'm succumbing. This is my street, my home a few blocks away. Things don't go bump in the night on my street.

A voice from somewhere echoed off the walls of the buildings and broke the silence.

"If you were the queen of pleasure,
And I were the king of pain,
We'd hunt down love together."

His nails against blackboard screech. "I am the king of pain. Can you return pleasure?"

I couldn't see him, didn't answer.

The voice again.

"The night simulates the dark hours of the mind.

That's when it's most beautiful,

Our kind of love,"

A passionate sigh.

"And it's almost time,

The dark hours,

For you and for me."

I calculated his presence to be somewhere up the street, but I still couldn't make out where. He appeared, in the shadows, about a half block up from me. I couldn't make out his features, but definitely the blue suit and hat. He tipped his hat in a rakish manner, and began in a sing-song fashion, "Ta-da-ta-da, ta-da-da -da-da," while performing a soft shoe. "He jumped so high," he sang. "Then he gently touched down."

The little freak was good. Bojangles good. I couldn't stop myself from applauding. He bowed. Stopped dancing and waved at me.

"Catch me if you can," he yelled and headed up the street in no particular hurry.

You bet I'm going to catch you, little shit. He was in trouble. I had my cross-country running shoes on, still unused for their original purpose —running. But, I was a speed demon when a Marine, I figured I still was—I wasn't. Still, at the pace he moved, the distance between us shortened. He stopped, looked at me, and ran into a passageway between the Pier One store and Dilani's "overpriced" treasures.

I wasn't far behind. I grabbed the edge of Pier One to stop me from running into Dilani's and turned into the passageway. I became the recipient of a well- placed and vicious kick to the shins. The shin bones felt shattered and pain roared up my leg settling in my thigh, causing my leg to buckle. He jumped by me before I could react. He headed up the street performing an intricate tap dance, where he jumped up and clicked both heels, coming down and tap danced from one side of the sidewalk to the other.

"It looked as if a night of dark intent
Was coming, and not only a night, an age
Someone had better be prepared for rage."
He yelled over his shoulder.

At the moment, all I could do was sit and rub my leg trying to get blood to circulate. The pain ceased, I rose and started after him. The pursuit would have been much easier if I was able to run on more than one-and-a half legs. If he reached North Avenue, I would lose him. There were always people on North Avenue, he could blend in with them, not counting the numerous bars and eclectic shops he could hide in.

He stopped at Goethe, a block down from North and the street my condo faced. He turned then headed west toward Wieland. I took time to fill my lungs with some badly needed air. Wieland is one of the few streets left in Old Town that hasn't succumbed to the condo builders wrecking ball. It is lined on both sides by Queen Anne and Victorian framed-houses, erected on postage stamp lots. An excellent street to find cubbyholes to hide in, if we were playing kick-the-can or hide and seek   But, I was certain games were not the prevalent reason for this chase.

   Still, why Wieland instead of North Avenue where I would lose him? Confusing, but so was he. Halfway down the block, the faggot bolted off a gabled porch, ran across the street where he scooted between two houses and headed for an abandoned Catholic grade school. He reached what was once a school asphalt playground, and stopped and checked behind him. He spotted me and took off running across the grounds.

   The chain-link fence that once stopped baseballs and children from emerging into the path of oncoming cars, was now a remnant of itself. I found easy access onto the playground. The street lights from North Avenue cast crisscrossing shadows on the grounds. And as if decreed by grand design, clouds moved in to block the moonlight, casting the perimeter of the school into obscurity.

   I caught the brassy squeal of rusted hinges forcing a door open, the movement to my right of a shadowy figure, wearing a hat, entering the building. The last place I wanted to be was inside. There had to be several generations of rats calling it home.   The rancid odor of human waste took my breath, and I stayed in the shadows of the entrance while I adjusted to the smell. The building, long now a refuge for the homeless, and the cops turned their backs. Why a pisshole of a place like this should confront me? Why did I want to go in there? Of course, if the doors opened on this side, they would open on the other side.

   A cold chill told me stop, stay where you are. The chase was all too easy, no real attempt by him to escape, to hide from detection. Tomorrow's another day; but, was this the blind chess game he'd challenged me to? If so, then I wanted to play. He was within reach. Soon, my life could be mine again. I closed my eyes, cleared my mind, and listened for the evidence of a presence. Nothing presented itself, only silence.

Every intuitive alarm that cries danger set off sirens. But it was hard to listen to them. I wanted my pint of blood, and it waited for me in this building.

If I was so self-assured he was easy meat, why were the short hairs doing a rap number on the back of my neck?

Everybody's got to be somewhere, the odds even on left or right, I chose left. I stayed close to the wall, allowing the darkness to screen me from view. I tried not to think of what I might be stepping on, rotted food, human waste, rat shit, rats, certain I could hear them, sure I felt the occasional brushing of them against my ankles. Hard to see where I was going. Why had it been so easy for him? No idea how far I traveled down the hallway when I caught movement. I let go a right jab straight from the shoulder. My fist hit glass. I looked at the dusty refection of my face in the glass of a door to a school room. You're letting him get the better of you. Get hold of yourself. Let the police and Marine training take over. You're bigger, better than he is. I headed down the hall.

The sound of laughter came from somewhere ahead of me.

"What depravity we will know this black night. What pain and pleasure in the black hours await us."

I moved further down the hallway, checking recessed doorways. Shadows seemed to dance in each one. Ahead, I made out an alcove, camouflaged in the darkness. I slowed to a more cautious pace. I listened for a sound, a warning, short, quick breaths, footsteps, anything.

"If you're in there, why don't you step out and we'll see about that pleasure."

"Tis now the very witching time of night,
When churchyards yawn
And hell itself breathes out."

He chuckled, it sounded like something small and vicious trying to chew its way out from inside him. A shaft of dim moonlight made its way through a dirty, old-fashioned, casement window. I made out a stairway. It also showed the ghostly outline of a man. I did my best with the poor eyesight offered, and double checked his hands and saw no weapon. My advantage. I edged up and put my foot on the first step.

"How now! A rat?
Dead, for a ducet, dead."

"Christ, Shakespeare wasted on a sick and twisted mind. Have you no shame?" I asked him.

He laughed. "You know Rik, we will make love before you die. My kind of beautiful love. But not here. This place is too nasty for my beautiful love."

He was seven or eight steps up from me. I slowly moved two steps closer. I had nothing else going for me. "I saw Sam today."

He screamed, it sounded like it came from the deepest hellholes of the insane. "My Sam, no, no. Not my beautiful Sam. Sam is mine, mine alone."

"Men have died from time to time, and worms have eaten them, but not for love."

I got a step closer and put my right foot down on the step below me for leverage, pushed off it and lunged at him. He jumped back and let go a drop kick. It was a good one, from a strong leg, catching me right under the chin. It snapped my head back and lifted me off the stairs, sending me backwards. The back of my head landed on something hard and metallic and I entered into a deep, dark cavern of thoughtlessness.

And it no longer mattered anymore what I would lay on.

Chapter Twenty-Six

I woke to whatever twilight state my brain registered as consciousness, and found myself lying at the bottom of a stairway. The senses slowly blossomed into reality as they peaked, steeped in the stench of human waste and rotted food. Picture highlights of last night's encounter with the fag reeled through my mind.

Rats! I could hear them. Has to be hundreds, all over the place, all around me. I found the railing to the stairs and pulled myself up. I shouldn't have. My skull fragmented into large pieces. A flotilla of every color associated with a bomb explosion danced before my eyes. I went to my knees, my stomach convulsed uncontrollably, and I threw up.

Legs unstable, but couldn't stay here. Rats! I shuffled like an old wino without any knowledgeable direction. Broken rays of dusty sunlight made it through dirty window panes. Daylight, Christ! I'd spent the night here. My stomach fought the stench of filth, felt as it coated me.

I stumbled over debris, but refused to fall. By pure chance, I recognized where I'd entered this shithole, and made it outside. The sunlight blinded me. My legs refused to go any further. I leaned against the building and slid down to my buttocks. Time passed without notice until my skull reconstructed itself and I weaved my way home. The few people I passed avoided me, no one asking if I was hurt or needed help.

I should have headed for a hospital, but then I would have to explain what happened and that would bring in the police and Captain Mac. No way Mac would ever hear about last night. I made it to the condo and my cave, where I did the sensible thing. I went to the bar, and poured a drink. Maybe I should have dumped the whiskey and filled the glass with pansies. Beat up by a fag. The clothes hit the garbage and I hit the shower, showering first hot, then cold, for about an hour.

Cleaner and definitely more human, I viewed my reflection in the mirror. A red welt beneath my chin, a half-moon of deep purple forming under the right eye, but detected nothing resembling rodent nibbles. No blood from the bump on the back of my head, but it certainly was noticeable. I did a twice over of my reflection. "You have to get smarter, tougher. Fine tune your reflexes, and fast, Rik."

I dressed, went to the kitchen, and filled two baggies with ice, one for the bump, one for the eye. I noticed Jim, and joined him on the balcony. He was leaning on the railing, looking at the skyscrapers.

"How old this coffee I microwaved?" He didn't wait for an answer. "You have a nice view. All I gets is the bottoms of balconies on the floors above me." He turned, looked at me, concentrated on my face, then returned to looking at the skyscrapers. "You look like shit."

"Thank you. I have a good reason. What's your excuse?"

He breathed deeply. "Nots sure I'se wants to talk 'bout it."

"Then don't."

"Two young guys come look at Joe's place. Dale and Winthrop they's names…"

I interrupted. "Winthrop?"

He shrugged a shoulder. "Everybody's gots to have a name. They come see if they wants to buys his place." He didn't continue.

"So?"

"So's after I shows them everything, they's axt me I want to go out with them. I gots nothing better and say why not." He reflected. "We's hits some bars, have fun. Then they's takes me to a party someone's apartment. Place jumping, sex heavy, but no girls, all guys. Then not sure I having fun no more. Think I shoulda left, things that going on there, but didn't." He said no more, stared at the skyscrapers.

I felt , "And?" might be appropriate, but let it slide.

He turned and looked at my face again. "You have some weird S and M sex with a woman where you face be the sexual object?"

"Car accident."

"Not Baby?"

"Cab. Got tail-ended."

He stared at my face. "Must been some tail. Knock you out the back seat into the dash board?"

"No, I was getting out of the cab. Smashed me into the door and made me fall back onto the cab."

He took another sip of coffee, made a face. "Uh-huh, cab." He looked over my face again. "Uh-huh. Don'ts like you coffee this mornin,' so gonna leave." And like that he was gone.

I went back to the kitchen, listened to the phone ring. It could be Mac, but I doubted it. I gave in on the eighth ring.

"Good morning, Rik. You're alive. Oh, good. For a moment I was afraid I'd killed you. And that would be a shame, you're not yet primed for death." The effeminate, smoky-sounding voice of the gay spoke to me. I started to hang up, but knew he'd just keep calling until I listened to whatever was on his sick mind.

"Why do you hide behind the phone? Why not come out and face me?" I asked.

"Me, the one who's hiding? You're the one hiding. Hiding from life. You're afraid of life, Rik. Now you're hiding behind the police. To be more specific, a Captain Mac. Such foolhardiness. He can't help you."

That hit like an uppercut right below the ribs. Getting my name would be easy, but Mac's? Had they met. Did they know each other?

A belittling laugh. "Gotcha, didn't I? Think of me as a spider, Rik. I collect things in my web; interesting things about you. I am the spider, you are the fly, soon to be entwined in my web. For… forever. Forever."

I rubbed the back of my neck. Head throbbing again, pain shooting from the center of my forehead down to my spine. "I have no idea what you're talking about. Wrong fly, unless you're looking for one big enough to beat the shit out of you."

"Rik, Rik. You have yet to grasp the meaning of all this. We are playing a game. A game of life or death. Your part of the game is to discover who I am. All you have to do is move the chess pieces to the right square. Which will lead you to me before I get to you. Then, it's set, match, checkmate, and you win. Or, if not, you die." A mean, nails across the blackboard, sounding laugh. "But, I can't make it easy for you, or there's no fun involved."

I searched for a really deep-digging comeback, but there's not much you can say when you're standing knee deep in shit and sinking fast.

"Let me make the first move in the chess game," he said. "As I said before, we've met. We are not strangers. You know who I am."

"I meet a lot of people," I answered feebly.

"Not like me, you haven't. No one ever like me."

"How fortunate for me. When do I get the honor of meeting you again?"

He laughed, it was always dirty sounding. "Soon. Sooner, you will find, than you wish it to be." He sighed, as if bored. "I am so clever. It was your lucky game day Rik. LSD Lover, not poison." A dirty little laugh again. "An acid trip for Rik. Unfortunately, it was not a happy one. A night in the hospital. How good for me, how bad for you."

"Fuck you, shit bag." I can always rely on my superior knowledge of the English language coming through for me in crucial moments.

"So crude. Really, for a writer you're originality with words is very limited. You could be dead now. But, do you thank me for letting you live? No. 'Shit bag', you call me. Not nice. Really, Rik."

He giggled like a girl. Enjoying himself way too much, and it was pissing me off. But, I figured he knew that.

Something tickled his fancy and his laughter became uproarious.

"I am so much more clever than you. You really don't stand any chance against me."

My right hand cramped, knuckles white from grasping the phone too hard, for too long. He started humming something in a classical mode, maybe Beethoven. Then in a voice so low I could barely hear it, muttered.

"Poor baby." A dirty laugh. "I scared you shitless. Oh good, goody for me."

There was a long silence, accented by his breathing coming in rapid, deep intakes. I realized he was mimicking my breathing. I picked up the odor of perspiration on my body. Controlling me, he was actually controlling me over the phone.

When he spoke again it came out in a frenzied rage. "But make sure you understand, it could just as well have been poison. The same poison I used on the rat. I want you to feel the terror of not knowing if you're going to die. Of dying like a poisoned rat. Don't forget that feeling." He hung up.

A beeping sound made me realize I was still grasping the phone. A slight tremor moved from my hand up into my arm. My chest cramped from being unable to take in much needed air. Controlling me, on the phone, controlling me. Mac said he would try and control me. Well he'd succeeded, but for the last time. I would find him, and it wouldn't be pretty.

If I ever had a legitimate reason for a drink, it was now. I refused to give him that satisfaction. Besides, while fresh in my mind, I wanted to write down the conversation for Mac. I went to the den.

So, you want to play a game? I obtained a sheet of paper, and I wrote:

GAME
Was he leaving clues to his identity with his phone calls? Beethoven?
HE KNOWS MY NAME:
No real lead, easily accessible
KNOWS I'M A WRITER:
How? I don't even know I'm a writer.
CLAIMS I KNOW HIM:
Pretty vague.
SAFE HAVEN;
Used by him and Mac. Home is a safe haven. Does he believe he has, or can obtain access to my condo?
FLY AND THE SPIDER:
Hopefully, just a metaphor. Scared shitless by those big rat eating ones in Iraq. How would he know that. Jim the only one. Footnote: Jim tell someone?
RAT:
Thinks I'm a rat because I stole his Sam. Knows I'm afraid of them? How? Who knows outside of Mac and Jim?
CHESS:
Why chess? He plays, knows I do? Has played chess with me?

So far, I hadn't accomplished much. Almost as a doodle, I wrote the word OBSSESSION.

The gay hadn't used the word, but Mac had in explaining the drive compelling him. Who do I know showing any traits of obsession toward me, or dealing with anything concerning me? The thing skittering across my consciousness in pieces came together. I knew who was behind the calls. It had been obvious from the very beginning. Too late today to do anything about it, wanted my mind clear. But first thing in the morning, I was going to pay a visit that would make the Gestapo look like choir boys.

Chapter Twenty-Seven

I sipped my coffee. Who the hell gets up at seven o'clock in the morning to do anything? If I had her phone number or knew her last name, I could settle the whole thing over the phone. Thrown off by thinking it was a gay blinded the obvious. If not for the rat in Baby, I would probably still be puzzling over a bunch of maybes.

Take away my friends, and that leaves a very short list of people who know I possess Baby. Take away Jim and Captain Mac, and you have only one other person who is aware of my fear of rats—Connie. On a shortcut through an alley one night, we'd encountered several of them. Still, it was difficult giving her credit for the creativity needed with the notes and phone calls, but in her witless view of things, there was no doubt she felt she had the right to harass my ass off.

She would have no difficulty knowing what she wanted to say. But, putting those feelings into written word was beyond her abilities. She was, however, popular with an eclectic assortment of customers, including two gays, who for whatever reasons, seemed overly fond of her. Both, highly educated, could easily provide the words needed— and would probably get a high out of harassing a straight.

Connie, too weak to stand up to confrontation, would confess all to me. And I wanted to see how well her fag friend talked on the phone when it was shoved up his ass.

Seeing her again didn't leave me overjoyed. But, as they say, "shit happens."

It took a moment to register, a bright, red rose, stuck by its stem, protruded from my mailbox. A message taped to the flower.

EENEY MEENEY

Eeney meeney, meiney mick

You despicable stealing prick.

Watch the shadows when your feet hit the brick.

Someone may be waiting to cut off your dick.

I stuck the note in my shirt pocket, and headed for her place of employment. Somebody was going to eat it. Took the rose, I might compare the two red colors—her two fag's blood and the rose. I was mad, no longer needed my head cleared, and Baby would get me to Connie faster than my feet.

Connie worked at a glorified Greek spoon, called Charlie's. Jim and I gave it a try, but stayed loyal to Gus's. Convenience of location caused us to stop in again and bring Connie into my life. I parked Baby in the free parking lot across from the Goose Island Brewery, and walked the short distance to Charlie's.

Three waitresses were working the spoon, I didn't see Connie. I noticed a washed-out blond of twenty-something, going on forty-something working the counter, and picked a stool in her station. She looked at me with empty eyes. She had nervous fingers and rubbed them over her left ring finger, which no longer sported a ring.

I gave her my cute schoolboy smile. She looked like a woman whose man's good intentions didn't stick around long. I doubted a man had smiled at her without there being a hook involved for quite a while. She accepted mine and laughed with a tingle that surprised her.

"Connie here today?'

Connie's name drew a blank. She shrugged and her eyes showed a tinge of disappointment. "A red rose," she said. "Lucky girl."

"She usually works mornings."

"I'm new here," she said. "The name Connie ring anything with you girls?" she yelled at the other waitresses.

One shook her head, the other shrugged. "Worked with her, didn't know her well. Haven't seen her in a couple of weeks."

The blonde gave me a timid smile. Her eyes a little brighter. "I'll check with the boss."

Her return was quick. "Charlie says she's gone, quit showing up for work and she's done for. Claims he still has her paycheck."

"By chance, does Charlie know where she's working now?"

She went back to Charlie like a good retriever. I could hear him yelling. From the tears swelling up in my retriever's eyes, I figured she was the recipient of the yells. She sniffed and fought back the tears as she returned to her counter. "Says he doesn't know and cares less."

I thanked her for her time, left a dollar tip and the rose. The rose brought a smile and a look asking me to stay. I'd had enough Connies for a lifetime and passed. The last place I wanted to see her was in the apartment. But, I saw little choice. I found a parking spot near her building, happy for Baby that squad cars were roaming the area.

An apartment for rent sign was taped across the glass of the entrance door. Connie's name slot on the directory was blank. I rang her bell anyway. Got no response. Continued finger pressure on it for a while, resulting in a waste of time.

I took a chance and buzzed the apartment next to hers. I was about to give up when I got a response. From the sound of his voice, I'd just awakened some uncivilized member of the male gender.

I told him I was a lawyer, looking for the occupant of apartment 302 so I could deliver an inheritance check. He told me he didn't care who I was or what my problem was, though not exactly in those words. The girl had split and the apartment was vacant. And I should split while he was still in a good mood. I asked him if he knew where she'd gone. He replied he wasn't banging her, so why should he?

I asked if he would mind buzzing me up so I could verify the vacancy. But, apparently my question addressed the speaker box only. I decided against pushing his kindness and tried the other apartments on her floor with no results.

I was slowly losing heart anyway. There'd been a definite demonstration of thought and intelligence behind each call and note. Both of which Connie totally lacked. Also, the stalker was not a well person. Connie was a lot of things, but she was not certifiable. But, I had nothing else. I memorized the phone number of the management company.

I walked across the street and looked up at her windows. On her salary, she wasn't going to find a nicer place to live. I'd expected her place to be decorated in weld wood and chrome. A sofa bought with no money down, and ten dollars for the rest of your life. Instead, I was transported back into the opulence belonging to my grandparent's house.

I entered into a rich and feminine interior, Oriental carpeting covered the living room floor. A large Venetian glass mirror resting over a burl wood Empire cabinet with a bombe' front, caught the reflection of my lust. The room definitely feminine, expensive prints of John Sargent's women watched as I walked by. A showroom, more than a place to enjoy. Shelves congested with Llador porcelain period pieces.

That the decorating taste belonged to someone other than Connie was confirmed as she expressed neither pride nor knowledge of the room. It was just a place to walk through on her way to the bedroom.

I never saw the rest of the apartment. And, to whom the furniture or the taste in decorating belonged to, I never found out. As I said before, she didn't ask me to contribute to the cause, so I let inquiries remain unasked.

The windows were now bare, stripped of the rich cloth that once covered them. The blank windows signaled an emptiness to the insides behind them and an ownership to the for rent sign on the entrance door. Something definitely wasn't right. The emptiness of her apartment came too fast. It hadn't been a month, since I saw Connie. The décor of her place demonstrated not only taste, not mine, but, caring and love. Even if she had been kept, and wasn't anymore, it should still be furnished. Lying in wait to seduce the next inhabitant willing to pay her rent by laying on her back.

I shook my head. Another missing piece in the current mystery puzzle known as my life. I turned to go, taking one more peek at the windows. A shadowy form, only for an instant, caught in one of the windows, stared back at me. At least I thought I saw it, couldn't be certain. It didn't appear again. Sun probably playing tricks with my eyes. Or, maybe my imagination, only something told me it was neither.

I crossed the street and tried Connie's bell again. Pressed the bells of all apartments, using two hands at a time. The building refused to let me enter. I walked to the emergency door, it begrudgingly remained shut. Crossed the street, stood in the shade of a florist's awning, and watched the blank windows. No shadowy forms appeared, no movement in the apartment. No one left the building. Only the sadness of solitude stared back at me from Connie's blank windows.

The air-conditioning in Baby blew my body dry, leaving a pungent odor of tension and perturbation. I pulled her into the garage, patted her, and headed for the elevator.

Where the hell was Connie?

Chapter Twenty-Eight

I called the management company. They had no listing or knowledge of a Connie at the address and apartment number I gave them. The apartment was leased to a man, which didn't surprise me. His name was their business and none of mine, which didn't surprise me either. My theory of Connie as my stalker faded fast. The caller exhibited an intelligence totally lacking in her, and from what I'd observed, that of her devoted fags.

I was on the verge of giving up. I didn't have enough for a judge to give Captain Mac a search warrant for the apartment. The morning, so far, proved completely unsatisfactory. Nor could I conjure any way to try and upgrade it. So I spent the day nursing my bruises and the bump and went through the motions of trying to write. My perspicuity seemed lethargic at best. The phone rang. I hesitated, picked it up.

"Anything?" Mac's gravely voice asked.

"Just the gay calling to let me know he put the LSD on the letter. Otherwise it's been pretty quiet. Can you just put LSD on paper?"

"Yeah, doesn't take much. Just enough to go through the pores of your skin. Anything else?"

"Not really."

"Good," he was gone.

Connie and her apartment kept borrowing my brain to play with . A man's name was on the lease, yet none of the decorating showed a man's touch. The design totally feminine, meant to bathe a woman in elegance. Obviously, nothing that beat Connie's drum. But then, she may not have been the first female occupant. And if she was being kept, he was doing a half-ass job. She still worked. The whole picture presented a maze with too many dead ends for my addled brain to absorb today.

The pool was mine alone. I claimed a chaise lounge, and dove into the pool. The water too warm to give that instant shock of temperature change to the skin and exhilarate the heart to pump life into the body, but it soothed my jarred nerves. I did eight laps and got out before fatigue caused me to drown, and collapsed on my chaise.

Margo stood on tiptoe smelling one of Jim's roses, a picture worth filing in the album of my mind. Renaldo must be home. She wore a one piece swimsuit, though cut high on the hip. She ambled over to me. The fluid movement of her body accented every curve. Damn, she could boil a man's hormones.

My mind was still contending with rats and faceless gays. I wasn't sure I wanted company. I had no choice. She settled down on the edge of my chaise. I smiled; she didn't. Her eyes fixed on the blood red rose in her hand. Her lower lip protruded in a pout. The melancholy of it matched the sadness in her eyes. She offered me the rose.

"Beauty has no space in my life today," she said.

I took the rose. "You know messing with his roses is reason enough for Jim to kill?"

"It was hurting, its stem was broken. I put it out of its misery, Jim won't be mad as long as I was the one who did it." She fixed her sad-looking eyes on me. "I wish someone would put me out of my misery."

My shoulders were far from pillars to lean on today, but she wasn't providing any options. "Anything you want to talk about?"

She looked down at the space between her feet. "No, but I need to."

She didn't continue, probably a clue I was supposed to say something. "Think you can discuss it with me?"

She took a moment. "When men look at me," she paused, stared at her hands. "Do…do all they see is some sort of sex object?"

Hell of a question. "I doubt they can picture you as a nun." Wrong answer, her lower lip protruded further. I tried again. "No, not all men. Especially those of us who really know and care for you." That made absolutely no sense to me. If it didn't to Margo, she didn't let on.

"I think it's a very small group that don't picture me naked." Her eyes grew moist. "Sometimes men make me feel dirty. I can put up with that, but not when they try to make me feel like filth. Like Joe made me feel."

I hadn't gone to her with words of comfort or arms open to sympathy over the whole Joe situation. Whether she was sincerely filled with doubt about herself, or just trying to make me feel guilty, I had no way of knowing.

"Joe was an asshole," I assured her. "Most men are assholes when it comes to women. You can't judge yourself by the thoughts of assholes."

"Why not?" she asked.

Come on! I was short on adjectives today. "You have much to offer a man. Don't lower yourself by the thoughts of throwbacks."

She thought on that for a short period. "Then my only gift must be to turn men into animals. Joe was a gentle person. And…and he was one of us."

Not exactly..

"Look what he tried to do to me." She lowered her head, when she lifted it, tears showed. "Did Joe die because of me?"

A definitely maybe, depending on how pissed-off Jim might have been. After you told him. I reached over and gave her a hug, awkward from my position, not much of a hug.

"I could have gotten that from my brother. What I don't need today is another brother."

`"What exactly do you want me to be?"

"Why should you have to ask?"

I played dumb. It didn't take much effort. My lounge was going co-op whether I wished it to be or not. She rested her head on my neck, cuddled me. I decided a little space between us might not be a bad idea, she didn't agree. A leg wrapped around mine, a thigh located my crotch, nails traced my back as an arm pressed against my stomach, breasts warmed my chest.

"It's okay," she said. "Friends can do this. Just let your mind think of us as friends."

Easy for her to say, it wasn't my mind I was worried about. I laced my fingers through her hair to keep my free hand from getting any ideas, attempted pure thoughts. The wind blew, the silkiness of her hair spread like a spider's web, entangling my fingers in it. A web meaning forever, if I didn't get her off me, free my hand. I pushed away from her, almost tipping over the chaise.

Her eyes grew wide. "Rik! What happened, what's the matter?"

"Arm. It fell asleep."

"What? Your arm fell asleep? YOUR ARM FELL ASLEEP!"

I had no capacity for explanations. No room for her temper tantrums that most likely would soon arrive—I needed air, bad, lots of air. Without looking at her, I walked away, she called after me, I didn't respond. I was sweating profusely, not from Margo's passion, not from the sun. From almost being forever.

Jim was seated at my bar, sucking on a beer. I didn't acknowledge him, went to the bathroom and sponged off the perspiration, lowered my head beneath the faucet and let cold water run off the back of my head. I discovered an old Marine t-shirt on the closet floor and started to put it on, stopped, and let it reside in the closet again. I had no right to wear it.

"Semper Fi, to you too, jerk-off. Big, macho Marine, held captive in his own home by a faggot. What would John Wayne think?"

Jim was still at the bar. He looked put out and ornery. He gave me silence and a glare.

"I'm thinking something stronger than a beer. What you thinking?"

"Margo is still a little girl, Rik."

I poured a scotch. "Don't know as I would go that far. Thought you wanted me to knock her up so you could be an uncle?"

His sigh was leonine. "She a child, and she a innocent…"

"I might go the young bit," I interrupted.

Jim continued. "….'sperminting with womanhood."

And doing a fine job with her experimenting. "So, what's your point?"

"Next time you help her 'spermint, don't do it so all can see."

"I take it we're talking about the pool?"

"Damn right." He was working into a good one. Jaw muscles pumping, scar crimson. "Margo ain't one you barfly cunts. She ain't to be used as a relief station." He slammed his fists down on the bar top. "Quit playing with the child. Commit or leave her alone. And I ain't waiting long for you to commit. Don't mess her, Rik," fist hard on the bar top. "Or I mess you…real bad." He left.

****

Life can take a lot of turns, normally ending up joyous, or sad, or just plain confused. Mine was so disconnected, it didn't belong to any of the above. The elevator doors opened to the garage. Not entirely certain what brought me down here, except this is where the intrusion by the gay started. Maybe the missing pieces of my life could be found here.

No footsteps, a muffled sound of a television, tiny creaks of the building still settling, water running down pipes, the hum of a ventilating system, everything but my life coming together—no footsteps. "How did he get in here?"

I walked over, patted Baby, checked first, no surprises, and climbed in. The world made sense inside Baby, as it used to when I was still young and full of wonder, filled with promise and a future. Before the real world scarred me, leaving nothing but cold and emptiness. I left Baby, faced the garage. No way he got in here without help. Listened—no footsteps, no rat, but they had existed, here, in the garage, no matter what Jim said.

They'd been as real as the question—why?

Chapter Twenty-Nine

I thumbed through my clothes, not certain what casual meant to Laura. I decided on tan slacks, loafers, recently shined, no socks, and a chocolate colored knit shirt would have to suffice and found myself taking extra time primping for tonight. An exercise in futility, although highly amusing. I checked the damage to my face. Everything had faded to almost skin color, the bump on the back of head only evident if she planned on running her fingers through my hair. When finished, I had to admit the product looking out at me from the mirror allowed me to do a little cock-walking in front of the lady.

For me, dating is a barbaric social custom, sort of a department store for human beings. I definitely have become a fan of the fast in and out method of meeting women. Now, all the excitement of the first boyhood date came back. I felt like asking myself if I could borrow the car. I re-checked my deodorant and left.

I took the chance of beating a ticket and parked in front of her building. Somewhere in the short walk to the elevator, I gathered a fluttering of nerves. So far, Jim was wrong, she didn't leave me feeling outclassed. I smiled at my teenage first date syndrome.

Laura was waiting when I arrived. Her dress was hot to look at, but stated cool and comfortable for the ninety- plus Chicago heat. A simple, oatmeal colored, tank dress showed her curves and stopped two inches above the knees. I liked it and it apparently showed. She smiled in appreciation, but still kept me out of peeping distance of her apartment.

"Wow."

She smiled. It highlighted the soft, liquid brown of her doe eyes, and my nerves came to rest under their gaze. To my disappointment, she didn't invite me in. Later. She took my arm.

"The movie, Fatal Attraction okay? It's supposed to be fantastic.

When I was a kid, Captain Mac took me to see every John Wayne western. He always said the same thing after every movie, "That's when the law of the land meant something." I grew to idolize the image the man projected on the screen. When he died, so did my going to the movies, and I predicted the decline of America with his demise. I figured I was about to be tortured with a chick flick.

Laura checked out the inside of my car. "I don't think I've ever seen a car like this."

"She's an oldie but goodie. Baby's a 1968 AMX. My grandfather collected muscle cars. He bought Baby and stored her to be mine upon my return from the Iraq war."

She tilted her head, her eyes smiling at me. "Baby?"

I'm sure I blushed. "A boy and their toys," I answered, and attempted a manly laugh.

She ran a finger over the dash. "No, you're not a boy and she's not a toy. I could tell by the inflection in your voice that she holds a special meaning for you. It must be nice having something special in your life."

I questioned her with my eyes. "You don't?"

She took a moment. "Not at the moment. I guess I've let business get in the way." She paused. "Maybe my books. I love my books." She colored slightly.

"Fatal Attraction" was not a chick flick. It presented a psycho chick who thought a cheating husband belonged only to her. She threatened not only him, but his family. It really didn't fit into my current situation, but caused the hairs on my arms to do the rumba. I did notice quite a few nervous spouses. So did Laura, as she commented after the show.

"Boy, did that movie make some men squirm?" She laughed. I didn't.

We ended up at Gino's East for deep dish pizza. I ordered a red wine with no idea of its quality. The waiter seemed impressed with my selection though. But then, it was probably his job to look impressed if I'd ordered vinegar. The candlelight played off the radiance of her hair, the flickering of the candle flame highlighting the beauty of her facial features.

She caught my gaze and smiled softly. I felt something like a slow possession taking over parts of me that had forgotten how to feel, I became suddenly and strangely alive. Whoa Tonto, we're galloping into unknown terrain here. The lady is supposed to be a conquest, nothing more.

The conversation in Baby on the way to the movie flowed easily, Laura confiding anecdotes of her day with customers. I figured my episodes with a gay stalker wouldn't turn her on, so I fabricated working on a new chapter to my novel. Laura kept the conversation flowing at our table.

She asked what I would have been if not a writer. That was stump city, I wrote for two reasons. I hated honest work, and had little talent for any other endeavor. "Maybe the guy that rides the caboose of a train."

That tickled her. "I don't think they have cabooses anymore."

"Then I'd better stick to writing."

"Having the talent to write always fascinated me because I love reading so much," she said.

The classics still filled most of her time, although there were some new women mystery writers she was getting into. Arts and psychology captured her moments with non-fiction. She lowered her eyes, a slight hint of blush on the cheeks.

"But, I have to admit my favorite thing is to curl up with tales of gnomes, magical trolls, wizards, and chivalrous knights. My volumes of Tolkien, Morte D' Arthur, Mabinoqion and, of course Mary Stewart's works on Merlin and Mordred are well worn."

I smiled with her. "Yes, the world of magical dragons and brave knights is easy to escape into."

She laughed. It was at herself. "It lies deeper than that. I was taught to believe." She tilted her head and laughed again. "Not in dragons, but chivalrous knights."

I wondered if some of her beauty lay in the fact that part of her still lived in the world of fantasy, and if so, how my mutilated view of reality would fit in. I took her to a hideaway near the magnificent mile called the Clusters. It's a restaurant/bar place that still enjoys the flavor of being for, and belonging to Chicagoans. The English character of the courtyard welcomes you with a small dance floor and the piano artistry of an old friend, Mark Nicholls, is the main attraction.

We lucked-out and sat at the piano, and I introduced Laura to Mark. He engaged her in that trivial, flattering talk club entertainers have as part of their repertoire. He then dedicated a soft rendition of the song "Laura" to her. She shyly acknowledged his selection. It was nice flattery, but her reaction showed it wasn't the first time it had been done. Mark had a whiskey voice and his fingers continued to waltz over the keyboard as he came on to Laura. And friend or no friend, he was coming on a little too heavy.

I decided this was a good time for Laura and me to try the dance floor, but I never got the chance to ask her. Mark started playing some melody with sugar- dripping lyrics about misty roses. A low "Ooh," emitted from Laura. Her eyes took on a dreamlike quality, and she raised her head slightly as she touched my arm. I looked into eyes focused on another time, a passed caress. A passion I could only imagine. The green tentacles of jealousy wrapped around me.

She slid off the bar stool and held her hand out to me. I took it and guided her to the dance floor. She came into my arms as though molded to fit into them with a warmth that penetrated my shirt. I had no idea who she was dancing with at the moment, but I intended to enjoy the benefit of the rapture within her and make it belong to me before the night was over.

The beauty of the moment lingered long after the last refrain, and we circled the floor as the song faded into silence. She turned to be led back to the piano, I pulled her back into my arms. Mark took the hint and played something as syrupy as the last song. This time she danced with me.

She let me know it was time to go. "I'm glad we stopped here, it made the last minutes before the bewitching hour enchanting."

"No," I said. "Anything but the dreaded bewitching hour."

"Unfortunately, tonight yes. Tomorrow's a busy day, and I can be as distasteful as the sisters ugly when faced without enough sleep to function at work."

Leaving here was fine with me. I was ready to be introduced to the inside of Laura's apartment. Mark performed his rendition of "Fly Me To The Moon," as we left. She leaned over and gave me a light kiss. I wanted to taste her fully, but it had been a kiss of appreciation not an invitation. Hope still lay at her apartment.

We arrived at her building, and eventually her floor, and apartment door. For a moment, I thought my teenage syndrome hit me again. Then I realized it wasn't a syndrome, I honestly didn't know how to play this lady. Right now, I was out of my league. I decided to see if her actions would give me a clue. They didn't.

She found her door keys and looked up at me. I couldn't tell by her eyes if I was receiving an invitation or not. "This is always the awkward moment after a first date, isn't it?"

Not usually with me. But then, I'm not usually with someone like you.

She smiled. "No lines, no moves to get into my apartment?"

I smiled back. "Unfortunately, nothing that would be new or clever to you, or particularly charming."

She tilted her head and looked up at me.

"Disappointed?" I asked.

She leaned against her door and reached for my hands. "On the contrary. You have no idea how refreshing a change this is."

Maybe for her. She looked more radiant now than earlier. I wanted to reach out and capture her in my arms. But, I also didn't want to destroy any chance for later. She made my decision for me.

"Would you like to kiss me?" she asked.

"I thought you'd never ask."

"Then please do," she said.

Her kiss was warm, her lips full, sensual. I put my arms around her. She responded for a moment, then slowly pulled away.

"I'm sorry, Rik. But, I think it best if I go in."

I looked into her doe eyes. "Don't be. I think I understand." Jeez, what a bunch of crap that was. I didn't understand at all. And my manhood was screaming for completion.

"Thank you, Rik." She stood on tiptoe and gave me a quick, but warm kiss. "I'm sorry, if I disappointed you." She stepped backward. I reached out for her. She came back into my arms. Her face said she was fighting her emotions. Indecisive how to handle them, I made her decision for her.

"May I see you tomorrow?"

She inhaled deeply. "No, sorry, dining with clients tomorrow night." She looked up at me, then down at her hands. "I was hoping though you would be free Friday night to escort me to the opera."

That was like a fastball to the mouth. The Opera?

She gave me a coquettish smile. "It's opening night at the Lyric Opera House. "Barber of Seville." If you don't take all the pomp and circumstance in the lobby seriously, it can be a lot of fun." Her eyes played little girl "please" with me. "Have you ever been to the opera?"

I was still recovering from the initial onslaught of going to the opera. It took a minute. "When a boy, my grandparents took me there. I liked the grandeur, but didn't like not being able to understand what they were singing."

She put her hands on my chest. "Now they flash English across the top of the stage."

"Opera for idiots?"

She laughed, all honey. "You're not an idiot. Most of the people attending have no idea what the words mean. It's opening night, anybody who's anybody, or thinks they're anybody, is forced to attend."

"Is that why you're going?"

"No, I love the opera. But yes, even if I didn't, I'd be forced to go. Lawrence's token showpiece." She stood on tiptoe and gave me a quick, but warm kiss. "Please, will you accompany me to the opera?"

I would accompany her to an afternoon of chamber music in Hell. "Yes."

She placed her forefinger and middle finger to her lips, kissed them, and placed them on my lips. "It's a black-tie affair. Pick me up by six o'clock?" She offered a look that stated perhaps the inside of her apartment wasn't off limits tonight. Then as my knees became dispersive, she disappeared behind her door.

    I stood for a while and stared at the door. Much of the last two days were spent in erotic fantasies of climaxing the evening in Laura's bed. Instead it ended with three kisses, none of them my doing. All that fantasy, and all that waited for me tonight, was Ms. Rosie Palm. I smiled. I'd just met a girl who wasn't more anxious than I to get her pants off. And, I was all turned-on about it. "What the hell is happening to you, Rik Burns," I asked myself.

    The Opera?

    I headed for McCabe's.

Chapter Thirty

Bobby's was crowded. I grabbed a barstool away from the action. Bobby looked at the clock, looked at me, checked the clock again, then made his way over.

"Thought you had a hot one tonight?"

"Claimed who?"

"Jim. Said you been in heat since you met her."

"I had a date."

Bobby looked at the clock again. "Then either you played minute man or you cherried. He wiped the bar and stared at me. His eyes began to sparkle and his cheeks grew red. "You cherried!" He burst out in uproarious laughter. "Jesus B., you virgined out. All loaded up and no place to pee." His eyes watered and he bent over with laughter. He sucked in air and tried to gain control. "Ho-haw! Lardy, this has to be a first."

By now we'd picked up the curiosity of most of the bar.

"You decide to change professions and become the town crier, or can I still get a drink in here?"

Bobby inhaled and tried to control his laughter, couldn't stop one last burst. He poured me a shot of malt liquor, backed up by a Heineken's.

"The malt's on me. It will help curtail your juices from backing up to your gizzard." He thought that was funny, and again let go with uncontrolled laughter. "Sorry.' He left to take care of some customers. I took care of the malt.

He returned, resting elbows on the bar. He gave me a serious stare before his face wrinkled in a full grin. "So, tell me, what's the story on this new talent?"

I returned his grin. "Not sure yet, but I sure like the prose.

Bobby smiled with the knowledge of a man who'd been there. "Got yourself a lady, huh? Hard to find that kind anymore." He refilled my glass, took a look at the bottle. "Why not? Been a long day," and filled a shot glass. "If I remember correctly —a lady— they're the most dangerous. A good broad, now there's a different story. They know how to keep your ass pleased and walk away without leaving a rash on it." He stopped and seemed for a moment in memory. "Now a lady... they have a way of getting under your skin and can cause an awful, incurable itch." He raised his glass. "Here's to ladies and here's to poison. One as dangerous as the other."

I figured I could drink to that. I had another beer, played gentleman and escorted a local, over-indulged, bar chippie to her apartment on Wieland Street. Summer rain clouds shadowed the moon and put too heavy a burden on the two street lights on Wieland to illuminate the neighborhood. The distinctive outline of gabled porches and roof cornices stood out from the Victorian style houses, set away from the street lights, and shadowed by the dusky darkness, leaving a serenity hinged on the poetic.

Where the hell did that come from? Perhaps because the whole street scene played with one's mind, induced one's imagination to wander. And mine did, only not in poetic avenues, in capturing sounds, like footsteps. Coming from no definitive direction, causing me to turn, circle.

Footsteps—first behind me— then possibly across the street—now, somewhere in front of me, and then they would go away. Quiet now, too much.

Close, definitely from behind me, the silence broken by the sound of footsteps. I slowed my pace, so did they—I stopped, so did they. I spun around, nothing. I closed my mind to the familiar, synchronized it for the unexpected. Again quiet, I waited, only silence, I moved slowly ahead. Movement across the street, between two houses, caught in the shadows, the outline of a man.

He appeared slight of frame, five-eight or nine. I didn't need to see him, I knew who he was. He moved toward me. If nothing else, I had to respect the little shit had one set of cahones. It left me feeling a bit uncertain.

He stayed out of the light, slowly walking toward me. What was the game tonight? I waited, let him come to me. He took his sweet time. Stopped, leaving about twenty feet between us. Something warned me closing the distance wouldn't be a smart idea. Shadows hid his facial features, so I couldn't read his face. Adrenalin pulsated through me. Felt the light chill of the primal instincts of the hunter and the hunted.

"I have so much pain, Rik," he said. "I can't stand the pain much longer."

I let go a breath I didn't know I was holding. "I'm so sorry to hear that. I may not be able to sleep tonight."

He let out a cold sounding laugh. "Don't worry, Rik. I just might enable you to sleep like a baby forever."

I never saw the move. It was slick, fast, and practiced. A gun pointed from his right hand. He didn't say anything, just stared. I sure as hell had nothing clever to say. What the hell? The freak was going to shoot me. Right here, just like that, shoot me. What kind of a game is that?

It wasn't supposed to play this way. The upper hand should belong to me, or at least the odds stacked better than Vegas. But, they weren't, and I had some fast thinking to do. I saw a muzzle flash and a bullet came close to grazing my left ear, slamming into a tree behind me. Christ! The little shit wasn't even going to give me time to think. Not that I had any idea on the subject anyway.

"Yes, beautiful. A beautiful night to explore the splendor of death. Don't you agree?" he asked, through a chuckle.

He lowered the gun. I did what Captain Mac instructed me to do. "When you have no other alternative son, you run."

The houses in Wrigleyville, as this area of Chicago is called, are built on postage stamp lots, almost one on top of the other. A concrete walkway, approximately a person and a half in width, separates the buildings. Any walkway became my destination.

The gay laughed. Actually it sounded more like the excited giggle of a girl anticipating her first experience with foreplay. Shit-for-brains. Did you expect him to go up against you without the advantage being on his side? Size equals size when one man has a gun and the other doesn't.

The houses were dark, asleep. His gun only produced a pop sound when fired, not loud enough to disturb anyone. I gauged his weapon to be a .25 automatic. Deadly at close range, losing accuracy at a distance. I put distance between us, hoping he was a bad shot.

"Death on your mind tonight, Rik? It should be," he called after me.

I kept expecting the searing heat of a bullet ramming into my back. It didn't come. Only his laughter chasing my heels.

It's two steps down from the front of the houses to the walkways. My left foot caught the edge of the bottom step, enough to twist me off balance introducing my mid-section to the walkway. At least my face escaped punishment, not so lucky for my cock-walking pants, I could feel a wide tear to the left knee. Shit, I was going to be shot in the back on somebody's walkway. Left for dead so feral cats could piss on me.

The walkway led to an alley in back of the shops on Wells. No idea how close the gay was. I picked myself up and ran. A bullet ricocheted off my right rib cage. Fortunately a small caliber bullet, it just burned eliciting no damage. I continued running. His laughter followed.

What the hell was his game tonight? He said I wasn't ready to die. Obviously, he must have changed his mind. A four-foot high cyclone fence faced me a few feet away. I slowed my pace, grabbed the top of the fence, high kicked and vaulted over it. Just like the old days in Marine boot camp. Only my back, not my feet, greeted the alley, thanking me with the agony of convulsions from my stomach trying to consume air, and a cloddish attempt at running.

I found a doorway covered by shadows. Not deep enough to conceal me, but it gave me something to lean on and suck in some badly needed air. I tried figuring my next move. So far, figuring hadn't been too successful. I could only hope he was a very bad shot. What did he want? To corner me, try and make me beg? I looked for any sign of life in the houses, giving me a place to run to. If anyone had seen the incident or heard the shots, they were not about to get involved. I was on my own.

Where is the little shit?

Basically, I faced the old six-of-one distance wise to McCabe's or my condo. Even in the shadows, I was open game. Where is the little shit? Hiding? Waiting? Has to be waiting somewhere. Where?

I was easy meat standing here. Not much difference in whatever direction I took. McCabe's should be closed by now. I headed for the condo. At first I took it slow, hoping to see him before he saw me. And if you do, then what asshole, yell 'ole, ole, ocean free?" He has the gun. You're a rotating duck at a carnival rifle shoot. I took off in a zig zagging run. Where is the little shit?

No matter how fast I tried to run, my legs felt weighted, my pace agonizingly slow. The length of the alley increasing with each step as the condo moved farther and farther away. The pounding of my heart was so loud, I couldn't hear myself think. When's the last time you did that, Rik? Sure he could hear the beat, beat, and follow its sound.

There are two kinds of sweat. One is honest sweat, the hard work kind. It cleans the pores, is acceptable. The other is stench, and comes from the armpits. It's caused by fear. Mine was a stench. It would linger. Everyone would know I was afraid when I died. Faggot scared him to death before he shot him.

Can't see him, did he pick McCabe's to wait for me? Doubted it. My luck wasn't running that way tonight. I leaned against the building and tried to control my breathing so I could pick up sounds of his presence. Nothing. Quiet. A bullet hit about a quarter of an inch from my left foot and skipped down the alley.

Get going feet. I flew down toward the end of the alley where it turned onto Wells Street and my condo. Remains of the alley brightly lit from street lights. If he was near, I should be able to see him. No freak, just the shadow of a hand with a gun pointed at me. A bullet hit the pavement directly behind me. I instinctively dove for a wall and kissed pavement. His laughter felt like shards of broken glass on a bareback. Gonna get up and beat the shit out of the little fucker. Who was I kidding? I was in a frigging alley, flat on my face. There was no, "From The Halls of Montezuma," music playing in the background, no John Wayne to lead me to safety. No native girl with long legs waiting behind a palm tree to caress my crippled body.

I was in an alley being shot at by a fag. John Wayne wouldn't even spit on me. I stood, a little late, but time to show some manliness. If he wanted me dead, I would have been so already. What the hell was the game? Wells Street was deserted, empty, like I felt. My pride badly bruised, maybe even bleeding. And while I was not entirely broken, I was bent pretty bad. So, I ate shit, tucked my tail between my legs, and humbly walked to my condo. I could hear his laughter.

I didn't exactly walk backwards to the condo, but I didn't turn my back to the possibility of his presence either.

Macho Rik.

I called Captain Mac.

Chapter Thirty-One

A shattered self-image and a bottle of scotch is not a good combination. So, I settled for a microwaved cup of stale coffee and the kitchen booth. The coffee tasted as bitter as my deflated self-esteem. Even if he was the worst shot in the world, he couldn't have missed me in the alley. So, he had to be so good he could miss me. But why? The total picture of the purpose of tonight remained a negative to me. I did know a complete reassessment of my life as it stands at present, was in order. I'd definitely underestimated the madness and ability of the gay, and obviously, the seriousness of my situation.

I finished the coffee and waited for the phone call. I let it ring ten times just to aggravate the little freak.

"You're a bad shot."

"On the contrary, I'm an excellent marksman. Was tonight as good for you as it was for me?" He giggled.

One shot, just one shot to his mouth. That wasn't much to ask. Then if he got up he could have his due. He was inflaming open wounds, but after my performance tonight, it would be a little pretentious to try and flaunt my manhood.

"You're not very smart you know?"

He had me on that one too.

"The expression on your face. You have no idea the pleasure the memories of it will bring." He paused. "A question. Have you lost the desire to fight, the valor to take a bullet? I mean, it's your life. Do you always intend to run away from it, rather than to stand up for it?"

"Life must be one big pisshole for you," I said."

"Speaking of life, have you realized yet how meaningless yours is?"

He had me again. "Does this phone call have a point?"

"Did it ever occur to you I may be your best friend?"

"Not lately."

"Think about it, Rik. Can you think of anyone but me who'd really miss you after you're dead?"

I would have liked to have bored him with fifteen or twenty names, but I couldn't think of one. "What's your name, best friend?"

"Name, name. What's in a name? Besides, that's the problem. You should know my name by now." He hung up.

I went to bed.

****

Mac stated I was to be at Gus's by seven-thirty Thursday morning. I worked on how to present last night to him. No matter, I would probably get a heated lecture on my actions from him either way. Mac occupied his usual corner booth, his back to the wall. No law enforcement officer likes to sit with their back to the door. He motioned for me to join him.

He was working on his usual breakfast fare, ham steak, three sunny side eggs, yolks runny and crisp hash browns. He ate from memory, eyes never straying from the door or patrons. I ordered two slices of Gus's homemade Greek bread, toasted, and coffee. Mac had yet to speak, and I was not quite ready to volunteer. His beverage this morning was tea, Boston style; a taste he'd acquired from my grandfather. He took a sip, added a half-spoonful of sugar, stirred and eyed me hard.

"It never fails to amaze me the atrocities humans can think of to perpetrate on their fellow man," he said. "I do believe that over the years I have witnessed just about all of them."

He paused, tasted his tea and gave a low, "umm," satisfied he'd achieved the right mixture of cream and sugar to tea. "So," he continued. "You would think by now that I would be used to anything the city streets dish up."

It took a moment for me to realize he'd stopped talking, and was waiting for a comment. I nodded agreement. "One would think," I said.

"Well, I have," he proclaimed. "It's the eyes. Sometimes I can't help it.

The victim's eyes get to me."

I nodded once again.

"Another corpse was discovered in a garbage bin this morning. On Belmont. Not far from the station. Like whoever is doing it, is throwing it in our faces. Second one this week." Mac stopped and smiled. "The rookie who found him heaved all over himself." Mac laughed. "I remember my first corpse."

Mac finished his tea, refilled his cup, and went through the cream and sugar ritual again. "First murder victim was about a month ago. Didn't get much play in the papers.

But, now two in one week. All three in different locations, but all in my district. What a bitch. Media's gonna have a field day with this shit." His attention went to someone who just entered Gus's. Whoever it was didn't keep his interest long.

"All the same M.O.," he said. "Lays them nude in the garbage bin. Face up. Lower legs propped over the end so they're certain to be discovered. We figure it's some kind of ritualistic message to someone, only we have no idea what the message is, or who it's directed to." He sighed and stirred his tea.

"All three cases, nice good-looking young men, early twenties. Fresh killings.

Blood not dried yet. Their right hand holding their severed genitals. I mean everything—penis and balls."

He sliced a bite of ham, portioned the right amount of yolk and runny white of egg on top of it. Added some hash browns, dipped them in a dab of ketchup and chewed contentedly.

"Shoots them in the stomach. Uses a small caliber weapon." He gave me an intense stare. "You know what a gut shot is like, Rik?"

It really wasn't a question. He was going to tell me whether I knew or not.

You don't die right away. You writhe in pain while your cavities fill up with blood. Actually, you don't die from the bullet wound, you choke to death on your blood." He let that set in. "Of course, we figure he shoots them first; can't imagine anyone lying still while a guy cuts their dick off. Then he bathes them. Can you imagine that?"

I noted I couldn't.

"He bathes them with some heavy-scented soap. Smells like some kind of flower. Corpse smells real good. Even after lying in garbage crap. What kind of nut gets his jollies of doing shit like that?"

"Not my expertise, Mac." I remembered my coffee and toast. Neither one appeared appetizing at the moment.

Mac finished his breakfast, pushed his plate aside and worked on Gus's toast. Dipping about an inch in his tea and biting off about two. "Sperm found in the victims anal orifices points to the same person in all three cases. No sign of a struggle during sex, although he did ream the boys pretty good."

He sat and stared absently for a moment. "Their eyes, Rik. Young men, their eyes talking to me of their terror. Pleading to me to stop it." His fist came silently down on the table top. "And I'll be damned if I can answer them."

"You'll find him, Mac."

He didn't acknowledge me, kept his attention focused on the door. "So, what's the story on your gay stalker chasing you with a gun?"

"Yeah, he shot me last night."

Mac pulled out a cigar and chewed heavily on it. "You don't look shot."

"He missed me on purpose."

He took the cigar out of his mouth and studied it. "You want to explain that?"

I recounted last night's events and the gay's phone call. Mac chewed a little heavier on his cigar. His eyes green ice as they concentrated on my face.

"Didn't you tell me the gay threatened to kill you?"

I wasn't fast enough with my answer.

"Didn't you?" he repeated.

"Yeah, I did, but, I wasn't expecting a gun."

"What did you think he had in mind, beating you to death with his purse?" His eyes remained stone cold. "You got shit for brains. Doing everything, reacting, just the way he wants you to. All the things you promised me you wouldn't do."

I shrugged. Mac didn't leave me much to respond with.

"When's the first time you noticed this fag?"

"At Joe's funeral." I recounted, to the best of my memory.

"Joe? The guy from your condo? Died in your garage a few weeks back?"

I nodded.

"Yeah, now I remember. Coroner couldn't figure how the broken neck fit in." Mac stared at me through half-closed lids. "By chance, you wouldn't have any idea?"

I did my best to hide any suspicion I might have. "Why should I."

Mac grinned. "Yeah why should you? This Joe, he gay?"

"How would I know. He never approached me if he was, but I had my suspicions. Why?"

"Later. You like him, pal around with him?"

"More like Jim and I tolerated him. He buddied more with Renaldo."

"Yeah," he said. "I can see him and Renaldo being buddies. Come on, we're going to my station."

I studied his face. "Why?"

"You'll find out."

Chapter Thirty-Two

I followed in Baby. Mac waited impatiently for me. Mac's place of employment, Area Six, was located off Western Avenue at 2452 W. Belmont. Another Chicago neighborhood changing for the worse, currently offering a mixture of every nationality and race available, along with every crime known and possibly unknown to law enforcement agencies.

Nobody really wanted this precinct. Mac once told me his promotion to Captain wasn't as much a promotion as a sentence to Hell for being Scottish in an Irish-dominated police department. His jailhouse isn't the most depressing institution housed in Chicago. A one-story edifice, cheery on the outside, modern, clean and efficient on the inside, it beats the other police stations to hell in appearance. Mac hated it.

Police stations were supposed to be housed in old, two-story brick buildings with tortured wooden floors and steps. Banisters polished over the years by sweat from palms reaching out for support. The monotonous Army green walls forever scented with the coppery odor of blood. And of course, the ever present gnarled desk sergeant, cold to the needs of anyone but himself. At least, that was Mac's ideal police station.

At Area Six, police activity was partitioned off from the public. Criminals escorted through back doors only. Metal rooms manned by women in civilian clothes, protected by bulletproof windows. A receptionist asked what you wanted, then took her sweet time in directing you on procedure.

Mac led me through a secretarial pool to his office, oblivious to the few women who dared look up at him. He pointed to a chair in front of his desk, I sat. He settled into his high back, black leather chair and sifted through some reports on his desk. He deposited what remained of his battered cigar in an ashtray, located a pair of eyeglasses in a desk drawer along with gum. He popped two pieces in his mouth. I wasn't offered any.

Mac's office was spacious. Photographs on the wall behind his desk depicted his history as a cop. The other walls were bare. His desk scarred and battered, a remembrance piece from a station long torn down. A cheap green vase with four daisies protruding from it, slowly withering away, captured a corner of the desk. Front center, a brass nameplate engraved with:

        Angus I. MacDonald
           CAPTAIN

I had no idea what the 'I.' stood for, but I did know I'd never met anyone brave enough to call him Angus --outside of my grandmother.

"So far, this has been hilarious, you got more fun lined up?" I asked.

He gave me a stare that stated if I wanted to walk out of here with my balls in place, shut up and sit until he told me not to.

"So, the only description you have of this fag of yours is he dresses all in blue and has a pencil thin moustache."

I nodded.

"Then forget the mug book."

He fooled around with some papers on the top of his desk and then peered at me over the top of his glasses. "Before I get into why you're here, I need to know something straight out. " None of your bullshit." He took his glasses off and concentrated on my eyes. "Just what is Baby to you?"

"What? What does that have to do with anything? Besides, that's personal."

"Not today. It may be more important than you realize. When I took you to where Baby was stored, you reached out for her like she was a living being. Shed some tears." Mac's eyes said, talk.

I sighed, hesitated, but knew I had no choice. "When I came home from Iraq, the world glasses the one I'd left. It was a stranger to me, and I to it." I played with my sunglasses, wished for scotch. "My grandparents were dead. Strangers lived in the home I grew up in. I had nothing and no one, until you took me to Baby." I stopped. "What the hell does this have to do with me being shot at?"

"Maybe nothing, maybe a lot. You keep talking, and we'll see."

"I discovered everything I wanted to come home to was in Baby. All the love my grandparents had given me. All the good things I remembered about my life. Everything I'd cherished about the world.' I smiled sheepishly. "They came to me in voices, in smells, in memories and spoke to me. Surrounded me with their presence." I took a breath.

"And they still do every time I get into Baby." I looked up at Mac.

He was intently staring at me.

"So, what does any of this have to do with my gay?"

"Nothing. I knew Baby was more than an object to you, and now I know why."

I got up. "You brought me here for this bullshit? I'm going home."

"Sit,' he ordered. I didn't. His fist came down on the desk. "I SAID SIT!" I did. "So, now let's get to why you're here." Mac drank some more of his coffee and made a face. "A psychopath had to make this shit."

He didn't say anymore. He left me with nothing to say. I stared at him.

"Going to go get a soda." He returned, opened the can and took a swig, stared at the can. "At least this piss is dissolving the taste of the coffee." He looked up and stared at me long enough to make me fidget. "Sammi Swain."

I didn't respond, stared back at him.

"I said Sammi Swain."

I shrugged. "I heard you, back at you."

"Name doesn't mean anything?"

I tilted my head, opened my arms and shook a no.

"You sure?"

I sighed. "Positive, why?"

"We picked-up a nude floater Tuesday in the North branch of the Chicago River. Been in the water a long time. Couple weeks at least. Bloated all to hell, fish been eating at him. Face beyond recognition." He paused, concentrated his greens on me. "What drew my interest was that he had been shot in the stomach, and his genitals were cut off."

"I surmise then, that he was dead," I said.

Mac gave me a look saying smart ass not appreciated.

"With all this new technology forensics has, they identified him yesterday. Kid's name was Sammi Swain." Mac eyed me. "Still nothing?"

I shook my head and sucked in a noticeable sigh. "How many ways can I say no, I don't know him, never heard of him."

Mac grunted, "As many as you can think up until I believe you."

"Know what. Don't worry about it. Maybe I'll grab my gun and take care of Blue Boy by myself."

"And do what? Get yourself thrown in Cook County jail where you can hope those are ping pong balls your fellow inmates are sticking up your ass?"

He gave me an intense glare but didn't wait for an answer. "SHUT UP AND LISTEN. All you do from now on is think. Quit spinning your life with your hand wrapped around your dick, and you think. That's what you do. You think hard about the last four weeks of your life. You think about every guy you might have talked to at a bar. Deep, concentrated thinking of every minute of your life for the last four weeks, hear me? Think about this Joe, did he introduce you to anybody? Renaldo, Jim, they intro you to anybody? Any male at Bobby's show any special interest in you? You got it? You relive every minute of your life over the last four weeks. Got it? Now get out of here."

Chapter Thirty-Three

I made it home on automatic pilot. Anger and frustration battled over control of 'where the hell was Mac coming from; and deep seated self-pity. Nothing made any sense. How did a gay named Sammi get a match book with my name on it shoved down his throat? What I needed was some female understanding and TLC. At the moment a chat with a friend would be acceptable. Did I still have any?

What I had for sure, was a bar and a bottle of scotch. Margo stood by her door, wearing a bright yellow dress with a short, flared bottom. She held a large leather carrying case. Her lips pursed as she rummaged through its contents. Margo keeps me aware of women in general, but to-date, I have been able to keep her from becoming one woman in particular. Today I wouldn't have minded a little particular.

"May I be of assistance?" I asked.

She acknowledged my presence with a cool resolution. "No, thanks, I'm accustomed to allowing only men with whom I'm familiar to assist me."

It was let's stab the bastard and see if his blood runs free of guilt. Swords at one pace, me with a pen knife. She gave my face a frosty onceover.

"Oh, surely you remember? The man who lives across the hall from you."

She tapped a finger on her cheek. "No, no, that would be Rik. And the Rik I know would never treat me like I was one of the guys."

I was waist-deep in heap, and it was going to take a heap of heaping to get myself out of it. Only I had no heap to give her.

A flame large enough to burn Yellowstone ignited her eyes. "All those memorable evenings treated as one of the guys." Her hands went to her hips, legs slightly spread, hair swirled from a head toss. "Tell me your Wednesday night bimbo was treated as one of the guys!" She didn't give me a chance to answer.

"Do you have any idea of the deep-seated complex one of the guys can give a woman?"

I didn't. Then in one motion, she twirled on one foot and her dress flared out like a ballroom gown, revealing one eyeball sucking set of legs. My fantasy proved correct. She was wearing lace panties the same yellow color as her dress.

"Does this body look like it belongs to a man?"

None I could think of.

She started for the elevator. "Unlike one man." She pronounced the masculine singular like it was warm pig droppings. "Some men are aware it doesn't. Quite seriously aware."

I knew that, for as long as I knew her. Something that didn't please me much more than it did Renaldo. Though for different reasons.

"It's too bad you hadn't taken the time to notice."

If I'd done any more noticing, I would be in a padded cell doing strange things to myself.

"Renaldo is introducing me to some very interesting men, men who find me interesting also. Men interested in asking me out."

It was a warning, and we both knew it. I had two options. Make her mine alone, or take the chance she was twisting my nuts. We reached the elevator.

"Do you like my dress?'

"Very much."

"Good. I bought it with your appreciation in mind. So remember it. I guess now some other man will admire how I look in it." She gave me one of her seductive bedroom stares. "Or, out of it." She disappeared into the elevator.

Seated at the bar, sucking one of my beers, Jim motioned for me to join him. By my calculations, the day so far definitely owed me a drink. I fixed one and sat next to him. He gave me a cold stare.

"Margo hurt, very unhappy. Caus' you."

I stared back, not as cold. "Didn't know it was my job to make her happy."

"Ain't you job make her unhappy."

"I saw her in the hall. She said she has a date."

Jim tipped the beer bottle, drained its contents. "No way Renaldo let her have a date."

He turned and grabbed my shirt. I didn't flinch or pull away. Jim can be one mean customer, but he doesn't scare me any more than I scare him.

"Don't like when you make Margo unhappy. Don't like it you not working on making me a family."

With that, he was gone. I took my drink to the kitchen booth, putting a distance from glass to scotch bottle. The phone rang.

"Speaking of life, the more I see of yours, the sadder it becomes. Are you aware of how totally meaningless it is?"

"I'd like to say time flies when you're being annoyed, but you're doing nothing to help the afternoon pass by at all," I told the fag.

"You only say that because you have no imagination, my dear Rik.

Honestly, I can't make up my mind if your life is total absurdity or planned obsolescence. Can you see the irony in all this, Rik? Both of us betrayed by life. You by your country, me by you, but see the delicious difference is that I can get even, you can't. Doesn't that just fry your balls?"

"You know, even watching the Cubs try to play ball is more exciting than talking to you. Are we through with your mindless babble yet?" *Come on, I'm not talking to you for kicks. Who are you? Slip-up. If you're giving me clues to who you are, I'm missing them.* "I almost feel sorry life is so shitty for you."

"Ah, Rik, my love, as I have said, life doesn't work. It hasn't been fair to me. Certainly the fairest of all. But then, it's the same for death. Everyone dies, whether they're ready or not. I just hope you are ready." He sighed deeply. "Life can be cruel, even for a more deserving and just person as me. Here I thought going against you would raise the game, so I guess I have no choice but to help you continue to play blind chess."

His laughed crawled from his stomach. "So, be prepared, my dear Rik. Life as you know it will never be the same for you. Never! Until you beg me to end it." Some silence. "And as a post note, beware of whispers and echoes to come." He hung up.

"Whispers and echoes? Thanks, Thursday. What a great day." I glanced at the clock. "How many more hours until Friday and Laura?"

Chapter Thirty-Four

I'd finally figured where everything went and what to put on first. The tie might never make it. The damn tux was as confining and uncomfortable as I remembered. I walked down the steps gingerly, afraid if I didn't, things would start popping. Jim stood frozen in my hallway staring at me. I posed for him.

"Do I look good, or what?"

Jim continued to stare. Mouth open, jaw dropping. "You looks like a bouncer in a French whorehouse. What it is?"

I continued posing. "It's called a tuxedo."

"Ise knows what it be. The question be, what it doing on you?"

I jutted out my chin, raised it in my best aristocratic manner, and looked past Jim. "Bite on this bit. Opening night at the Lyric Opera. High society in attendance, invitation only."

"The Lyric Opera? So, Ise ask again, why you dress like that?"

"I just told you. I'm invited."

He broke out in uncontrollable laughter. "The opera?" He laughed again. "I mus' make wrong turn. What apartment this be?"

"Ah, my man. I'm consumed with fond recollections of youthful days sitting in the parlor, listening to recordings of the masters with my grandmother," I said.

"Uh-huh, maybe a youth spent masters-bating. Caus' none you grandmother rub-off on you." Jim walked behind the bar. "Ise needs a drink. Why you doing this?"

"It's something Laura wants to do."

He chuckled. "What this broad promise to do afterwards if you go?"

"Her name is Laura."

Jim nodded. "Right. You have any idea what's being presented, who's performing?"

"Not really, Laura is all excited about it. Besides, opera is opera, and a fat tenor is a fat tenor."

"Placido Domingo," Jim said.

It was my time to stare. "What about him?"

"He's your fat tenor. He'll be performing, Il Barbiere di Siviglia."

I joined Jim at the bar. If my eyes didn't reveal my total disbelief, they never would. "Say what?"

"The Barber of Seville." Jim leaned back, resting his chin on the tip of his fingers. "She has chosen well." His lips parted in a private smile, eyes softened, focused on something only he could see. "You have a hundred and sixty-two minutes of pure pleasure waiting for you."

I couldn't stop staring at him. "Okay, you got me. This is shitting time down South, right?"

He looked wistful. "It was a favorite of a lady I knew, and therefore became mine also." His smile broadened, it was for him, a memory. "The arias, 'Una voce pace far', and above all, "Large al factorum,' should please even you."

"Okay, you want to tell me who's talking right now?"

Jim gave me an irreverent stare. "A someone I once knew." He stared into his drink. "I wasn't always a janitor. I used to be a somebody with a prestigious job, climbing up the ladder. I shared my world with the love of my life, a beautiful lady named Jasmine." He stopped, his eyes seemed to reflect on his words.

"Where is she now?" I asked.

He shrugged. "Not in my life since prison."

"Did you go see her when you got out?"

He looked at me as though I'd gone simple. "She a classy lady, working her way up in corporate America. She don't need no jail rat trailing five feet behind her." The hurt showed in his eyes, masked his face.

"She tell you that?"

"Never went to ask."

"It wouldn't hurt to give it a shot."

He looked at me, shook his head. "The past never comes back the way it was."

"You'll never know unless you try."

"Yassir, Mr. Man, if you's says so." The memories must have passed, the street hardness returned to his face.

I brought my fist down on the bar top. "Why did you go back talking like that?"

He looked surprised. "Likes what? Ise a black janitor, that the way I talk."

"No it isn't."

"Here," he reached over untied my tie, retied it and smiled. "The drink and the tux, make my time here worthwhile." He laughed and got up. "So, you gonna be a beautiful folk tonight, huh?" He chuckled. "You…going to the opera." He was still laughing as he shut the door behind him.

I was in a tux, Laura would be in a gown, Baby was built to handle neither, I ordered a cab. At least the cab was clean, the driver not so much, and he spoke pigeon English. He agreed to wait while I picked up my date. I think I felt like I was in the South Side of Chicago trying to bargain with a pimp. Laura buzzed me up and responded to my knucklerap on the door.

"Is this my opera companion for tonight?" she asked.

"No, it's a bouncer from a French whorehouse."

"A what?" She asked as she opened the door.

She caught my immediate attention in her black gown, cut low to expose enough breast to make men drool. Tight around her waist and hips, the slit exposing most of one leg and enough of the other, if one wasn't enough to keep you busy. A jeweled choker of diamonds and emeralds graced her neck, that if real, would buy a whole lot of house.

I took longer than chivalry allowed to soak her in. She smiled.

"I take it you approve?"

"I would like to show you how much."

"And miss the opera? I know that's the last thing you want to do." She walked in front of me to the elevator, teasing me with a come-on swing of her shapely rear, as she stayed out of my reach.

"If those stones are real, I think we need some bodyguards."

"$280,000.00 price tag."

"Say what?"

She sighed. "Relax, not mine, rented for the evening by Lawrence, at a tenth of the value, and heavily insured."

Our cab waited in line at the Lyric as I watched the 'beautiful folk' parade out of one limousine after another pulled up to the curb. Anal jag-off. You brought Laura here in a cab. I turned to her. I already felt the discomfort of not belonging here, certain my tux had "rented," spelled all over it. Laura's face beamed with anticipation of the evening. And you brought her in a cab. "God, I'm so sorry, Laura. Sitting here in a cab has to be embarrassing."

She healed my bruised image with a smile. "There might be two people in that whole crowd who own a limo. The rest are playing the snob game. 'Look at me. See how elegant we look; notice my jewels.' I came to see the opera, not play the games." I received a brief kiss on the cheek. "Did I tell you how handsome you look tonight?"

The lobby had been set-up for entertaining. Masses of bored looking men and overdressed women controlled every inch of space. Couples moved about going through the formalities of discussing whatever was or was not important to them, all taking great pains to make sure the right people noticed their presence.

Laura appeared to know exactly where she wanted to be in this cattle throng. I followed sheepishly. Waiters mingled through the crowd, trays loaded with champagne or canapés. I wasn't particularly thrilled with either, but procured two glasses of champagne for us. Laura took my arm and directed me to a crowd of about ten people. I immediately knew I wasn't going to enjoy this.

The men all exuded the aura of the importance wealth brought. The women, gaudy in overpriced gowns and jewelry, masked the security of the social status their husband's money gave them. Laura received the lengthy eye from the male constituency and me the quick appraisal, which translated into little if any value in the choice of her companion for the evening.

The women took time from the importance of their own presence to smile politely at us, wave and coo at Laura, flashing their jewelry, as they nibbled on canapés and consumed dainty sips of champagne.

"Laura, what a pleasure your being here brings," the men offered. Whispers in her ear, a smile.

"If only my wife wasn't here."

A soft laugh from Laura, a coy smile, lowered eyes. She was playing them, and she was good at it. A few kisses on the cheek, a quick squeeze as their wives pulled them away. I froze a smile on my face and forcefully refrained from tightening their ties around their Adam's apple.

And finally. "Oh yes, and who is this you've brought with you?'

I was introduced and received cursory handshakes. "And your business?"

"I write."

"Really? Always thought that would be an interesting hobby. Laura, we expect to see more of you tonight. Oh sorry…er, Rich was it not? Nice meeting you."

A woman approached, five-two maybe, in height, five-six with her jewelry on. "Laura, love, so good to see you. And who is this?" I thought I was going to receive a pinch on the cheek. "Tall, and such big shoulders. Everything about him looks big." A raise of the eyebrows, a knowing play of the eyes. "Lucky you, my dear."

Laura smiled. "It's just started, Love," she whispered to me.

Her smile brightened. It was returned by a tall, lean, distinguished looking man who moved out of the crowd toward us. There was something in the smiles, the way they looked at each other, that put me on guard. I knew without introduction who he was, and the hairs on the back of my neck curled in anger.

He was all the adjectives—slick, suave, smooth and actually looked comfortable in his tux. A full head of hair, silver at the temples, stayed in place on command, and he was good-looking. He was everything I feared he would be.

"Laura, how nice to have you here. As always, you look lovely."

He took her hand and kissed her on the cheek. The kiss lingered longer than necessary, and his eyes made no attempt to hide I was only temporary. She was his possession. Laura introduced us.

"So nice of you to accompany her. It's a pleasure to meet you." His fifty-something looked not a day older than forty-something. His smile was genuine, his handshake firm, and his violet blue eyes stayed fixed on mine. It was hard to dislike him.

"Mr. Giordanian," I acknowledged.

"Please, Lawrence."

He'd sized me up, and seemed to make judgment, but gave no hint at his evaluation. He continued to return my stare, but his eyes searched me for some reason why it was necessary for him to do so. I realized he'd decided to stare me down. The old macho, I am more powerful, "I am more important than you game." Something I figured he usually won, only he'd picked the wrong person. It didn't take long for him to look away.

"I hope you two enjoy tonight," he said. "It should be a special evening. And of course, I expect both of you to join us after. Sorry, I'm in demand. You know that situation, huh, Laura?"

She smiled and acknowledged she did. He looked into her eyes. If there was a message, it was coded for Laura only. He shook my hand, but only briefly held his eyes with mine, and left.

Laura leaned her head against my shoulder. "You stared him down. I've never seen another man do that." She kissed me on the cheek. "I knew you'd win."

My tux turned red, a capital 'S' appeared on my chest. I'd just become Superman.

We were about to look for our seats when a woman approached. She possessed the direct self-confidence of someone accustomed to position and wealth. She was no-nonsense, no frills, but it was the polished, well-groomed look that made her stand out over the others.

"Evelyn, Lawrence's wife," Laura informed me.

She brightened as she reached us, her smile sincere in its warmth toward Laura. She either was an overly trusting wife, leaving a man like Lawrence alone with Laura every day, or, more likely, had some control that assured any desires on Lawrence's part would be relieved in the bathroom only. She took Laura's hand and patted it. "You look wonderful, Laura." She gave me a quick appraisal.

Her eyes smiled, whether from approval or skepticism, I could only guess. "Rik, is it not?"

"Yes," I answered- a little surprised she knew my name.

"Laura has spoken of you. He is a big one, is he not Laura?" I received a sly wink. "And you my dear Rik, how do you live?"

"Very well, thank you. And yourself?"

She stepped back so she could look me directly in the eyes. We stood fixed on each other for a moment, and then she laughed. It came from her toes, filled with warmth and made me laugh. She took my hands in hers. "He's precious, I'm happy for you, Laura. And may I add, long overdue." She squeezed my hands. "Take care of my girl,' she ordered me. "Later my dear," she patted Laura's hand then apparently spotted someone equal to her own status and left us to ourselves.

Laura looked up at me and smiled. "We can stay, you've been approved."

"How nice for me."

"These are the people I have to deal with every day."

"What fun for you."

The lights in the lobby blinked off and on, signaling time to find our seats. The main show was about to begin; the one here in the lobby had come to an end. The seating and leg space at the Lyric belonged to another time when long legs were not in fashion. With the help of a couple pinches from Laura on the sensitive part of my inner thigh, I stopped fidgeting.

The stolen glances at the beauty sitting next to me, and the expression of enjoyment on her face, captured my heart more than the opera. I never picked-up Jim's two favorite arias, but he didn't need to know. I brought Laura here in a cab, and she was going to leave in a limo. I found a driver hoping for a fare and overpaid him to escort the lady and I to her destination. She wished to stop at her place for a moment.

She directed me to a stark modern chair. She fixed me a drink, entered her bedroom and stated she'd only be a minute. I had no idea what a minute meant to a woman, but suspected more like an hour to a man. The chair wasn't that comfortable, the tux's cummerbund cut into my sides, the drink long finished. I was about to fix another when she appeared in front of the open bedroom door. I came to straight rigid, seated posture, like a ventriloquist's dummy with no one to operate my mouth.

Her hair looked unkempt like she'd just crawled out of bed, and combed it with her fingers. She captured my full attention, with a see-through white blouse, unbuttoned in front, no bra. Black satin bikini panties, thigh high black hose, six inch heels and that was it.

She motioned to the bedroom. "I saw no reason to dine with the others. I'm sure we can find something to eat in here."

I'm quite certain my response was clever and glib, but with all the blood rushing from my head to my groin, it sounded unintelligible.

She extended her arm and offered her hand to me. "Would you like to join me?"

I rose from the chair, not as easy a task as it would seem, and did the best to simulate the act of normal walking. She tilted her head as she watched me approach.

"You're walking funny, have you hurt something?"

"Not yet." I thanked God there were no steps leading up to her bedroom.

Chapter Thirty-Five

I woke to white satin and fluff. I reached for Laura. She wasn't there, and apparently hadn't been for a while. There was no trace of her body heat on the sheets, no head indentation on the pillow. Only the faint scent of her perfume belied the fact last night hadn't been fiction.

I wondered what time it was. From my vantage point, I couldn't locate anything that gave the room any sense of time or interval. White walls and ceiling, thick, white carpeting, captured me like a cloud with no depth. I called out to her, received no answer. I rose, found my clothes and dressed. I didn't feel right using her shower without permission. Still no Laura. I searched the rest of the apartment, Starbuck's coffee, a glass of orange juice, bagel with cream cheese, and a red rose, awaited on the coffee table. Coffee cold, orange juice warm, no Laura; only a handwritten note held secure by a coffee cup.

"Sorry I'm not here my Love. Last night was wonderful, maybe even a dream, but I need time to think. Give me a little space, then please, please, call me later today. My mind is so confused at the moment. The rose is yours to take home so you'll think of me when you look at it. Laura"

Think about what? We'd done the natural thing and slept together. She wrote the night wonderful. I thought "fabulous" fit better.

The lovemaking contained all the eagerness of new lovers, but unhurried, passionate, yet comfortable with all the ease experienced by old lovers. Yes, it had been wonderful. I'd awakened with the feeling I'd experienced something entirely new. It caused an unhealthy expectation. Perhaps Laura felt it too, and would want to linger in my life for a while.

Dreams of any merit don't last long around me. They seem to prefer to live in the subways of life so they can lie on the tracks and be squashed and wiped away by tons of moving steel. Hopefully, I hadn't driven Laura there.

An overnight lover once told me, "The next morning is always an awkward moment. It always is for new lovers. Difficult, only when you hope the lovemaking of last night means as much to the other person as it did for you." Then she looked at me, caressed my face. "A shame you'll never experience that moment. You can't when your heart is empty."

I felt somewhat awkward being here. Awkward, in that something inside me wanted Laura with me. Awkward, because I'd never cared about the feelings of the morning after, so why now? Awkward, because nothing written in black or white told me I really did care.

I took the warm orange juice and headed for the French doors and the balcony. Laura's niche of the world was situated high enough so that you received a great view of the city. It was going to be a beautiful summer day. The city sparkled, too early for city pollution to dim the effects of a bright morning sun illuminating the buildings.

Laura possessed one of the smaller condos, a one-bedroom model. Unlike the opulence of Giordanian

Imports, her living room furniture consisted of two chairs, a sofa, and a natural wood coffee table. All light tan in color, modern stiff, ergonomically-designed seemed to function as dividers between the kitchen and the great room that led to the balcony.

I noticed two framed pictures on the wall across from me that gave the otherwise monochromatic room its only touch of color. One, a quality print, showed a night street scene of two lovers, arms around each other walking by a café, oblivious to the rain and the reflection of streetlights off puddles.

The other picture, an oil painting, captured my attention with its sadness. It depicted a four-pane wooden-framed window with gray paint peeling away from age and neglect. Three window panes, showed only jagged remnants of remaining glass. The fourth frame remained intact, but was filthy and streaked. In a clay pot, in the center of the window, a blood red rose grew, droplets of water on its petals. On one petal, a droplet drooped like a tear waiting for gravity to make it fall.

I figured there was some sort of symbolism to the painting, but it was too early in the morning to care. I finished my orange juice and headed home.

I slowly walked toward my cave, my mind still on Laura and wishing I'd awakened with her next to me.

"Hello, stranger."

I turned. Margo stood by the open door, a white bathrobe her only clothing, hair still wet from a shower. It didn't take much imagination to realize the only thing under the robe was Margo.

She eyed the rose, but didn't question it. "Renaldo's not home, we haven't talked in a long time. Why don't you come in?"

You've got to be shitting me. How many times have you dreamed this, Rik?

"I'm not sure that's a good idea."

She pulled her robe open, letting it slide off her arms. All my fantasies of Margo had been photographs in black and white compared to her real beauty. I didn't pretend to look away. "Why? Why aren't we a good idea? Don't you want me? Don't you think of having me?"

"What my thoughts are, have nothing to do with it."

"I don't know what that means," she said.

I didn't either.

"Come to me, come to me," she groaned. She moved her hands up her body, cupping her breasts and letting out breathless, erotic moans. Her smoldering dark eyes filled with suggestive heat. "Look at me, Rik. Look at me."

What the hell did she think I was doing?

She shed tears, lots of them. "What does she have that I don't? What can she give you that I can't?"

The sound of elevator doors opening, followed by Renaldo's cough, made her grab the robe and disappear behind closed doors before her brother reached me. Thank You, I guess, God. Renaldo eyed me suspiciously.

"Talking to Margo?" He asked. "Did I interrupt something?"

"Thought maybe you two, Jim and I, could go out tonight." I lied.

He stared at me, luckily not below the waist, but didn't appear to see me. "She is beautiful, Margo, is she not?" He asked.

I nodded. "Very."

A strange look came into his eyes. Whatever it said didn't transpire in this world. "I hope you realize Margo cannot hide her discretions from me. I am aware of things in ways you would not understand." His words came close to religious fervor.

"What indiscretions are those, Renaldo?"

He didn't answer and gave me a condescending smile.

"What you think of me holds no real shakes in my life," I told him. "What I do care about is your apparent low opinion of Margo every time you see us together."

Anger flickered in his eyes. He walked past, then turned and stared at me. Flamelike intensity runs in the family. "She is my sister, my property!" He measured me with his eyes. "There is a place of great honor awaiting her, not too far in the future. She is not aware of it yet. Outside interference that could destroy that honor, is not appreciated." He stared directly into my eyes. "We must remain friends…most necessary we remain friends." He was off somewhere other than the hallway. "Margo's"…a pause, a look upward…"sacred, untouchable. Don't destroy our friendship. I have a gifted power, a gifted future."

He stopped, opened his door, turned. "You would not like your life if you anger the powers…if you anger me. Friends, we must remain friends. I ask you to leave. Leave the presence of Margo." He entered his apartment, closing the door to any further conversation.

I sat at my bar and tried to get pictures of Margo out of my head. Think of her with my big head, Jesus, could I ever look at her again and not see her naked? I didn't even bother trying to figure out Renaldo, except I didn't like being threatened. If he did it again, then he couldn't count on any powers protecting him from me. I called Laura.

"Hi," I said, always slick of tongue, when she answered.

"Rik?"

"Aha, maybe expecting someone else? Do you have a boyfriend, lady?"

She laughed. "I don't know, do I?"

"There could be a strong possibility." Classical violin played in the background. "Although you weren't too gentle last night."

"Poor baby, did I hurt you?"

"Maybe my ego, by not being in bed with me this morning."

There was a pause. "I…I'm sorry, Rik. Please try to understand. My bedroom has always been my private place. I've never shared it with anyone." Her voice lowered. "That must sound silly to you." Another pause. "It's been a long time since I shared myself." An uncontrolled burst of laughter. "Oh, God, Rik, I must sound like a high school virgin. You opened emotions I'd forgotten I had. I had to sort them out, so I just couldn't be with you this morning."

I let her sit in silence for a moment. "Perhaps I may forgive you, if your bedroom will be open to me again. Can I come over and help you see that your world might be much better if we shared it?"

She laughed. "You're a bad influence."

"Good, that's my purpose in life."

"I need today. Saturday has always been my day to be a slob, to do whatever I want to do. I know it sounds silly, but can you understand?"

It wasn't that hard. She'd given me a night, now she wanted her day. I gave it to her.

"But, tomorrow? Breakfast and the day ours?" She asked

"Sure, but how did food get into the equation?"

She giggled. "Be a good boy, and I'll let you show me how terrific Sundays can be. I sleep in late on Sundays."

"I'll start now, drive slow."

'"At least, let the sun come up."

"I don't know if I can drive that slow. Tomorrow?"

"Tomorrow."

I sat looking at the phone. Margo and Laura. Greed can be a dangerous thing. A knock at the door, Margo, dressed, stood looking at me. Without waiting for an invitation, she entered.

"Uh, does Renaldo know you're here?"

She was all smiles. "He sent me." She headed for my bar. Renaldo and Jim entered and joined Margo. What the hell was going on?"

Margo's composure bothered me. She was too assured of herself. Too much a woman of the world. I wondered if her little girl innocence was gone. If so, then something beautiful had been corrupted, and I couldn't help but feel most of the blame rested on my shoulders.

No one wanted a drink. I sure as hell needed one. Conversation flowed as if nothing had happened between Margo, Renaldo, and me. Jim was all smiles, glancing back and forth at Margo and then me. Renaldo noted how nice it was being with good friends again, and we had to do it more often. What the hell was going on?

As with everything, our little makeshift party came to an end. They turned to leave, still laughing and chatting, with another agreement to get together again soon. What the hell was going on? Maybe nothing out of nothing— nothing more—nothing less, than friends enjoying each other's companionship. Maybe it was just me trying to make something out of nothing. Maybe Renaldo hadn't threatened me. Maybe it had been my fantasies, not Margo who had disrobed. Maybe I needed help. Whose could I count on?

Chapter Thirty-Six

The rose leaned haphazardly out of the water glass. It was the tallest water container I had, but the rose was too long for it. I sat in my kitchen booth enjoying a real cup of coffee wondering how many minutes the rose had before it fell out of the glass. Not an overly exciting way to spend the morning, but it helped me think of something other than last night. I was having a difficult time not being immersed in every detail of it.

I jumped at the sound of Jim's voice. "Any of that brew left for me?"

"Just once, for the sake of me living to see forty, will you make some noise when you enter my place?" I asked.

He made no acknowledgement, filled a cup and joined me in the booth, eying the rose.

"Don't ask," I said.

He twirled the rose around in the glass. "Me, Margo and Renaldo had dinner out last night. We gonna axt you to come, but you not home."

'Why did you wait until the last minute to ask me?'

"We nots know until last minute we going. You be free?"

"No."

"See it make no difference it be last minute or not."

He stretched. You give him plenty of room when he stretches. "You with the bike broad?"

"Her name is Laura. Laura, remember that, Jim."

His eyes focused on something over my head. "Let's have a drink."

"It's only eleven-thirty."

"When that have anything to do with drinking?"

"It's supposed to."

By the time I caught up to him, he was behind the bar with two rock glasses filled halfway with malt liquor.

His eyes were cold and hard as he locked them on me. "This makes three times this week you out with Miss what's-her-name."

"Laura."

He nodded. "Not like you, three times same broad."

I laughed at his concern. "It was three dates, not marriage."

"Yeah, I forgot. You thrives on living with memories of midnight that ain't there with the dawn."

"That supposed to mean anything?"

"Just talking fact," he answered. "Something that don't make Margo happy."

I let out a deep sigh "Didn't know it was my job to make her happy."

"Ain't you job to make her unhappy"

"Then you want me sleeping with her?"

He slammed his drink down. "Don't even think, unless you ready to do it legal like, and gonna makes me a uncle." He left.

The phone rang. "Have you been to the garage lately? If not, you really should check it out."

Have I been to the garage? The phone rang again. I didn't want to answer it, but it might be Laura.

"Didn't you hear me? You haven't been to the garage yet."

"Why can't you talk like a man? Don't you have a dick?"

"A party-size one, my dear Rik. Would you like to play some games with it?" He laughed. "No, probably not yet. Besides, I have a headache."

I didn't reply, the conversation gave no clues to who he was.

He laughed again, this time, pinching, stinging, drilling laughter. "If you don't go to the garage, you can't see your car."

"What!?"

More skin-crawling laughter, and then he hung up.

I stood in the garage, letting my eyes adjust to the light. Couldn't remember getting here, didn't remember any action after the phone call. Only I was in the garage, wanting and not wanting to be. The lights were playing tricks with my eyes. Yes, yes, the lights, had to be the lights. Please make it the lights. I stepped back, viewed Baby from a different angle, it didn't make any difference.

Along the driver's side, from her headlight to her tail light, a continuous, deep gouge stared at me. About a quarter of an inch-wide wound, her skin completely removed, bare metal left to the elements. I knelt beside her, slowly placing my hand on her violation, feeling her pain transfer to my hand. A winter chill settled on my body. Rage boiled up in me, immediate and volcanic. I choked on it, my blood singing with implacable fury. I couldn't contain it. "You fucking piece of shit. You're dead! Understand? Dead, dead, dead. Hear me, DEAD!"

I couldn't stay with her, look at her. "I'll get him," I told her. "I promise, and it will be painful and deadly." It was cold comfort, like telling a terminally ill friend death is pastoral, his unfulfilled dreams only chaotic waste. From somewhere, a gut-wrenching scream filled every cavity in the garage.

Jim's steel garbage drum blocked my way to the elevator. What made it think it deserved to be there? Ugly thing had no right to be in my way. I came from the floor and delivered a solid, resounding, uppercut blow to it. The impact rocked the drum precipitously, some of its contents escaping imprisonment, and that gave me some thought it might tip enough to allow me to kick it in the balls. It wasn't until I reached my condo that the excruciating pain racing from my knuckles to my shoulder announced itself, and brought me to my knees.

Oozing blood existed where skin once covered knuckles, fingers swelled, stiffened. I acquired a clean wash cloth, soaked it with scotch whiskey, and washed the wound until I was satisfied it was sterile. Deciding I probably needed an antibiotic, I drank some of the scotch. Made an ice pack, and taped it around my hand. I'd forgotten how right-handed I was, though it didn't seem to interfere with my ability to make a drink. Didn't want to, but answered the phone.

"Want to know where I molested her?" His nails against blackboard laugh again. "Can't wait to tell you. So exciting, five seconds to guess." More laughter. "Time's up. In your garage. I did the dirty, right under your nose. In your garage. How delectable is that?"

In my garage? He was lying. I sat down. The rat in Baby hadn't been a lie. How did he get in? Only answer, someone's letting him into the building. Jesus, I felt like I lived in a fish bowl, only the glass was a one-way mirror, and I couldn't see out.

"Artistic rendering though, you must agree. My work was violent and beautiful all at the same time. The pinnacle of eroticism. A masterpiece done for love. Violence can be so beautiful when performed for love. But, you know that, don't you dear Rik."

My hands began shaking. I wanted this guy so badly I could taste blood.

"You are listening, aren't you?" He waited. "I can hear your breathing, I guess I can take that as a yes. I do wish you to know, dear Rik, I shed a tear of love for it. A beauty, scarred like that forever."

"You sick faggot, asshole mother…"

Laughter, biting, mocking, laughter. "Yes, yes, more, more, don't stop, please more." Mocking laughter again. "I am the harbinger of pain. She screamed. Screamed; screamed out in pain. Did you hear her? Huh, huh?" He hung up.

Having another drink would be exactly what he'd expect. What he wanted from me. I passed, besides I didn't need alcohol screwing with my mind. Unfocused pictures of the garage played with my thoughts. I could still hear his pricking laughter. It crept into the room like mist from the sea through a screened window.

Perhaps like the small boy who hopes his mother's vase he broke will go undiscovered, or that given enough time, he'll discover he didn't break it. It was only a bad dream. I had to go back to the garage and check Baby. It hadn't gone away. The scar loomed, looking wider, more entrenched than before. What he'd done had hurt, hurt a lot. But, by showing him it did, I'd left the door open for him to enter and tear at the fabric of my soul at will. I'd been betrayed by my own emotions as much as by him. He'd won.

Baby had been his last success. Never again would I allow him to make me play his game. And that meant never to allow emotions to enter my life again. I'd survived without them. They had no place in my life now. I smiled. Except for one—hate. That emotion I could let grow inside me, cultivate into a ripe fruit. Hate, the emotion of survival, of strength, not weakness. Hate would allow me to cause him deep, agonizing pain before I killed him. Hate would bring cold, sweet, detached revenge.

The message machine light on the phone was blinking. Laura had called, wanted me to call back. Laura, she'd dominated my thoughts until Baby. Now, I couldn't seem to get her focused in my mind, unaware of any twinge of excitement at the sound of her voice. If what I felt last night and this morning were emotions, could I handle them in my life right now? Can emotions be turned off and on at will or need? I didn't know.

What I did know, was the consummate degree of hate that I felt, would sour any relationship with Laura. What I also knew, was that I wanted to taste last night again. So, cutting off my dick while I made up my mind whether to rid myself of her presence until I made the gay history, lacked in common sense.

Laura— she wasn't aware of the gay, of the possible danger in associating with me. Though I had nothing that showed the gay was aware of Laura. So why stir the pot? Until it boiled, leave it alone, and let me enjoy life and Laura.

I should call Mac—screw it—I didn't need his approval to kill the fag. What I did know, was that I needed some answers.

Chapter Thirty-Seven

Getting falling-down drunk made no sense at all, but neither did anything else I could think of. I gave thought to going over to Laura's. And do what? Beg her to let me cry on her shoulder. I went to the den, but gave up on writing before I even tried. I turned on the TV, turned it off and called Jim-- no answer, I had a drink and went to bed.

I sank into a fitful sleep, visited by muddled dreams. Alleys filled with rats. Me, seated in a chair, in the middle of an otherwise empty room, where Laura, Jim and Mac would take turns entering laughing unmercifully at my distress over Baby.

Jim's voice shattered the dreams like they were formed from fragile crystal. Heart pounding, I sat upright.

"I say again," he called out. "What's the 'potant?"

By the time I made it downstairs, he'd turned the lights on and was sitting on a bar stool; most of him slumped on top of the bar. I checked the time, 12: 45. I sat next to him and he propped his head upright with a cupped hand.

"You look like something that should be flushed and chemically treated," I told him.

"You the one calls me, I don't hafta see if I pretty or not."

"Jim…Baby…she"

" I'se really could use a beer."

I got him one.

"Baby? What happen to Baby?"

"She was gouged all along her left side."

It took a moment, but he finally focused both eyes on me. "Baby gouged? Jeez, sorry Rik. But, both knew sooner or later, sumthin' gonna get her." He belched, made sure that was all he was going to do, and eyed me suspiciously. "But, that not why you call me."

"I need you to listen to me. Really listen." I waited until he nodded he would. "The gouge wasn't a random act." Jim frowned, but focused the best he could on me. "It was slowly and deliberately done. Done to psyche me out." I made sure he was still attentive. "And he did it in our garage."

That got his attention. Scar went crimson. "And you know this how?"

"It's on my answering machine, word for word from the fag's mouth bragging about it." I stopped, checked his response, whatever he felt wasn't visible. "I wanted you to hear it. That was the important."

Jim looked over at the machine. "A fag, you say. Why a gay, Rik?"

"Don't know, something about me taking away his lover." Jim's eyes spoke volumes. "Shit, just listen to the tape."

His eyes were clearing of the red, doubt replacing it. I played the tape. Jim listened. Retrieved a beer, listened some more. Iced me with his stare.

"You hearing something I can't?"

I rewound the tape, played it again. No sound, nothing, no voice of the gay, no message, nothing but the sound of the tape winding. "I'm telling you he left a message on the

211

phone." Jim just stared. "And…and someone must have let him into my apartment so he could erase it."

I didn't like what Jim's eyes were saying. He stared at me long enough to let me know I wasn't supposed to.

"You hearin' whats you saying?"

"I'm telling you Jim…" He held up his hand.

"Since I be you friend, I'se telling you getting' scary again. Gets help for' you goes back seeing heads in the garage." Commiseration took over his eyes. "A gay scarred Baby caus' you play with his lover? Christ, Rik, get some help." He turned and was gone.

Tomorrow morning was going to greet me with one hell of a hangover.

Chapter Thirty-Eight

Jim called Saturday, invited me to a stroll with he, Aztec and Margo, and grab a Chicago hot dog and cold beer. I bowed out as gracefully as possible. Laura called, offered pretty much the same menu as Jim. The weather outlook promised a beautiful day. Laura wanted to escape her dwelling. I succumbed to her wishes.

I stroked Baby, ran my hand over her wound. She wasn't helping me cleanse myself of emotions. But, she was Baby, and I could never shut her out. It was life and people I couldn't let in.

At present, I had no story to cover my swollen and bruised hand, or if noticed, Baby. But, I was unconcerned, since I was skilled at fabricating my life. So far, my whole relationship with Laura had been a lie.

I picked up Laura, fortunately the passenger side was her only view of Baby. No way to have only one side of my hand. She noticed it immediately. A juvenile loss of temper, I told her. So childish, I wished to forget it and enjoy her presence and the beautiful day. She hesitated, not fully ready to accept my explanation, but a promise of later curtailed her curiosity.

It was a great day for the River Walk on South Wacker Drive. A stretch of five blocks of sidewalk on both sides of the Chicago River, where you could sit in outdoor cafes, take in the artistic carvings on the back of business buildings, and people watch. I parked Baby in a city parking garage. Metered parking on the streets only covered an hour before the dutiful meter maid arrived at your car before you did. So, the solution lay in the parking garage, though a couple of hours there probably matched the cost of the meter and the ticket.

I realized Laura was staring at me. "You see, but you don't see, do you?" She asked.

I returned a puzzled look. "Where did that come from, and exactly what does it mean?"

"You looked up, noticed the carved stone art, the gargoyles on the back of the buildings looking down at us, but didn't question or acknowledge their reason for being there. You also glanced at the flowers at the Art Institute, but showed no appreciation for their color. You then commented on how busy the streets were, but didn't really see the people, or question their existence being there. How can you be a writer if you don't see life around you, question its reason for existing?"

I didn't have an answer, especially since I hadn't attempted being a real writer for years. She wanted one. We found an empty table, nicely located where you could view the passenger boats that acted as water taxis during the week.

"Maybe I do see, maybe my experience as a cop forces me to hide it." Pretty feeble, but the best I had. Before she could probe any further, I tried throwing the ball into her court. She beat me.

"Did you always want to be a writer, Rik?"

I ordered drinks for us. "Ever since I can remember wanting to be anything."

She concentrated on my face. "It must be satisfying, being what you dreamed you wanted to be."

"I take it then, that being an importer/exporter was not your first choice?"

She didn't answer right away, sipping at her drink and people watching instead. "I studied drama and dancing at Northwestern."

"You wanted to be an actor?" She nodded, but didn't seem responsive to the question. I thought of dropping any more reference to it. I should have. "Did you burn out before the breaks came?"

She sighed. "More like I grew tired of what a girl was expected to do to get the breaks." She looked for a smile but found only a bitter remnant of one. "I did some acting here in Chicago. I was good, Rik. Really good. I was discovered at the Goodman Theatre playing Tennessee William's, Maggie Pollitt." She reflected. "A must-see play. Best interpretation of Maggie The Cat seen in years, the papers printed." She smiled. "Broadway here I come." She laughed. It had a stinging, acrid sound. "Naïve, little Laura. I guess it's the same old story, told since women got bitten by Broadway, and Broadway bit them back."

She acted like she wanted to stop there, but couldn't hold back whatever was inside her from exploding. "They had no right. I was good, so very damn good." Her words were close to melodramatic and definitely encrusted with bile. "But, I refused to let them degrade me. God, how I learned to hate them."

It was a controlled rage, but still, I was happy it wasn't directed at me. Obviously, it was aimed at a memory of indignities forced upon her by men who tried to keep her on the level of a pet. On second thought, maybe it was directed at me. All men are hunters, and fresh meat out of college is always fair game. If afforded the same opportunity, would I have been any different?

"I'm sorry," she said. "It was a bad time in my life. I had no right forcing you to walk through it."

"No, I'm glad you did." I wasn't. We've all been dealt a road of bad times, but, it gave me a little deeper insight of where and how to tread softly with her. "And life for you now?"

A slow smile captured her face. I checked her eyes. The rage was gone, the smile real, though a tinge of sadness still reflected in the doe-eyes.

"Life is good now," she answered . "When I came back from New York, I met Evelyn and Lawrence Giordanian. Lawrence took an interest in me."

I bet he did.

"They took me under their wings and taught me the import business. I like my work and now confine my acting to mimicking the actors on film."

"I noticed," I said. She laughed.

We waited in the city parking garage for the car jockey to bring Baby down. I heard tires squeal and my muscles tensed. The jockey pulled Baby up and jumped out, a grin on his face like he expected me to congratulate him on his driving skills—his hand out waiting for a tip. If Laura hadn't been present, what he would have received was my hand firmly gripped around his throat. I palmed a dollar on him. Gripping his hand around his knuckles, palm and thumb pressing his thumb backwards, squeezing so hard he grabbed my hand, his eyes close to tearing from pain. He looked at my face, into my eyes. What they said was, if I wished, he was dead. His grin had long disappeared, he walked away muttering to himself.

I patted Baby, assuring her she was in good hands again. Laura grinned and assured her also.

We ended up at Chestnut Station Cinema on Clark and Oak to see some kind of foreign film Laura felt she had to see. The content of the movie either succeeded in enveloping me in total boredom, or left my mind wondering what the hell the film was trying to say. I kept a smile frozen on my face in case she decided to scrutinize my concentration. She showed little reaction to the plot, giving undivided attention to the actors. She passed on popcorn stating she was saving herself for pizza, as she was starved. I had yet to ascertain which consumed her more—movies or food.

The theater sat in what was once an exclusive residential area. It still struggles to hold on to that label, and will, until the city tears down the remaining brownstones and replaces them with mass housing. Entertainment around the theater limits itself to browsing in the Moody Bible Institute or giving or drinking blood at the Red Cross office across the street. Of course, with establishments offering every fulfillment from culinary to carnal needs on State and Rush Streets, there was little need for any entertainment around the theater.

Due's is a short walk away, so I told her to suck in her gut, as perhaps the best pizza awaits. We walked arm in arm down Clark. I graciously pretended not to notice the twenty-something twerps eyeballing Laura as we walked. She noticed the full moon and wanted to share it with me.

"Do you hear the moon, Rik?"

"Hear it do what?"

She laughed. "Then we can forget about the stars. Talk. The moon talks to you if you listen."

"Maybe when I was a kid."

She shook her head. "Ah, that's sad. If you can't hear the moon, then that means there's no romance in your soul. Women like men to be romantic every once in a while."

I stopped. "Wait. Yes I hear him. But, he's talking dirty."

She punched me on the shoulder and ran her fingers through her hair, fluffing it the same way she had the first time I'd seen her. I felt the same twinge of electricity.

"No way. Never!" she said. "The moon has never had a dirty thought in his head."

"Then why did he just wink at me?"

"You're going to need a lot of work." She slowed, almost to a crawl. I wasn't built to walk any slower than I already was.

"Do you know that strange little man?" she asked. "I swear he's been following us, staring at us the whole time. He really gives me the creeps."

I turned and looked where Laura's eyes were focused. Across the street was Washington Square Park. A block or so of grassy space between Clark and Dearborn, better known in the day as Bug House Square, a Mecca for anyone with a box to stand on and a philosophy or maniacal raving to voice. After they were chased away by the neighborhood folk, it became a meat market for both male and female purveyors of fantasy sex. Now, it just sits, neither attractive nor useful.

At first I didn't notice anyone. Then, in full splendor, eyeballing us, hand- squeezing his crotch; Blue Boy stepped out into the center of the Square.

Chapter Thirty-Nine

I lost reason and took off after him, forgetting Laura had her arm looped around mine. His eyes grew wide and he took off for State Street.

"Rik, stop!"

I did, she didn't, passing me, feet off the ground. I grabbed a lamppost stopping us from kissing pavement. I watched him run down Chestnut toward State Street. There was an outside chance I could catch up, but what was the program if I did? Beat the shit out of him in public? Have the police arrest him for eyeballing? All while Laura leaned against a streetlight faithfully waiting for my return?

"Goddamn him," I yelled.

I realized Laura was giving me an intent glare, with her eyes expressing more than just puzzlement.

"You okay?" I asked.

She took a minute . "Physically speaking, yes." She straightened her dress, stopping a few men in their tracks as she did so. She fixed on my face, didn't say anything, just stared like she was trying to read whatever she thought she saw on it. "Do you always react this way when someone stares at you?"

I was looking at her, but my mind was owned by Blue Boy, so it took longer than necessary for me to reply. "No, I don't. Sorry. But, it wasn't me he was staring at. I didn't like the way he was looking at you." I had my fingers crossed behind my back.

She didn't respond immediately, just continued to study my face. "Is this going to be a problem? Men do look at me, and I've learned to accept it. I suggest if we decide to spend time together, you do too. Especially, my dear, when you are the object of attraction, not me. "

I heard her, damn, I was hoping she hadn't noticed, but her observation registered somewhere between the space of, 'so what' and I want to catch the little bastard and kill him. She didn't care where I was, she wanted my attention. "Again, sorry. I'll work on not making it a problem. How about some pizza?"

We walked in silence. I worked at clearing my mind of Blue Boy. I could tell she hadn't swallowed any of my explanation, but apparently she wasn't going to push the incident.

She slid her arm underneath mine, laughed and shook her head. "Well, I considered you might be more than a little different. So far I've been proven right."

"I did overreact a bit didn't I? It won't happen again."

She smiled. "That's too bad. It was kind of fun for a change. Most of the men I know would have expected me to protect them."

She wasn't exactly staring at me, more like a soft study of my expressions. "If Baby belonged to me, I would have kicked the garage monkey in the balls. How long has Baby been in your life?"

"We go back a long time. To a world before Iraq."

"Then she represents your past to you." She looked over at me and apparently read something in my face. "I'm sorry, did I bring back unwanted memories?'

"No." I smiled. "They were good memories, I don't mind having them brought back."

We finished at Due's, and I had a mind set for Rosa's on Armitage for blues music and a cold one. Laura froze.

"No, oh, no, Rik."

The parking spot available on the street close to Due's left the driver's side of the car visible on approach. The night was proceeding nicely, I'd forgotten Baby and her scratch.

She walked over and placed her hand on the scar and ran her fingers over part of it. "I'm so sorry for you, Rik. This has to hurt you, seeing her like this. Did it happen while we were in Due's?"

I didn't want to talk about Baby. "Sometime this weekend. Some punk getting his jollies-off."

She moved toward me, her eyes moist by the time she reached me. She cupped my face, her hands sliding down to my chest. "She looks so sad. So vulnerable."

I guess Laura's caring should have warmed me inside; awakened the emotions I decided no longer belonged to me. But now, at this moment, I didn't want to feel. To appease her, I pulled her closer to me. "She's a car, I'll get her fixed."

Laura didn't respond. She just gazed up at me. I thought I caught a flash of anger in her eyes. But, if so, it disappeared as fast as it had come. The night no longer held the promise of fun. "Please take me away from here."

She rested her head against my shoulder and nothing more was said until we reached my apartment.

She pulled away from me and slowly traveled the walkway taking in the decor. I couldn't catch if she approved or was making some final judgment about me. She asked, and I agreed to her scrutiny of the rest of the place. I let her go on her own. She returned with a smile.
"A woman decorated your place."
"What makes you think that?"
"Oh, it's definitely a man's apartment, but she left enough subtle feminine touches to stop it from being overbearingly male."

"Is that good?"

"Yes, but she was expensive."

And not worth the expenditure it took to get her into bed.

"It's all you. She took time to get to know you."

I wasn't sure what she was implying, so I just dropped it.

Her mood changed. She took hold of my arm, held up my hand. "Explanation."

I shrugged. "Immoveable object beats flesh and bone."

She inhaled deeply. "You lashed out in anger over Baby, didn't you, Rik?"

I didn't answer.

She stomped her foot. "Rik?' I shrugged, she sighed. "Why are you ashamed to admit that you did?"

"You want me to admit I hit something harder than my hand?"

She looked at me—eyes flashing. "I'm asking you to tell me what happened to Baby. What hurt you so deeply and caused you to lash out and hit something?"

"Why would I admit to doing something dumb like that?"

"What? Admit you feel for Baby, which caused her violation to fill you with pain?"

When I didn't answer, her anger flared. Soothing anger hadn't been on my agenda today.

"Let the bitch do the crying for you, so you don't lose your manhood?"

"I'm not asking anyone to cry for me. My hand was the result of a natural reaction. A dumb reaction, but a reaction. A car, Laura. Baby's just a car. I don't understand what you're asking from me."

She sighed like she'd just lost an important argument and turned away from me. When she looked back at me she was crying softly. "Oh, Rik. Can't you see? Let me in. Please tear down that wall you've built and please let me in."

She moved into me, arms around my shoulders, head rested on the crook of my neck. "Would it be so bad to let me in? So we can share each other, enjoy each other?" She looked up at me. "Let me feel your pain, Rik."

We made it to the couch, arms around each other, side by side. We kissed gently, held each other, nothing sexual, just held each other, content in the warmth of being one.

****

Renaldo paced the living room floor. He had no choice, he must make his move. He could no longer trust either

Margo or Rik. He had to stop Rik before he defiled Margo, before Margo let him.

It was almost too late. Mentally, Rik had corrupted Margo, raped her. Vengeance against Rik was now his just due. Physically he was no match for him, but there were other ways to equate the game; pains more excruciating than those applied to the body. The thought of destroying Rik excited him. He laughed. Time to make a phone call.

****

I woke in the morning with no room to stretch out the kinks. Laura and I were still on the couch, still in each other's arms.

The phone rang. Laura stirred but didn't wake. I started for the phone to silence it, while looking down at the enticing body waiting for me. Screw the phone. I crawled back into her arms.

Chapter Forty

I went to the kitchen and made fresh coffee. Laura stood in the doorway. "I need a shower first, then feed me," she said.

"Good morning to you too. I bought a new toothbrush, and I have a hair dryer and toiletries. I can't help with a change of clothes, unless a man's large dress shirt will do."

She tilted her head rakishly. "Men's shirts button funny. I take it you would do with the buttoning?"

"Who said anything about the shirt having buttons?"

She walked over to me, ran her hand gently down my cheek. "Thank you for not making last night a sexual thing."

"It was difficult, but sex didn't seem to be what you were after, or, I've lost my mind."

She played my lips with her finger. She placed two fingers to her lips, kissed them and then placed them on my lips. "I shall return."

I headed for the fireplace. The phone rang.

"Pretty girl. No, pretty doesn't cover it. I don't possess the adjectives to describe her beauty. You must be most proud." A cheerless and foreboding laugh. "I can't help but wonder though." A deeply penetrating, bone-cauterizing laugh chilled the phone. "Would you be as proud if her face were scarred ugly? Beware of whispers of things to come." He hung up.

I placed the phone on its cradle. My feet automatically headed for the fireplace.—Why? Fire, Laura wanted a fire. Like a computerized family robot I mechanically lowered the thermostat, put firewood in the fireplace, lit the logs and closed the screen. Indulging only in myself, the possibility of the fag hurting Laura never was a consideration. Reality had just kicked me in the balls.

I went to the kitchen and gathered the needed ingredients required in Margo's Spanish omelet recipe. Laura joined me. She smelled like bath soap. No man's dress shirt. Damn, wasted fantasies.

"There's a record collection by the bar, or stay and watch a genius at work."

She smiled. "I intend to do both."

She returned and fingered the seasonings. "These little bottles contain no hidden surprises, right?"

"No hash omelets today. When do I tell her? Not today, this is my day; not his to spoil.

She pursed her lips in disappointment. "Probably for the best. You don't need help from drugs."

I finished chopping red and yellow peppers, mixed the ingredients together and added them to the egg batter. I added a touch of minced jalapenos, a pinch of finely chopped garlic, some sliced ripe olives and half a teaspoon of taco seasoning. Laura raised herself so she could look over my shoulder. Her breasts massaging my back as she did. I spilled some of the mixture on the stove top.

"All good chefs are messy," she assured me.

When the batter was ready, I poured it in a preheated skillet, added some slices of aged New York white cheddar, flipping the omelet and pouring in a little cognac, browning the top of the omelet as the liquor flamed.

"I was told ripe olives are an aphrodisiac," she said, as she popped leftover remains in her mouth.

"I heard, but never found out," I answered.

"No girls willing to test the premise?"

"Couldn't afford the olives."

We ate slowly, savoring each bite. I watched as she ran her tongue over her lips in appreciation of the flavors.

"I'm stuffed," she said. "Ready for R and R by the fireplace."

We settled on the floor, our backs against the couch. I watched the flames in the fireplace catch the gold shades in her hair, made her a second mimosa.

She questioned the drink with her eyes. "Are we playing the French Quarter?"

Close your eyes, and we can be anywhere you wish."

"I'm totally content here."

"Something strange is happening," I said. "My head is permeated with the sound of violins."

She laughed. "It should be. Your recording has just arrived at the Adagio movement of Rachmaninoff's Second Symphony."

"Oh, I thought something mystical was happening to me."

"There is. You're just not aware of what it is yet, my love." I prepared myself for a warm kiss. She moved to the fireplace. "It's time."

"I agree. It's just a little difficult you standing over there."

She returned a steely stare. "It's time for me to read your novel."

"What?" Her eyes stated I'd heard her correctly.

"Now? I thought…"

"Now," she said.

I knew it rested in my desk, but not certain where. "The story is out of order. I've been working on it and haven't lined up the chapters."

Her eyes narrowed. "Is your book a lie, Rik?"

From the point of her chin and the purse of her lips, I knew I'd better produce something. We headed for the den. She sat on top of the desk as I rummaged through the organized confusion that made up my drawers. I finally located the manuscript under a pile of forgotten short stories. The top pages of the manuscript had turned upward with age.

I hesitated. She stared. I handed it to her. She sighed in disgust.

"I've been busy making a living as a free-lance writer."

She looked at the desk top and typewriter. "Writing what?" She left for the living room, curled up at the end of the couch and started reading. I needed a refill on the mimosa. She didn't. I decided orange juice and champagne definitively lacked the balls to face an angry woman, I poured a scotch. She glanced up at me, I smiled at her. She didn't smile back. I went to the bathroom.

I returned and she was still reading—damn. I sat on the other end of the couch and drank my scotch. She continued reading—intently—brow knitted, I think I noticed fangs. I went to the kitchen and finished the two strips of leftover bacon, then spent at least ten minutes drinking coffee.

When I returned to the living room, she'd left the couch and was seated on a chair. Nothing showed that she'd noticed my absence or presence. I tried to gauge how much she'd read. Her face remained emotionless, except for an occasional twitch at the corner of her mouth. I gave consideration to another scotch, but thought best to pass.

She stopped reading and dropped the manuscript on the floor, staring at the smoldering embers in the fireplace. I wanted to say something but I felt too weighted by the heaviness of the silence.

She tilted her head, her eyes filled with a stern intensity. They questioned my being with the exactness of an x-ray. "Why, Rik?"

I knew the bottom of a drawer was the best place for my creativity, and should have remained there. "I never claimed to be a great writer."

She shook her head, brushed away a tear. "I never asked you to be, only that you just take pride in what you do."

I had no response for that.

She didn't add to her statement, but stared at me. "Have you ever been in love?"

That was a curve ball to the groin. "Where did that come from?"

"Can't you answer? Tell me about the women you've cared for."

"Isn't this sorta like men's locker room talk?"

"I didn't ask you to tell me about the women you've laid. I want to know if you've ever loved one."

I sat, stared at her, didn't answer.

"Haven't there been any?"

I laughed. She didn't. "Well sure, everybody's been in love." She waited. "I don't know, Suzi, I guess. At least I thought it was love. She didn't."

"Then you loved and lost. Did it hurt?"

It was my turn to stare. "Christ, I don't know. At twenty-one you're in love with love. What the hell does this have to do with anything?"

"Then someone from when you were older, wiser."

Bound by the lies that made up my life I tried inhaling them away. It still left me with no answers for Laura.

She sighed deeply, choked on a sob. "Oh, God, Rik. Don't you see how sad it is? You've never loved." She got off the couch, her back to me, and walked a few feet away. She turned to me, something close to deep sorrow reflected in her eyes, I didn't understand the why or where. I did feel myself hooked by the sadness of her distance from me.

"I'm sorry, Laura, but I have no idea what you want me to say."

"Oh, my God!" Anger and hurt seemed to be one in her eyes. "You've never loved. You claim to be a writer, but you don't write." She paused, stared intensely.. "And you can't reach out to me over what happened to Baby. I think it's best I leave."

"Whoa—can we hold on a minute here? Baby is a car, Laura. I didn't want to spoil what we have over the grotesque feelings that were spent on Baby."

She grew silent, her eyes seemingly trying to search inside me.

"I have no excuse for not writing. It…it just didn't seem important anymore. I didn't mean it to be a lie."

She continued to search. "You don't get it, can't understand any of it. Your writing is beautiful, your story cries out to be finished. Instead, you bury it in some drawer to rot away. You showed no feelings over what happened to Baby—two things that supposedly mean so much in your life. If you have no feelings for them, how can you have any feelings for me? What I'm about. What I am. How I feel?"

   I had no idea where to go with this. "I'm a little lost here." She didn't offer to find me a path. "All this came about over a book I have yet to finish?"

   She shook her head. "So sad. You're not living, Rik. You're existing. Minutes tick away from your life and you don't hear them." Her eyes moist, fighting back tears now. "Even the lowly caterpillar wants to be something better than it is, so it turns into a butterfly."

   A tear worked its way down her cheek. I wanted to brush it away, but her eyes told me my touch was the last thing she desired at the moment.

   "If you don't care about yourself, then you're not capable of caring about us." She fought another tear. "It's so sad. You couldn't have written what you did unless at some time you tasted and felt life. Loved and cared about people. When did it stop?"

   "I wasn't aware it had."

   She lowered her eyes, then looked at me. Her expression was tightly drawn, as if a fierce tension was churning inside her. "That's what scares me. You're not aware. Things have moved too fast. You've taken my control away from me. I need time to think, to know if I still want to be a part of your life, and if you want to be part of mine. I need to leave."

Christ, I'd apologized, what else did she want? She looked like she needed a hug, but not mine. We stood only a few feet apart, but it might as well have been miles.

"I know what I want from you, for us. It's up to you to decide if I'm worth the effort for you to give it to me."

"Could you be a little more specific about the want part?'

"If you don't know now, you never will." She headed for the door.

"Laura, please wait." She didn't. No choice now, she had to know about the gay, had to let me drive her home. "At least let me drive you."

She shook her head no. "I'll grab a cab." And she left.

I followed behind her, stayed out of sight. I waited until a cab picked her up, and felt she was safe. I was positive the gay had no knowledge of her address.

I returned to my apartment. "What the hell?" A few moments later, I heard noise outside my door. She'd changed her mind, came back. I opened it. Margo stood looking at me, her eyes flooding tears.

"Why, Rik? Why not me?" She turned and headed for her apartment.

Christ Almighty. Why the hell did your Father put women on the earth?

Renaldo stepped out of the elevator. He watched Margo, but did not call out to her. He walked closer to me. "Were those tears I saw on Margo's face?"

He looked at me as though his eyes were reading my soul, and he wasn't happy with what they saw. "So sorry about Baby, Rik," he said, before I could answer.

His eyes masked a sadness, I doubted it was real. "It must have been so difficult for you to look at her. So sorry." He turned and entered his apartment.

I turned to enter mine. Sorry about Baby? How did he know? He didn't drive. What was he doing in the garage?

The bottle of scotch was looking more like a friend every second.

Chapter Forty-One

Scotch is a good friend. It doesn't question why, or ask you to think, or judge. A willing, arms open, to a fault, unselfish friend—unless of course, you abuse its friendship. Go ahead, abuse the booze. He's controlling every other aspect of your life. Might as well control your drinking. God, you're a pathetic asshole. I let the scotch remain a friend in waiting, and stretched out on the couch.

The weatherman said sunny; it rained ,leaving in its wake an expanding veil of repressive ebony, matching the gloom that resided throughout my apartment.

I needed Laura, here with me. The exact why confusing, but I needed her, and it was as plain and simple as that. I fell into a fitful sleep. I awoke and looked out the window, the sky showed evidence of it being early evening.

My body screamed hunger, and I remembered McCabe's served homemade Irish stew on Sundays. That and a beer should solidify the insides. A beer's not drinking. I drove Baby to Bobby's—pretty good late dinner crowd. I made it to the bar, a local chippie let me know she was available. I thanked her for the offer but passed.

Bobby walked up to me and concentrated on my face. "If your new lassie is doing this to you, you better grab the chippie and say goodbye to the lady skirt."

Without asking, he delivered a Heineken's beer and a shot of malt liquor. The last thing I needed was the malt, but I sure as hell wasn't going to say no to a freebie.

He was busier than usual, and I received no more personal time than ordering my stew and a beer. I grabbed what conversation I could. None, however, led to the easing of my pains, the one over Baby, or the current one with Laura that I'd inflicted on myself. I had more beers than I should have—but who gave a shit, and headed for home.

Even with the lights on, if you're inclined to hear things that go bump in the night, our garage can be spooky enough to give credence to those who believe they do. I don't believe in bumps. But, with the definitive reality of the happenings to me lately, my inner voice was suggesting it might not be a bad idea to start believing.

Only, my bump wasn't a thing. It was a little man parading in blue. I listened. No bump. But, my inner voice warned me that maybe there was something else out of line in the garage besides the silence of bumps. Something you couldn't touch, but you knew was there. I turned and faced the bowels of the garage. The lights went out.

I froze, listened. Only the familiar creaks and groans of the building. Something new, something strange, something that didn't belong, like a susurration that filled the emptiness of the garage. At first one, then two, then in multiple propagation came whispers.

The lights came back on. I was on the balls of my feet, my left hand clenched into a fist, my right resting where my holstered gun used to be. I did a slow survey of the garage, revealing nothing except the morgue-like appearance it presented. The lifeless bodies of cars, lined up, awaiting autopsy. No shadows moved. Darkened corners revealed nothing. No whispers. No movement. Nothing that belonged to anything, or to an imagination that could make it belong to something.

Christ, Rik. Shit happens. The lights temporarily turned off. It wouldn't be the first time they did. I wondered if the fag was in the garage, hidden, watching me, laughing at me? I took a breath and pushed the up button. I refused to allow myself to look back over my shoulder.

The elevator didn't arrive. I checked the indicator arrow. It pointed to the third floor. I pushed the button again, and then again. I tried again, but the arrow stayed registered to the third floor. Who the hell would be tying up the elevator this time of night? No one—no one who lives in the building. Then who? Of course, Rik, the bogeyman with his whispers. The garage remained in darkness. They were out there. Whispers from the past—whispers from the alley—whispers from the last breath of the little boy. Stop it! Stop it! You're succumbing to him.. I pushed the button again.

The stairs. You can always take the stairs, three floors of them waiting for you. Well you wanted to get back into shape. I opened the emergency fire door to the stairway. Forty-eight steps plus six landings to my floor, I scooted my foot until it was firmly on the first step. The lights came on.

I took a breath and started my climb. First step, first step to getting back into shape. Might as well be positive about it, I headed upwards.

Four steps left to the first floor. Not even breathing hard. In better shape than I gave myself credit. Maybe start taking two steps at a time. The lights went out.

An inky darkness surrounded me. I stopped, afraid I might stumble, fall. I reached out, found the banister. I didn't move. I tried to allow my eyes to adjust to the blackness. Go back down? To what,? Inky blackness in the garage? An elevator that won't work?

It was far from pungent, faint really, but unmistakably there. An odor of something that registered familiar, but was totally alien to this building. Whispers, soft whispers, but resonant against the silence of the stairway, coming from behind me. The lights came on. I turned and looked, back. Rats. Big ones. Okay, get off on the first floor. Rats waited on the landing, bared teeth saying no.

I saw an opening, headed for it making the landing and two steps up to the second floor, past the rats. The odor grew stronger, the smell of putrefying flesh. I took a breath, the stairway a tomb, silent. A noise? What? Silence prevailed, hushed, expectant. I made three more steps up, away from the rats..

The lights turned off. A mother's warning to 'hush' came from dark corners. Ahead of me, the sound of clicking nails against concrete steps. Sounds like the wind whispering through grass were moving up the stairs toward me. The blackness grew heavier. Whispers filled the stairway.

I felt an icy prickling at the base of my spine, hands slick with sweat. Click. Click. Click. The lights came on. Piercing, black beady eyes stared at me. The stink of my own perspiration overshadowed the smell of rotting flesh. Long, naked tails, coarsely scaled, swished back and forth.

Rats. Jesus, big, black rats, big as cats, all over, at least one on every step now in front me. Afraid to look behind me. Rats, big rats, no place for me to go. I remained frozen in place. Pugnacious, quarrelsome, their anger heightened at my interruption of their feasting on a rotting carcass, their ill-mannered tempers at their worst.

Can I escape before they attack? Rip my skin off? Tear muscle from bone? Their movement became more frenzied, perturbed, excited at my presence. Sounds like whispers as they paced back and forth, eyeing me, smelling my sweat, my fear.

Come-on, Rik. They're just animals. You're a human, the superior machine. You can outsmart them, plan an escape route. That's it. Get away. Can't stand here. Have to get away. Yes, you can get away. All they can do is reproduce better. That's all, that's all. And bite better. Claw better. Rip skin better.

A sudden movement, a break in rank, several coming at me, certain they're coming at me. Can't let them get me—don't let them get you. Get away. Have to move—get away. Move where? Up, to the second floor, to the hallway, move, get away, get safe.

Fast. They're moving fast. Right at me, I kicked out at them. Missed. Lost my balance and almost fell. Around me, all around me, brushing against my legs, around me. I kicked out and missed again.

Around my feet. I felt them around my feet, walking over my feet. The lights go out. The walls close in around me, leaving an inky well of darkness— silence. Whispers travel down the stairway toward me.

Air heavy, can't breathe, the closeness suffocating. I can't see rats, just hear their whispers, all around me, whispers..

Have to get out of here. I move my hand slowly and find the banister. No quick movements. Get out of here. Whispers. Get out of here.

Can't see, can't judge the distance. Do it, get out of here. All I can hear is their whispers. Get hold of banister, and use as leverage. Swing leg backward for momentum, then bolt over them, over them to the second floor.

My foot lands on something wet and slimy. I pitch backward and lose control, hands coming off the banister. I fall, land flat and land on my back. The air rushes out of me and I can't suck it back in. Choking, I need air but it won't come. Whispers all around me.

Something's moving in my hair, on my head, on my leg, something big, something that smells like rat. It's on my leg, moving up, coming up my leg to my body. Off me! Get off me! Get up, Rik, get up, get out of here. I can't get up, my foot stuck in rungs of banister. Get it loose, agitated whispers around me. I can't get my foot loose. Get off me. Get off me!

A scream? Someone screamed.

My foot loose, but I can't get up. I crawl, I crawl forward, through something wet and slimy. I get to my feet. Run, don't trip, run to the landing and the door. The door is straight ahead, on the landing. I ran, sure that the rates followed. Get to the landing, find the wall. Can't find door. Jesus, find the door. The door is straight ahead.

Find the handle. Turn the handle. The handle won't turn. My hands slip around the handle, too wet from sweat, and slime. Turn the handle. Get out of here, Jesus, turn the handle.

A lighted hallway. I'm in the safety of the lighted hallway. No rats, no whispers. Laughing, God, I'm laughing. I don't recall getting here, but I'm in my apartment. I dropped my clothes to the floor. I never want to see them or wear them again. I need a drink. No, first a shower, a long cleansing shower, then a drink.

I must have heard the sound. It should have registered. It should have sparked a warning, long before I entered the bathroom, but, it didn't. Only after I entered. Water was running in my bathroom. Had the nerves not been ragged beyond the shattering point, I would have had some reaction. At least I would have experienced the element of surprise. As it was, I just stood and stared.

Someone was in my shower.

Chapter Forty-Two

There was no movement, no acknowledgement of my entering. I could make out the outline of breasts. Shoulder-length hair, a woman. A too stationary, a too still woman, doing nothing but letting the shower water cascade over her.

Laura—Margo? Who let them in?

The gears in my head moved like they'd been lubricated with peanut butter. "Hello?"

No response, no movement, stationary. No one can remain that stationary. It was time she moved; time to find out why she hadn't. I moved stiff-jointed toward the shower, my feet disconnected from my legs, unable to relay to the rest of my body where they were going. My brain remained somewhere in the middle of the room. No game plan. Against what? Open the shower door. I would have to eventually. See who's in there. Say hi.

I was naked. I doubted the person in the shower cared one way or the other. Too still. She was much too still. I grasped the shower door handle, and took a chance before opening it. I called out Laura's name. Nothing. "Margo?" Same result. Whoever you are, move. Please.

I opened the door, intuitive reflexes making me jump backwards, avoiding a surprise fist, foot, or possible knife slash. I shouldn't have bothered. I was in no danger of being attacked. Or, anything else for that matter.

"What the fuck?"

I stared at a mannequin taking a shower in my bathroom.

It was one of those new, lifelike models. Silicone made the face and body appear to look like human skin. Arms posed, reaching out for someone to come into them. The body was beautiful, inviting and the mouth full-lipped. The mannequin was adorned with a human wig, shoulder-length, auburn colored hair. Hello, Laura.

Only her facial beauty had been scarred by a sharp instrument. Water caused some kind of red gel to liquefy and look like blood running from the slits on her face to her breasts, and down the front of her body. I turned off the water, and found myself apologizing to the mannequin for the atrocities committed on her. I left everything the way I'd found it and headed for my bedroom.

The pants in the closet hung neatly from hangers; really too challenging a task at the moment to pick a pair. I noticed an old, forgotten pair of jeans lying on the closet floor, wadded up in a corner. They still fit around the thighs and butt, but had shrunk around the waist. My body started shaking, so hard I could barely walk. I made it to the bathroom and threw up.

I followed the next logical move and made it to the bar. I called Jim. He wasn't home. I left a message, "Get your ass up here. Now!" Then followed with a call to Mac, but not before I consumed two ounces of scotch neat, and had two more at the ready.

Sunday, Mac wasn't at the precinct, so I called his home. "Yeah what? This is my day off. And I have big plans." I could hear ice cubes clanking against glass and swore I could smell scotch on his breath coming through the phone.

I told him about the rats in the stairway, and the mannequin. He listened to my detailed report, and snorted. I could hear him unwrapping a new cigar.

"Rats?" He laughed. "You must have shit in your pants." And he laughed again. "Sorry, are you still enough of a cop that you didn't touch or disturb nothing?" Mac's words, gruff as usual, but still providing a warmth that reached out to protect me from the ills of the world.

"Think he knows about your fear of rats? How?"

"Don't know. I just don't know right now. Mac, the mannequin, it was meant to be Laura."

"Who? Never mind, I know. You told her yet?"

"Not yet.

"Would be nice if you did. No, don't. Best I did. Have her come to your place Wednesday, at six thirty. The mannequin makes your bathroom a crime scene. I'll send some people over. Use your guest bathroom." He was gone.

I finished the second scotch, then took a sponge bath. The phone rang.

"Pretty girl. No, pretty doesn't cover it. I don't possess the adjectives to describe her beauty. You must be most proud." A cheerless and foreboding laugh. "I can't help but wonder though." A deeply penetrating, bone cauterizing laugh chilled the phone. "Would you be as proud if her face were scarred ugly? Always, always beware, the whispers may come again." He hung up.

Mad at me or not, and no matter what Mac thought, I had to reach Laura. She couldn't be alone. The gay had never mentioned her before. Why now? He didn't know she existed until Saturday. I called. No answer. If her phone allowed her to know who was calling, she probably wouldn't answer anyway.

Dark clouds dominated the sky, presenting an expanding veil of repressive ebony, like February in Chicago when it's hard to remember the days of summer. It left an appropriate gloom throughout the apartment, matching how I felt about life at the moment.

I would have liked to complain to someone, but it was my hurt, and it belonged to no one else, was caused by no one else. That was not exactly true. Laura had something to do with it, but the hurt was mine,. A hurt I'd brought upon myself. I was finding it hard to accept, mainly because I didn't understand it, its origins, nor why I felt it so strongly.

I tried Laura again. No answer. My mind pictured the mannequin's scarred face. But, how could he be aware of her? She was too new for him to be aware of her. Too new for him to know where she lived. Then why didn't she answer her phone?

Where the hell was she? Where are you fag?

There was a knock at the door.

Chapter Forty-Three

I let the crime scene techs in. They weren't friendly, and made me feel like dog shit in my own home. They looked over the bathroom, and had me show them where I'd encountered rats. I said I had to leave. They told me maybe it would take them a couple hours, so don't hurry coming back. I parked illegally in front of Laura's.

She wasn't home. Where the hell was she? I sat in Baby and waited. I was about to give up on ever seeing her again when a cab pulled up and she got out. She started to close the cab door but grabbed it for support instead. She pulled her shoulders back, lifted her chin, and tried not to weave her way to the building door. I let her make it on her own.

I waited until she was almost in the foyer and joined her. "Hi."

She greeted me with a roundhouse hook that landed her into my arms. I cupped her face, tilted her head back and kissed her as passionately as possible without it being lewd.

She broke my hold and pushed me away. "I'm intoxicated, you know."

"Yes. It's very becoming on you."

She looked at me, with one eye, as the other kept closing. "If I wasn't drunk, I wouldn't let you touch me. If you were a gentleman, you wouldn't take advantage of my situation."

"Did I ever make claim to being a gentleman?"

She found the doorknob and held on to it. "Then, you admit to taking advantage of me because I'm drunk?"

"Yes."

"Don't you feel guilty?"

"Absolutely not." I pulled her back into my arms. She didn't resist.

I got her into the elevator, and with a lot more effort into her apartment.

"Then every time I get drunk, you will willingly take advantage of me?" she asked, through enunciation that could have used a lot of help.

"You betcha."

She focused on my face suspiciously. "Then why aren't you taking advantage?"

I woke, it felt early. She lay next to me. Our lovemaking still warmed her body. I immersed myself in the beauty of her nakedness.

She woke with a start, turned her head to me and glared, her eyes sparked. "You!"

I smiled. "Yes, me. You ready to be taken advantage of again?"

She scooted away from me as far as possible without falling off the bed. "What are you doing in my bed? You know, I don't like you anymore!" There was no tenderness expressed in her face, or her eyes. "Oh, Rik, I really thought I'd found something real. Damn you, get away from me!" She made fists and pounded me on the chest. "If I hadn't been drunk...get out, get out. I hate you!"

I grabbed her hands, pulled her on top of me. "No, you don't. You're just disappointed that I lied to you, and…overstepped the boundaries of what's right. I'm sorry—forgive me…it won't happen again. I promise. No more lies."

"You have no right being here. I walked away from you." Her eyes reddened. I wrapped an arm around her and offered her my shoulder to cry on. She did more than cry, her body lightly convulsed with each sob. "You hurt me so bad," she said between sobs. "Why did you lie?"

"Because I didn't want to lose you."

The tears stopped, she looked long into my face. "Oh, Rik." She exited the bed without touching me, and walked a few feet from the bed. "What time is it?"

I took my eyes off her ass. "I don't know. Some time Monday morning."

"What! What happened to Sunday?" She pointed at me. "Don't answer. I don't want to know."

"Need breakfast?" I asked.

"Of course," she answered, as she headed for her bathroom. I could hear shower water.

She returned shortly, wearing a full length, terry cloth robe, her hair bound in a towel. She made me get dressed and leave the room. I went over to the bookshelves. A book hadn't cradled my hands for a long time. Her young adult section caught my attention. No use rushing the brain into trying to understand Hemingway.

 She joined me, shorts, sandals, tee shirt, gym bag. I looked at the book, 'Gulliver's Travels.'

"That's really a novel written for adults, and I doubt you qualify being one." She walked toward the door. "First breakfast, then I need to jog."

I choked, audibly. "You mean, like run?"

"I need to detox. Jogging will do that." She stared at me. "Don't you jog, or is taking advantage of drunk women your only exercise?"

It sure beats the hell out of jogging. "When I get my cross-country running shoes on, you're in trouble, missy."

We ate at Gus's. Gladys rattled my chain by asking Laura how she'd picked such a big spender taking a piece of class like her to Gus's. As we left, she let me know my companion was too good for me. Laura turned so she could look into my face, smiled, and let her eyes tell me she totally agreed with Gladys.

Margo's door was ajar, I caught her looking at us before she quickly closed it. I noticed Laura standing very still, staring at it.

"Though I imagine it's an impossible situation at the moment," Laura said. "I think I would like to be Margo's friend. I feel sorry for her."

"How do you know Margo?"

"I don't. I've caught her watching us coming or going more than once. Saw the sadness in her eyes. I checked her mailbox to get her name. Who's Renaldo?"

"Her brother." I held her in my arms. A pleasant task, so I kept her there. "I want you here, in my arms, not her. Not being your friend is her decision, and one we can't let guide our lives."

Laura sighed, and nodded. "Still, it's sad, being the instrument of a broken heart."

Right now, getting Laura back into the fold was my main concern. Margo's feelings were a spill on the back burner. "Can't be helped."

In the apartment, Laura headed for the bedroom. "Me first."

I didn't know what, "me first" entailed, but I waited; waited for what seemed like an inordinate amount of time. When she finally appeared, the shorts and top were gone. A black spandex jogging suit adorned her body. Yellow and orange stripes ran down the front. The outfit highlighted her every curve.

I smiled. "We going to do something kinky?"

"Only if you consider jogging kinky." She looked disappointed. "Don't you have something to run in?"

Laura made it to the bottom of the stairs, and pinched about an inch of skin from around my middle. "The jogging will make me feel extremely physical. I fear your body may not be able to sustain the TLC I intend to give it later."

I joined her, wearing an old pair of red, workout shorts, a tee-shirt advertising Uno's Pizza, and cross country training shoes that had never trained. We walked to Lincoln Park. The way the spandex accented her tush should have been classified illegal. There were other people in the park, with the same concept as Laura's, that jogging and health were spontaneous. Several young things jogged ahead of us. Like Laura, spandex covering tight backsides.

Laura noticed me noticing them and smiled. "See what you've been missing?"

"Just a short run today. We'll go slow, just a couple of miles. I don't want to burn you out," she said caustically.

I nodded. "Swell."

Laura set the pace. I think she forgot about the slow part. I ran behind her. Not a bad place to be, the view was fantastic. First sweat, profusely, then a painful burning sensation in the calves and thighs. My lungs screamed for air. We must have covered two miles, though it felt like five.

Laura's stride was smooth, fluid. No show of perspiration. She breathed effortlessly. She turned, ran backwards and faced me. "How we doing?"

I would have responded quite colorfully about smartasses, except my lungs didn't have enough air to waste on words. "Two miles, yet?"

She turned forward again, slowed and pointed. "See that bench ahead. It's about three-quarters of a mile from where we started," she said behind a hidden smile. "You can stop there, and rest. You did good," she said, no longer able to contain laughter.

I really hate smartasses. I used the bench for support, Laura jogged in place. My whole body said, 'screw pride.' I did, unabashedly sliding my butt onto the bench.

"You earned a rest. I'm going to go a little further. I'll come back for you."

I nodded, and she took off. I watched her until I lost sight of her around a curve. I ran my hands down my legs trying to stretch out some of the kinks. It sucker-punched me. I'd let her out of my sight. I'd left her alone. Alone in Lincoln Park; a park full of trees and places where all kinds of people hide. People like Blue Boy who blend out of sight.

So many hidden places available for him to surprise her—hurt her. *I swore to myself. Have to reach her, get to her before he does.* I got up, a calf muscle turned into a Charlie-horse. I grabbed the back of the bench and tried to stretch it out. The calf muscles screamed. I can't leave her alone. Run. My legs are totally spastic. *Run, damn it! Muscles or no muscles, I have to run. I have to catch her. A scream? I swore I heard a woman scream. Run. I have to catch her. I swore I heard her scream.*

Chapter Forty-Four

I might have made it three yards when I saw her rounding the curve. Only she wasn't jogging. She was running, as fast as she could. I rose above pain and stiffness and closed the gap between us. She ran into my arms. The way she gasped for air and the perspiration on her face signaled she'd run at a fast clip for a good distance. Her heart pounded, her eyes a mirror of panic and alarm. She tried speaking, nothing came out.

"What? What happened, Laura?"

"A man," was all she could get out.

"Where?"

She pressed her face against my chest, fought for control over the shaking that consumed her body. "On the path, He appeared next to me. All of a sudden, from nowhere, right next to me. Next to me, Rik. He jogged with me." She turned. "Back there, back there. He was waiting for me. Oh, God, Rik." She squeezed against me, secured her arms around me.

I scanned the grounds, the path, but no one appeared to be following her. "How far away, Laura?"

She tightened her grip on me. "No! No, don't leave me. Please don't leave me, Rik. Please."

I assured her I wouldn't. I knew trying to find him would be futile. He wouldn't make himself available to me. Still, that I made no attempt to find him, let him terrify

Laura without retribution, chafed my balls. "Did he hurt you?"

Her rapid breathing had returned to normal. "No." She looked at my face, as if looking for guidance. "He ran along side of me for a short distance. His eyes were focused on my face the whole time, smiling." She paused. "His smile was so sinister-looking, so evil." She rubbed her face across my chest as if cleansing it of something vile.

"Then…" she sought more protection in my arms. "Then he looked at me and laughed, while he ran a forefinger, like it was a knife, down his face. Repeating over and over the words…slice, slice."

She shivered, a small sob escaped her. I wrapped her in my arms. "It's okay now, you're safe. It's okay." I wasn't sure I believed it, I just wanted Laura to.

"Why would that man do something like that? It was like he was imitating slicing my face. Why would he do that?"

"Because he's a freak." It was my turn to take control, but I did not choose wisely.

"Maybe we should wait here to see if he comes to us, so I can break his bones."

Temporarily, her eyes appeared to question my sanity. "Rik, I don't want to be here anymore. Can we please go to your place?"

"Sure." Damn it. Best place for her. Best place for the both of us. But the man in the park had to be Blue Boy, and he would take away any pleasure or warmth my apartment offered. I looked down on her.

She seemed so small, so vulnerable. She wasn't going to let the incident in the park go, especially the 'why' of why it happened. Leaving me with no choice but to expose the hidden truths that made up my life. It left me no choice but to tell her sooner than I had intended about the gay—bringing him into our lives way too soon for her to be able to accept, or understand.

Joggers brought me back to reality. Running around us, cursing as they did, voicing an occasional snide remark. I refrained from taking out my frustration and anger on one particular asshole and permanently crippling him.

We walked off the path, away from the joggers, making our way back to Clark Street. She stayed as close to me as possible and still be able to walk. I kept my arm around her. I felt some of her tension ease as Clark Street neared. Her neck and shoulder muscles relaxed as we left the park.

She inhaled deeply, making us stop so she could analyze my face. "Rik, the man who ran with me was dressed all in blue. He looked just like that horrible little man you chased Saturday."

I hesitated, I'd hoped for later, but I could definitely rule that out. What a fun day this was going to be. "You sure?"

"Yes." She waited, that's all I gave her. "Who is he? How do you know him? Why does he know you?"

I kissed her on the forehead. "Let's take a deep breath and try to enjoy the walk home. I don't know about you, but I could use a drink. Maybe even a little laughter at Bobby's."

Her nostrils flared slightly. Her eyes burned into mine. "I want to know, I have the right…"

"Yes and yes. And you will, but not right now. At the moment I refuse to answer on the grounds that I don't want to. First, Bobby's for a drink. Let's get our lives back into perspective."

I used Mac's pay phone to bring him up to date on the park. He wasn't happy.

Mac's sigh was leonine. "I told you I wanted her at your place on Wednesday. Couldn't you wait until then to fuck up?" I could hear him opening a new cigar. "I'll be at your place in an hour. Have her with you."

Bobby was leaning, elbows on top of the bar, face cupped in his hands, eyes sparkling. "Well now, and who are you Lassie?"

Laura gave him a smile. Bobby blustered a little and blushed from his receding hairline all the way down his face I grabbed a stool next to Laura.

Bobby turned from Laura and shook his head at me. "This one's too good for you, Rik."

"Thank you, I wish he would learn that." Laura leaned over and laid a kiss on Bobby's cheek. From that instant on, she owned him, and our drinks were free.

We left, Laura's body language said she wasn't sure she wanted to. She moved into my arms again. I focused on doorways, and alleys. I noticed her doing the same. I wished Jim, with his brawn was by my side, just in case. She moved out of my arms and faced me. "I had no idea how paralyzing fear can be," she said. "To come face-to-face with it, especially when that fear belongs to someone so strange and frightening…God, Rik, I'm so scared. I have never been so scared. What waits for me at your place?"

I kissed her on the forehead. "The truth—which will probably frighten you more." I couldn't hold back a culpable sigh. "I'm so sorry, Laura."

She grabbed me by the shirt, stopping me. "Then why should I want to go there?"

I reached deep down but found nothing that justified not taking her home, giving her the safety of being out of my life. She continued questioning my face. "Because I don't want to lose you."

Jim was sitting at my bar, enjoying one of my beers. "So's I asks," his back to us. "What the 'potant? Why's you bother my phone yesterday wanting my ass up here?" He turned, saw Laura, and glared at both of us. "Mos' sorry, missy. Not spectin' prickhead have company." He set the beer down, his eyes icing Laura, scorching me. "I'se be nice caus' womans here.

Laura was focused on Jim's face, stiff in her stature as though frozen by his eyes. She reached for my hand, moved to me, leaning into my body, seeking shelter.

"Talk goin' roun' building, somes official looking mens." His eyes like ice now as he eyed Laura and then me.

Laura moved tighter into my arms.

"Like po-lees official-looking mens. Be seen other day, carryin' a dead woman outs the building." He eyed me suspiciously. "You maybe knows why that?" He finished his beer. "Only problem be," he said. "Everybody live here, not be dead."

He got up, walked close enough to slam his shoulder into mine. He made sure Laura was aware he was eyeing her up and down, frosting her. He did the same to me. "Margo not happy." He headed for the door. "That make me not happy. I'se wants everybody happy, 'specially me."

He gave me a glare job "You best be ready to 'splain stuff, fores I break you neck."

Laura remained stiff, frozen, her eyes wide as she searched my face, avoiding Jim's stare. He left, I picked-up an exchange of words in the hallway.

Mac entered. He looked pissed.

Laura looked up at me. Eyes showed fright, tears.

Mac's suit looked like he'd slept in it. "Again, I ask. You ever hear of a Sammi Swain?"

Chapter Forty-Five

There is never any visible movement of his eyeballs, but Mac never enters a room without taking it all in and making himself aware of everything and everybody in it. He was looking directly at me, but before I could answer him, he was standing next to Laura. He pulled the chewed cigar out of his mouth and handed it to me. I took it gingerly between thumb and forefinger.

"Dispose of that for me, and bring your 'old uncle' a toddy. I'll be with the lady."

He took hold of Laura's hands. "You have to be Laura?" She nodded. He patted a bar stool. "Why don't you join Uncle Mac and let's get acquainted?"

I retrieved a Heineken's beer and a shot of Scotch whiskey for Mac.

"Pardon an old man, but looking is about all we have left. My God, you are exquisite."

She tilted her head. Her eyes stating she'd fully appreciated his appraisal.

"Did numbnuts ever tell you about me," he asked her.

She smiled, and then gave a short laugh. "Not enough, I don't think. And I can't imagine why."

"He tries to keep me a secret. The ladies usually find me cuter than him and much more charming."

Laura did a little girl giggle and touched two fingers to his face. "Definitely more charming."

"You two having fun?" I asked, as I joined them.

Mac concentrated on Laura's face. He downed his shot and motioned to me for another. He took Laura's hands and wrapped his around them. 'I'm so sorry my dear, what you're about to hear is not pleasant." He patted her hands. "But, I find it necessary that you do."

He gave me his penetrating stare. "Now," he said. "I'm going to ask again. Have you ever heard of or know a Sammi Swain?"

I could tell by the tone of his voice the questioning was going to be relentless. Laura had seen the last of 'Mr. Charm.'

"As I said before, nothing rings a bell."

Mac's stare x-rayed into me. "I think it should. And if you'll concentrate, you'll think so too." He prepared another cigar for chewing. "A bartender, someone you talked to in a bar? Someone, someone you were introduced to?" He finger-poked me on the forehead. "Think man, because you know him."

Laura looked at me, then Mac. "Does this have anything to do with the man in the Park?"

Mac shot me a stare, then concentrated on Laura. "What happened in the park, dear? Come close and tell your Uncle Mac all about it." He was giving her his, 'you can trust me, tell me all, routine he uses on the naïve when starting an interrogation. Laura laid out in detail the happening in the park.

Mac looked at me, a shit-eating grin on his face. "Jogging?" Then his face took on a less than friendly demeanor."

He inhaled sharply and kept his eyes burning on mine. His interest in Laura seemed to have waned. "I'm asking again. You ever hear of a Sammi Swain?" He methodically tipped the shot glass, followed by a swig of beer while he waited for my answer.

"Damn it, I'm telling you, no, never."

That was not the correct answer. "Sammi Swain was his stage name. How about a Lester Hamburg?"

"You're kidding, right?" He wasn't. "A definite no."

"He entertained in gay bars. Sang. Did female impersonations."

"Why the hell would I know someone like that?"

Mac grunted in disgust. "How am I supposed to know? Give me something, Rik."

I shook my head. "Can't help."

"Shit." He sipped absently at his beer. "Too bad. It would have tied-up some loose ends." He sighed and leaned back on the bar stool. "Couple days ago, this fruit of the loom comes in to the precinct all excited. Claims his partner is missing and he's sure he's come to bodily harm. No one gives a shit and pays him little attention. He's persistent though, so I bring him into my office." Mac paused and shook his head. "Should have seen this guy." Mac took another minute.

Laura gave me a questioning look, and one that said I had a lot of explaining to do.

Mac continued. "I made sure my door was open." I laughed, Laura gave an uncertain grin. "Sorry, Laura, been around bigoted cops too long." He nursed a sip of beer.

"Anyway, fruitloops claims his partner has been missing for a month and is sure he's come to bodily harm. Of course I have to ask why? "

Mac stared at me. "So you tell me why I'm telling you this?"

I shook my head. "No idea."

He shook his head. "What made me think I was talking to Mr. Sherlock Holmes? Apparently, his roomie had a hang-up that made their relationship less than perfect. A taste for masochism. He got his jollies-off having it stuck in his ass. Hard and hurting. The rougher the better."

Laura grimaced, looked away. Mac noticed it.

"Sorry, not nice, but necessary. So, he would stray looking for variety. In his quest, he met a man fitting the description you gave me of your stalker. At least that's the same description my fruit gave me of the man obsessed with this Sammi."

"Stalker?" She fastened her doe eyes on me. "What stalker?"

Mac stared at Laura. "He fits the description you gave me of the man who harassed you in the park, my lovely." He turned to me. "The same description you gave me of your stalker. Follow where I'm going, Mr. Sherlock?"

I'd wanted to tell Laura about Blue Boy on my own, maybe over a drink, by the fireplace, something classical on the recorder. I could forget that scenario now, and from the look in Laura's eyes, any time in the future, "I don't get the connection with Laura and me." I told Mac.

Mac gave the cigar a hard chew. "Supposedly our mutual friend is not only scary, weird city, but possessive of the boys he's performed his skills on. Especially, according to his roomie, totally toward this Sammi Swain, to the point of being obsessed. Sammi apparently couldn't get studly to leave him alone, and feared for his life if he didn't give in to your Blue Boy's demands." Mac finished his beer.

He looked at me like he was expecting some sort of brilliant offering. When he didn't get it, he shook his head and concealed a disgusted sigh. "You told me your stalker kept blaming you for stealing his Sam, right?" I hesitated too long. "Damn it, right? And he wants your ass because you stole his Sam, right? His one and only love, right?"

I nodded. Laura was burning holes in my shirt with her eyes.

"The floater I told you about was fruitloop's roomie. As I told you, my interest in him peaked because he fit the M.O. of my serial killer. His genitals had been cut off and he'd been shot in the gut."

Laura covered her mouth and coughed. Mac noticed and apologized to her.

"Last time he'd been seen alive, he was with Blue Boy."

I studied Mac's face, and let him know I was really pissed he'd thrown this shit at Laura. He didn't care what my emotional state of mind was. "So, you have another murder that matches the M.O. of your serial killer. What's that supposed to mean to Laura and me?" I asked him.

Laura was studiously gauging both Mac and me.

Mac snorted, looked at me like I'd just gone simple. "The floater turns out to be this Sammi Swain. Sammi, Sam? Gay Sam, Blue Boy's lover, got it?" He gave this time to soak in. "Which," he continued, "leads me to figure your stalker and my serial killer are one and the same person."

That leveled my Adams apple with my nuts. "What? Bullshit! I told you I don't know this Sam."

"His partner put out a missing persons flyer on him. He was twenty-one, from Iowa. Worked at a gay bar on North Clark called "The Eighth Square." Mac checked his cigar, put it back in his mouth and worked it heavy. He concentrated on my face. "You familiar with the place?" I slipped him the finger.

He acted like he didn't notice, "You sure about this Sammi character?"

"Damn it! I said I don't know him."

"Think you do. In his prying around, the coroner found something very strange lodged in Sammi's throat. A matchbook."

"So what?"

The expression on Laura's face, was less than reassuring.

Mac sighed heavily and ran his hand over his mouth. "Matchbook was pretty much destroyed, but eventually they brought up a legend on the cover."

He looked at me like I should know what the legend was, acted pissed that I didn't. He waited for me to enter the conversation. I had no idea what to enter. "Right in the middle of the card, in capital letters, the name, Rik. Underneath the name, 'Call Me'. He paused. Laura shot darts at me with her eyes. "Now, I don't know anyone but you that spells the name Rik without the 'C'." He waited, I let him. "They couldn't come up with a phone number is the reason why you haven't been bothered by the police. I figure Blue Boy found your card on his love piece and in a jealous rage, killed him." He shook his head. "Did you find the cards successful?"

Laura looked at me like I was fast becoming something vile found squashed on the bottom of her shoe. She rose, walked behind the bar and fixed herself a drink. She didn't ask if either Mac or I wanted one, which was probably just as well, as I wasn't sure this was the moment to trust what she would pour in my glass.

"Help me here, Rik. How did this Sammi kid get your card?"

"No idea. A small time printer hangs out at Bobby's. He came up with the idea of the matchbooks as a way to break the ice with a girl. He printed some up and passed them out." I laughed, though Laura didn't think it was funny. "I never used them."

"You sure?" Mac asked.

"Maybe one at the Angry Pickle. I lit a girl's cigarette." Laura's eyes said things meant to be left unsaid in public.

Mac looked tired. He rubbed the back of his neck. "You don't know shit. Have no answers to anything." He looked over at Laura. "And you haven't told this lovely dick-squat have you?"

Laura's eyes flared. This could be a long day. "Gay! Stalker! You put my life in danger, but couldn't find a reason to tell me?" Laura finished her drink, looked at Mac. "I want to go home, will you please take me?"

"I was going to tell you everything today. I was just waiting for the right time." I said. She looked at me like I was lower than whale shit.

She looked over at Mac. "Is it okay if we leave now?"

"Yes. It really is best if you come with me dear. I need to ask you some questions and give you some fatherly advice about not coming back to lover boy here, any time soon——ever." He looked at me. "First thing in the morning, my office." He took Laura's arm and led her to the door. She didn't look back.

"Christ, Rik. Really? A calling card? Tell me. If you didn't know this Sammi character, how did it come into his possession?" Mac asked.

Nothing I could say now would bring Laura back. And I couldn't help but feel Mac might be correct. Best for her, if she walked out of my life.

Chapter Forty-Six

I watched as the door closed. "Swell."

Laura hadn't turned around, hadn't said call me later, or screw you, or fuck your momma for bringing you into the world. I was left sitting on my ass not knowing what she expected or didn't. I could however, justify it was time for a drink. The phone rang. Too soon for it to be Laura—still I picked-up.

"The bitch is there again. You're so wrong, She's so wrong, so very wrong. You will pay for her intrusion, pay heavily for your indiscretion." The phone slammed brutally into its cradle. Something had been placed over the mouthpiece to distort the voice. Whatever, it successfully stopped me from recognizing who was on the other end, or defining the gender. The only certainty was, it wasn't the gay. I didn't need this, and I slammed the phone down.

"Wonderful, another voice heard from that wants my ass." Time to evaluate my situation—but the only constant presenting itself in this picture was the malt still waited.

Knowing Mac, his fatherly advice to Laura would amount to her staying out of my life until they caught the freak. He would be insistent and present a cop's lifetime of what a sick mind could do to her if she presented herself as easy pickings. Leaving her frightened, maybe scared shitless, hating my guts, and making sure her heart and soul stayed too far away for me to reach them. Not even close to being a satisfactory solution to my problem at hand—'nobody knows the trouble I've seen'.

I'd attempted to find the gay without Mac's help. I gave up after a week, letting the gay move the chess pieces of our lives at will, hoping to look weak and draw him to me. Instead, he'd invaded my life, sucking something very precious and very meaningful out of it. And with the possibility of Laura being in danger, he had me close to being checkmated. I could no longer take the chance on Mac keeping her safe. He was a good cop, but he was handicapped by regulations and had nothing legally to hold Blue Boy on. My only regulation was me. Not good for the gay, and an arsenal of resources unavailable to Mac. I would find the freak, and when I did, I would cut his balls off.

I went down to the garage and Baby. Still, unable to stop myself from running my hand over her wound. I told her I would take away the pain, make her as good as new.

My destination was an area of Chicago known as the Far North Side. My specific interest, was called the Edgewater Community. Once inhabited by prominent and moneyed city citizens, it was now suffering through the throes of ethnic change. Edgewater's Senn high school boasts students from fifty different countries learning English as a second language.

Among this change is a large constituency of Asian nationals, and one Tommy Dao. Tommy is one of Edgewater's successful businessmen, if you consider prostitution and drugs a business. Dao knows those who walk the dark side of the streets and hide businesses in lightless corners. Nothing happened on the streets that escaped his notice. And while he hid it well, he was also as gay as they come.

I reached Foster Avenue, took a right off Broadway and turned onto Winthrop. A residential street, once consisting of red brick, single-family-owned, three flat buildings, now turned into multi-family subdivided slums. Tommy Dao's place of residence had escaped the conversion. I parked Baby in front of it. A large stone stairway, and brick and stone porch adorned the front of the building.

On the top step, in miniskirts and braless white tee-shirts, sat three Vietnamese girls. They smiled as I approached. It was hard to tell their age, but I figured tenth graders wouldn't be too far off. They sat with their legs stretched out over the lower steps. Slowly raising them to a sitting position as I drew closer, and even more slowly crossing them. They brought back sensory memories of dank smelling rooms, sweat, and the overpowering odor of garbage and death. I forced myself to look at their faces. If they were Tommy's girls they would have nothing on underneath the minis.

A hollow-looking, ancient wisp of an Asian man sat in a rocking chair on the porch. A non-filtered cigarette dangled from the corner of his mouth. He smiled with toothless gums.

"Hello, Joe," he said. "Want to make nice-nice with pretty girls?"

"How do you know I'm not a cop?" I asked.

His smile widened. He took a drag from his cigarette, the smoke sucked deep into his lungs before he exhaled. "Cops like pretty girls. Especially when they free. You want?"

"What I want, is Tommy Dao," I answered.

His smile disappeared. "No know him."

"Tell him 'Spider' wants to see him."

"No know him."

If I wanted, no one here could stop me from going into the building, but there would be a fuss, and depending on what business was being transacted no telling what might be waiting for an unannounced intruder. I pulled a twenty out of my pocket and gave it to one of the girls. "Go tell Tommy, 'Spider' needs to see him."

She smiled and glanced at the old man. He gave a low nod. She got up and went inside. The other two girls continued to stare at me seductively. The lure of their come-on differed from that of most working girls. It was one of childhood innocence and purity, while their eyes screamed of deep carnal pleasure.

Young girls giving sex—a perversion in the States, a religion in many parts of Asia, was based on the belief that young girls transfer their youth and vitality to an aging man during sex. I turned my attention to the old man.

"You Tommy's hawker in Nam?"

"No know this man," he answered.

The girl returned and nodded for me to follow. I entered a short hallway. She left me and returned outside. The outside of Tommy's building remained aged and in disrepair, the inside completely refurbished in Art Déco. Expensive reproductions of Erte pictures lined the walls. An attempt to present a sense of class to a classless business. I took a deep breath. I dreaded having to renew acquaintances with Tommy. He was part of history I was trying desperately to forget.

The sweet scent of pot reached my nostrils. Somewhere, in another room, the rustle of string bead dividers reached my ears. All the memories I'd attempted to push from my mind came rushing back. Days spent here, my mind fogged in the haze of alcohol, drugs and sex. An escape, although temporary, from the alley and the boy's dead eyes looking up at me.

The rustle of silk on silk caught my attention and I brought myself back to the present. A young woman stood looking at me. I looked into the deep, almond colored eyes of an exotic beauty, her facial features showing the mixed blood of the Khmer Rouge.

She wore a blue silk sheath dress, bound skin tight around her body, very short, and leaving nothing to the imagination. If you desired this beauty, you better be ready to fork over a thousand dollars for an hour. She motioned for me to follow her. I walked behind shapely legs and a tight, rounded tush. We came to the end of the hallway and into flashing neon signs. A Tommy Dao trademark.

A young man during the Vietnam War, he realized a fortune was there to be made if he could lure the GI's out of their money. He told me his place in Hanoi could have competed with Broadway. 'Neon Father Sin,' the GI's had called Tommy. Neon signs signified Western culture and money to him, he'd told me. Apparently they still did. He spent a great deal of money trying to bring class to his establishment, and then whored the whole thing with neon signs of every imaginable design.

I followed the woman through string-beaded curtains into what once served as a living room; now a display room to show his girls to customers. A red velvet cushioned couch occupied one side of the room and faced black-lacquered chairs. Customers would sit and watch as the girls strolled in and sat on the chairs. Drinks served from a small walnut bar as the 'john' made up his mind on his choice for the evening. Free sex and drugs kept the police away from his operation. We walked to a mahogany stained wooden door. The girl knocked, opened the door and ushered me in, closing it behind me.

The room was a small office. Unlike the other rooms, plain, Thai dance and theater masks decorated white walls. Tommy sat behind a large desk, a straight- backed wooden chair placed in front of it. He motioned for me to sit.

He stared at me through disbelieving eyes. "Be still my heart," he said. "Spider. To what do I owe this honor?"

I doubted I was able to hide my shock. Facing me sat a shadow of the virile man who'd been there for me, when the world I knew couldn't be. His Armani tailored clothes hung on him, the skin on his arms and face covered bone, eyes sunken.

The Vietnam War ended in 1975. Tommy's American agents had sneaked him into the States   two years later. I met him in 2007. I thought him aged then, now he looked older than dirt. He tried a liar's smile. "Not as bad as it looks, Spider."

"You lie like shit."

He coughed a laugh. "Can you believe it? Bitten by the big "C."

"I'm sorry," I said.

"Not as much as I am." He stared at me, his eyes still sharp and keen. The jungle stalker and the killer animal instinct, still very much alive in them. "Did my Father give you a hard time?"

I shook my head. "Father? I never would have guessed you had parents."

He laughed, followed by a deep cough. There was a knock at the door and the woman in silk entered. She carried two small silver plates, each with a marijuana cigarette. She set the plates down, opened a small vial filled with a white powder, and poured its contents onto one. With a razor blade she made two straight lines of the powder and handed the plate and a short straw to Tommy. She offered to do the same for me. I shook my head no. She smiled, bowed and left.

Tommy nodded approval. "Ah, good Spider. For a time there I feared you might get addicted to my drugs, especially when opium seemed the only way your mind could escape the alley."

His eyes passed to another time. "Sorry for this wanton display of dependency, but it helps ease the pain. And the pain is severe today." His eyes reflected memories of times memorable and worth cherishing. "Your true opiate was sex," Tommy continued. "Although you refused to taste the young ones."

He attempted to hide a cough. "Are you aware that you talk in your sleep after strenuous sex, answer questions?"

I wasn't. The look on my face tickled him. "Something to be aware of my friend, if you wish to hide secrets from a woman." Bony fingers with a slight shake, reached for the straw. He bent over the desk and sucked the powder one at a time into each nostril. The effect of the dope visibly hit him. He leaned back in his chair, rested his head on it for a moment.

"I sat in and listened once. Mostly what you spoke of were images of your conscience." He smiled the smile of secrets kept. "Strange analogies. Webs that held you. Spiders trying to bind you forever into a life of commitment. Thus, the name I blessed you with." He stared into my eyes. "I wonder why I remember all that. I guess because you feared so much having to face life, for it meant having to commit." He shook his head. "Is commitment still that scary?"

I shook my head. "If what I have is real, perhaps not as much."

"He pouted his lips. "I noticed right away. Your eyes could not hide the joy you feel for another." He reached for the cigarette, lit it, inhaled deeply holding the smoke in his lungs. I needed some sunshine in my life today, even if drug induced. I lit mine. We sat in silence for a while.

"But here, you come to see me and what do I do? Reflect on the past while your soul cries out for answers to the future." He stared off somewhere. "The past is for those who have no future. You are young, you need to forget the past. Only the future should guide you."

I shrugged, but didn't reply.

"But, I digress. You did not come here today for a high. You sit with furrowed brow. Trouble haunts you. How can I help?"

I hesitated, uncertain how to tell him.

He stared, shook his head. "Life is not fair. I treated my body as if it were a temple. You treated yours like it was a garbage dump. And look, decaying skin, rotting organs, while you sit in glorious health. But my status is not your problem, what concerns you so?"

I described Blue Boy, and told him the story of his invasion into my life and Mac's conclusion on who he was.

Tommy studied me. "A gay?" He smiled. "Oh, my poor heart. All those years trying to convince you to walk on the wild side with me. Now, when it's too late, you tease me with the possibility you've considered it."

I looked hard into his eyes. My silence and probably my facial expression brought laughter from him. "Obviously he has the wrong man, but does not yet know it."

"Agreed," I said.

He took another deep drag from his weed. "Do you fear this man?"

"Have you forgotten who you're talking to?" I asked. "And if so, do you really think your question needs an answer?" I told him about Laura. "I need your help finding him, Tommy,"

He bowed his head, like in prayer. "Have you forgotten, when you were a rookie cop, what I taught you?" He leaned back in his chair, closed his eyes against the pain. "Discover who your enemy is. Become one with him. Feel him, and you will know his mind, and where he hides will become your knowledge."

I nodded. "No, but I have no time. I have to act fast."

He leaned forward, rested the palms of his hands on the desk, looking somewhere beyond me, and remained silent.

"Can you help me?" I asked.

Tommy took time to reflect. "I don't see much, as I used to, of the streets anymore. This Blue Boy of yours is unfamiliar to me."

The exotic-looking girl brought in an alcoholic drink. Tommy's eyes reflected a passion, a caring toward her. Some sort of pride of ownership brought life to his eyes. "But, my friend. I have an adult version of Sherlock Holmes Baker Street Irregulars, who keep me informed of the activities happening out there." He expanded his chest with an attempt to fill his lungs with air. Facial muscles contracted with his pain. "Give me a few days and he will be yours."

I nodded a thanks.

"Are you sure you would not like the pleasures of my Cambodian beauty? She will be my gift. A trip back in time to what could have been?"

"And a gift it would be. And as tempting as she is, I'm afraid I need to pass."

Tommy smiled. "I have always been aware of this woman you call Margo in your life. I thought by now you two would be one." His eyes looked into me. "But still, you would never pass on my beauty because of her. This Laura girl must really be something. At least your eyes say she is when you speak her name." His face softened. "I'm happy for you. But remember, for a loving relationship, always give a woman the right to love and control your soul, but make her a slave to your groin. Take good care of this woman my friend." He reached for my hand. "Now please leave, my body cries for sleep."

I grasped his hand, let it go, and headed for the door.

"I will call," he said. "But a favor."

I turned and faced him.

"Don't stay away for so long, Spider. I may not be here the next time you honor me with your presence."

Baby and I headed for home. I should have felt some exuberance that soon Blue Boy would be mine. But, I didn't. For all he was—for all he'd been, I liked Tommy Dao. And sadness filled every inch of my body that soon I would see the last of a friend.

Chapter Forty-Seven

I called Jim to see if he wanted to take in a movie. No answer. I garaged Baby and walked to McCabes for noise and some cheer. There was lots of noise, no cheer, a bunch of twenty-something's, celebrating whatever twenty-something's celebrate. I tolerated the senseless babble until the booze worked on the anger part of the brain and left before I got into trouble.

I picked the phone up four times, and replaced it each time before dialing. I had my man card to consider. She walked, not me. I turned on the TV, watched a movie where John Wayne played an Irish cop from Chicago sent to London, England to beat up a bunch of crooked Brits. If the movie had starred anyone else, I wouldn't have watched it.

A man card offers little substance to a lonely man. I decided to swallow my pride, but the phone rang before I had to. It was Laura. She seemed hesitant, unable to form the cognizant thought she was looking for. The words came out hollow-sounding, practiced, lacking the sincerity I was looking for. "Can you pick me up tomorrow?" Her breathing uneven, nervous sounding.

"Nine o'clock too early in the morning?"

"At your office?"

"No, at my place."

"I'm certain I can arrange it."

"You can buy me breakfast."

No apology. No words to endear the heart. I felt a bit cheated. But it had been a day of moody gray without her, and tomorrow offered a hint of sunshine. I wasn't going to push the chance of pissing her off. "Nine o'clock then. See ya."

****

She looked good. Her mood wasn't. She was a little removed, but not cold. Mac had brought the danger she might be in closer to home than I had. Her smile was meek, her eyes reflecting a low that captures people as the holidays dissipate. She didn't speak, just stared. Then she was on me, fists pounding my chest and shoulders.

"You bring me into your life but conveniently forget to tell me there's a maniac after you, and then you let Mac tell me my life might be in danger?"

"I planned on telling you.…I have no excuse except that I was afraid you might walk. And I can't blame you if you do."

Laura sat rigid in Baby. Tenseness and anger lined the features of her face. She stared ahead, without seeming to focus on any one thing. The trip, so far spent in silence. I parked Baby in a city garage and we hit the sidewalks.

Her breathing was on the nervous side, uneven. "Why does a gay want to kill you?"

I looked at her and shrugged. "I can't answer, because I don't know."

"Captain Mac told me it would be best if we broke up. He told me quite a story about your stalker and you. Did you think it unnecessary to inform me?" Anger caused her eyes to flame. "You didn't give a shit? Didn't care about the danger to me? Was I just something convenient to share your bed?"

I found a street bench to sit on. She turned from me, hiding her tears. "How could you do this to me?"

'Because I didn't want to lose you." That did nothing to erase the fire in her eyes. "Is this the best place to have this conversation?"

She focused hard on my face. "Does it really make any difference where? Lies seem to be the territory you're most comfortable with." she answered.

"I didn't lie to you. Maybe I just hid the facts." Her focus was on people traffic, not me. "But, Mac may be right. What we're dealing with is a psychopath. Through his insanity, he stays a step ahead of me, because I'm unable to think as he does. You could be putting yourself in the middle of his madness if you stay with me."

Her eyes showed her pain. "Do you really think you deserve to be in my life?"

I took in some needed air, looked into her eyes. "Only you can answer that."

She rose, looked down at me. "I want some breakfast."

I passed on Gus's. We grabbed a cab that took us to the Gold Coast and a restaurant that catered to the snob element. It specialized in ambiance, overrated food and prices, and did nothing to change her mood. After breakfast she announced she wanted to escape the ugliness of our world and would I take her to the Art Institute? I did, but culture seemed too heavy to be a pick-me-up. She needed hustle and bustle.

We headed for the section of Chicago known as "The Loop,' or better recognized as 'State Street,' that great street, once considered the hub of activity, shopping, eating and entertainment-wise. It was not so great anymore. Undesirables now tested everyone's patience, as more and more desirables abandoned State Street for North Michigan Avenue.

There was hustle and bustle though, and her mood picked up, but I still received the silent treatment. I discovered a fruit stand on the corner of Monroe and State and bought a bunch of grapes and a banana each. With no plan, we continued down Monroe to Dearborn and the First National bank. A sizeable crowd sat on the steps of the plaza eating lunch and waiting for live entertainment the bank provided at lunchtime.

We made our way over to the Chagall Mosaic Wall. Our conversation was forced and prepubescent. As most Chicagoans, I'd made a point of viewing the Chagall upon its arrival. My conclusion being like an exotic woman, it had style, but contained a mystery not entirely understandable

"Do you like Chagall?" Laura asked.

I answered with a non-committal shrug. "As much as any non-student of his work can like him."

"I adore him." She said.

"I am afraid I'm a dilettante when it comes to his work. I'll have to bow to your expertise."

The sound of classical music came from the plaza, catching Laura's attention and gratefully diverting her away from Chagall. Four ballerinas gracefully ascended to a temporary stage in front of the bank entrance. Laura grabbed my arm and we made our way through the crowd to a good viewing point of the dancers.

Laura was enthralled by their performance. "Nice variation on the *jere*," she commented. I nodded. "They're good. I wonder which dance group they come from?"

I was the wrong one to ask. Laura intently gazed from one dancer to the other, lecturing on the execution of certain steps. I would grunt agreement perfectly content watching long legs and cute asses. I realized Laura was watching me.

She shook her head. "I give up on you." But I noticed the corners of her mouth concealed a smile.

Still engrossed by the dancers, there appeared a serenity surrounding Laura. She rested her head on my arm and sighed in contentment. Maybe I should study the ballet. Just enough so I could converse with Laura—just enough where I could hide my studies from Jim and Mac. I almost exploded with laughter.

I wondered if the beauty she saw in ballet was part of her magical world of dragons and knights? I scanned the crowd to see if there were others as lost in the ballet, as the one next to me. Laura grabbed my arm, holding on with all her strength. She stood next to me, alone, no one near her. Her eyes were wide, filled with abject fear—fighting back tears, her face held frozen by total panic.

"What?"

It took time before she could form words.
"Him…bumped into me…ran his finger… down my face. Oh God, Rik!"

I pulled her against me, her face ashen, even through her tan. I looked over the crowd and saw nothing to cause alarm. I looked again, with the crowd blocking almost all but a blue fedora from view. A man made his way up to Clark Street. Too far away for me to catch him and rip out his lungs, I concentrated on Laura.

"He's telling us again!" She studied my face for reaction; it gave none. "God, Rik! Don't you see? He's telling us he can be anywhere in our lives." She stopped, her breathing coming in hard, short spurts. "He's anywhere, everywhere, we are at his biding. There is nowhere safe!" Tears welled and fell with abandon. "He controls our lives, to play with as he wishes, to own and destroy as he desires."

"Not for long," I assured her. "I know people who know how to find him. When they do, it's over; he's history."

She didn't speak --just looked out the window at whatever activity interested her on the ride to my condo.

"It seems so silly being afraid of such a puny man," she said.

"The size of a man doesn't measure his madness." Christ, I was beginning to sound like Captain Mac.

She didn't respond. We ended the trip in silence that continued in my apartment. I guided her to the fireplace. She pulled her legs underneath her, and leaned tightly against me. She studied my face for an inordinate amount of time.

"What's happening to my life, isn't something I planned. It happened, and I don't have the power to change it."

Finally she spoke. I wished she hadn't. "What are you feeling right now, Rik?'

"About What?"

She sighed. It sounded more like disgust. "God. About anything. Right now, you seem so outside the realm of having feelings."

"What do you want from me? To tell you not to worry? That everything is okay? I can't tell you that. I can't tell you anything you shouldn't be able to tell yourself."

"And what do you tell yourself? That you are above being afraid? Above having feelings?"

"We all have feelings. I was trained not to react to them."

"Does that include life and love?" She started to add something, but shook her head instead. Appearing to give up on whatever point she wanted to make—or possibly me. A couple of tears showed, but she fought them, then gave up as more followed.

"What are you afraid of, Rik?"

I didn't see where any of this mattered. She was going to leave me, and as much as I didn't like it, it was the right thing to do. "I don't know, I haven't given it much thought."

She shook her head, looked at me as if I was totally unacceptable. "Everyone is afraid of something. That's how we know we still care. Are you afraid of me? Of us? Is that why you want us to split up?"

I walked toward her. She backed up. "Splitting might be the best thing for you, but I never said I wanted us to split."

"I don't know whether to feel sorry for you, or hate you," she said. She turned and headed for my bedroom, closing the door behind her, leaving me alone. I fluffed a couple of floor pillows and fixed a strong drink. The bedroom door opened.

"You can't get any sleep there", Laura said. "Come in please. Protect me."

All proper like, we shared the bed—she on her side, me on mine, like married couples do. Sometime during the night, she laid her arm across my chest, her head using my shoulder as a pillow. I put my arm around her and we stayed that way until morning.

Chapter Forty–Eight

She woke me early in the morning to take her back to her place for a shower, fresh clothes, and a ride to her office. I didn't like leaving her, Lawrence or no Lawrence. I poured her a cup

"How are you doing?" I asked

"Fine."

"No, you're not, you're still angry."

"More afraid than angry."

"You should be, he's scary."

She fidgeted with her hair. "I'm angry for allowing myself to get involved in your life. But, I'm not so much afraid of him, as I am of us."

"Sorry, you left me on that one," I said.

"Then you need to do some serious thinking about it, and, decide if you want me in your life." She turned her back, and then turned and faced me. "And you better decide fast, because you need me in it."

"Are you sure you want to belong in it?

"Mac did everything possible to make me want to break up with you"

"You could be in serious danger, that's why. This isn't a movie you can mime."

She paced, fought back tears. "If you can show me you care, really care for me, then I won't listen to Captain Mac. I'll stay."

"You're not using your head. My feelings shouldn't play in your decision."

She breathed in deep gulps. "God, that makes me mad. Yes, I'm frightened, but I'm not scared. You can protect me. I'm safe with you. Why should I leave?"

"Because it's the right thing to do. You're thinking with your heart."

Anger flashed in her eyes. "It's my heart. Mine. Mine to do with as I please. If we break up, he's won. Is that what you want? Do you really want me to leave?"

I only had the answer she wanted to hear. And she made sure I knew I'd made the right one.

We were a bit late arriving at the Mart. She tried to assure me not to worry, she'd be fine, and to pick her up after work. Her smile said she believed in what she said, I wasn't so sure.

I drove around the City with no direction or destination. I desperately needed info from Tommy on how to find Blue Boy. I headed home to wait his call. I waited for what seemed an eternity. He didn't call. I knew better than to call him. He would reach me when he'd obtained what I needed.

I tried reading, I listened to Jimmy Reed sing about bad women and lonely nights. I gave up, and went to my den and actually worked on my novel. I stared at my phone—it slept. I thought about calling Laura, and didn't, but instead walked to McCabes for lunch. I window shopped on the way back to my apartment, and didn't see anything I couldn't live without. I decided to buzz Laura the instant I got back home.

The elevator doors opened. Jim stood in front of my door, his passkey in hand. When he turned to see me exiting the elevator, I spotted Laura. His broad, six-foot four body had been dwarfing her from view. She had no idea how good she looked to me, though from the expression on her face, I looked much better to her. She looked nervous, frightened.

"She be all yours," he said in a brooding voice of someone having been put upon. "I finds her hanging in the foyer." He looked over at Margo's door, and then scowled at me.

Laura thanked him for escorting her. He gave a quick nod and headed for the stairs. Laura allowed me to collect her in my arms. "Can we please go into your place now?" She asked. She turned and glanced at Margo's door.

I took her inside, held her face in my hands. How could anyone want to slice it away, destroy its beauty? She tilted her head questioning my concentration.

"I thought you were still at work. When did you get here?"

Her eyes were haunted, and her face was strained. She laced her fingers around the back of my neck, and stood on tiptoe. "I really would like a kiss now."

I fulfilled her wish, doubling it.

"I convinced Lawrence it was slow enough for me to have a half-day. I wanted to surprise you. I think now, it would have been better if you had picked me up." Her eyes masked an uneasiness, as she headed for the living room. I didn't know what was troubling her, and was almost afraid to find out. She attempted to hide whatever it was, and forced a smile. We were here, together, but something separated us.

I turned her head toward me. "What?"

She inhaled heavily and fidgeted, and slowly found my eyes. "I know he's your best friend. But he…" She stopped, hung her head. "Why doesn't Jim like me?"

That caught me off guard. "Jim? Jim likes you," I answered without conviction.

She shook her head, and looked down at her hands. "You weren't there, and didn't see his eyes when he spotted me in the foyer." Tears formed. "I'm not sure dislike even comes close to describing his feelings toward me."

Trying to make light of her concern wasn't going to knock it. "I'm sure you just misread his eyes. It takes Jim a while to accept new people in his life."

She was still looking at her hands. "So, he scares them to death until he does?"

"What did he do?"

She shook her head. "He definitely made me feel like I didn't belong here." She shivered, I took her into my arms. "I didn't ask him to escort me to your door. It was like I had no choice. Like he couldn't wait to conceal me."

"That's not like Jim. Inside, he's puppy dog."

She looked at me like I was five bricks short of being a mile. "No, Rik, puppy dogs don't flash hate in their eyes, or have scars that flame scarlet red. He'd look at me, then at the door across the hall, then his eyes and scar flamed hate. I've never seen a face so cold-looking. It was even colder than the gay's." She choked on a sob. "You can't believe how glad I was to see you step out of the elevator. I'm sorry, your friend or not, he frightens me."

I got up to start a fire. Any more discussion concerning Jim could wait until later. She stopped me. "Who lives across the hall, Rik?"

Oh good. Let's bring Margo into the picture and have a party. My turn to fidget. "A brother and sister." Her eyes said keep on keeping on. She wasn't swallowing that this was all there was. "Okay, in a nutshell." A little more fidget. "The sister's name is Margo. She thinks she's in love with me. Jim thinks I should be in love with her. He wants a family, and Margo and I fit his idea of family. That's why he doesn't want Margo to see you."

Laura's eyes looked like they were losing ping-pong to disbelief. "You've got to be kidding!" When I didn't respond, she stood up. Her floral-designed blouse was no longer tucked in, nor buttoned, compliments of me. "Then you're blowing up my skirt, right?"

I shrugged and raised my eyebrows. "No, but I'd like to."

She attempted a laugh, but a smile was the best she could come up with. She was doing her best to be cheery, bouncy, as though nothing had happened. But her eyes expressed troubled thoughts. She reached over and grasped my face, gently kissed it. "I didn't come here to let Jim ruin our day. And I won't let him. I brought you a present."

It certainly wasn't big enough to be contained under her dress. "Yeah, where is it?"

She batted her eyelashes, and began a teasing demonstration of cheesecake. "If you want it, you have to find it." I reached for her. She backed away. "But, you can only have it if you can truthfully answer my question." I waited impatiently.

"Since you've known me, have you fooled around with this Margo?"

I smiled, raised my eyebrows, her eyes narrowed. "I can't lie that I don't look, and that she doesn't give me thoughts of silk sheets—but she's really not worth the trouble."

Laura looked at me suspiciously. "And when you think about it?" She asked.

"Well, I don't play with myself, if that's what you're asking."

She broke up laughing. "Good, I'd be very upset if you wore it out without me."

I eventually found my gift. Some places were more interesting to search than others. It was a Mont Blanc pen, so I would think of her when I wrote.

We lay in bed. Physically she took up space beside me, but mentally she wasn't present. She raised to a sitting position. "I want to meet Margo."

Chapter Forty-Nine

The next morning I tried convincing Laura that life for her would be so much better if she stayed at my place. My powers of persuasion fell on deaf ears. I tried assuring myself there was nothing to worry about Physically, I doubted Lawrence could stand up to cream cheese, but he would do anything to protect his Laura, and the Mart boasted above average rent-a-cops. Plus, with the glassed in showrooms, most of the businesses on the same floor could view all the activity going on in the others.

I entered my apartment. The phone rang. I recognized a voice way too familiar.

"I was close enough to nibble on her ear. Did you know that?"

My hand froze on the phone in a death grip. "Outside of the fact that I have no desire to talk to you, I haven't the foggiest as to what you're talking about," I said. "Who's ear?"

"Oh, Rik, Rik. Come on now. Of course you know." He laughed. "You're fearfully aware. The ballerinas? The girl who makes your dick hard?" A dirty, bone chilling, laugh. "Close enough to her for us to be one, I was, my dear, Rik."

My stomach soured. If he could get that close to her in public, how much closer could he in private. I tried responding, and couldn't. The words stuck in my throat.

"Nothing? Really, Rik, a big disappointment. You have to be thinking about her. Is she safe ? Has she been hurt?" He laughed. "I bet just the thought of her gives you an erection. Right, Lover? Can I come over and see it?"

Silence, all I could hear over the phone was his breathing. I didn't need to see his face, to see the pleasure engraved on it, see his scorn. I steamed.

"I love her perfume," he said. "Please, do me a favor and get its name. It would dangerously enhance my sexuality. Bye, bye Lover."

Come on, Tommy, where do I find this asshole?

I drove to the Mart. No game plan. I just had to check. The office door was locked. A note said back by three o'clock. I faked window-shopping other showrooms. No sign of Blue Boy. Several security people pretending not to be, walked the halls with me. I continued the window game until I drew the interest of the toy police. I left, feeling somewhat more secure about Laura, but more upset that she insisted on staying at her place alone tonight.

"I will not allow him to control my life."

I intended to case her building before she arrived there and remain out of sight as I watched the entrance until I felt it safe enough to leave her. I entered my apartment. Cold greeted me on the back of my neck, a slight bristling of neck hairs—I turned. Slowly. Nothing. No one behind me, no movement anywhere, the living room empty. I stood like some psychic practitioner, trying to pick up vibrations.

That left the bathroom, den and kitchen on this floor for someone to be in hiding, waiting. This made no sense at all. My apartment was secure. It's my home, my safe haven. My apprehension had to be nothing more than nerves. Then I noticed it. On the edge of the chess table lay a single, blood-red, rose.

My senses heightened to the silence of the apartment. My hearing was tuned in to any sound that would break it. I stood, not sure how long, and stared at the rose. Finally I walked over to it. I didn't touch it. No note. It just lay there as a wordless messenger from someone.

The rose lay in front of a pawn-mine. The last one I had left from a chess game played over the phone with Captain Mac. It had been guarding my king. Someone had moved it to my opponent's eighth square. My first thought was Jim. He'd been pissed the round robin had been called off, but he wouldn't have moved my chess pieces to give me the advantage over Mac; and he certainly wouldn't have killed one of his roses.

The other option was unacceptable, and I tried to dispel it, but my anger kept it present. Like a bad dream, a sixth sense arose from my apartment. It was sending a warning. Intruder—I am no longer a safe haven. I've been violated.

I went to the kitchen and heated leftover coffee and called Mac. He was tied up. "Unless this is to tell me I checkmated you, I'm too busy for idle chit chat."

I told Mac about the chess table. He said to stay put, and he'd be over shortly."

Coffee didn't hack it as a time killer. I walked out to the balcony. Jim could spend hours gazing at clouds, but in five minutes I was bored. The intercom buzzed. It was Mac. I left the door open for him. His face was drawn, haggard looking.

"Over on the chess table," I said.

"Yeah, the rose, I saw it."

I walked behind the bar and hefted a bottle of scotch. Mac shook his head.

"I have to go back to the station. You discover anything else besides the rose?"

"Not that I've found."

Mac rotated his neck, massaged his temples. "I can't wait until school starts. Kids are killing kids like the streets are a video arcade game." He studied me. "Outside of like shit, how do you feel?"

I decided a drink was a marvelous idea. "Violated. No, worse. He entered my home, violated my home. Me. He defiled me by doing it."

Mac nodded. "Usual response."

"Do you realize," I asked. "As of now, I can no longer ask Laura to spend the night with me. Hell, any woman as far as that goes."

Mac spread a smile. "You're probably the only victim I ever talked to that is more worried about their sex life being screwed-up than the possibility of getting their throat slit."

"Sex has nothing to do with it. This is my home and he raped it." I slammed my fist on the bar top. "I feel like my life is a dark corridor enmeshed with spider webs, and I keep getting more and more entangled in them. I want this son-of-a-bitch, Mac"

Mac gave me his fatherly stare. "I don't like the look in your eyes. Don't go playing macho citizen on me."

"I'm not a little boy anymore. I don't need you by my side every time this freak does something."

"And just how do you intend to retaliate, and to whom?"

I sucked in some air. "I have to do something.'"

"You listen to me, and listen good. Your world is no longer made up of sand, and people hiding behind the Koran. Your world now consists of streets and alleys and cars and garages. Habitats for predators like you've never seen. A jungle—albeit a concrete jungle, but still a jungle. The only difference from the war you knew and the one you're in now." He paused for emphasis. "Your enemy is a psychopath. Do you understand?"

He waited. I nodded.

"Good. Because this jungle is my turf, not yours. Stay out of it." He glared at me. "If that makes you feel like a little boy, tough shit. The fag does something, you call, and I keep coming over. GOT IT!"

He waited, I nodded. "Good, now talk to me."

I went through this morning from beginning to end. Mac would nod and chew on his cigar. He headed for the chess table. I followed.

"Door wasn't jimmied. How many keys to your apartment?"

"Two."

"Laura have one?"

"No, I have both."

"Jim has a passkey, right?"

I nodded.

Mac admired the chess table and ran his finger over an edge. "I don't see any damage. That's good. I wouldn't like it if I saw any damage."

Mac and my grandfather spent hours playing chess on this table, accompanied by a glass of Glenfiddich. The table was transported from its original Scottish home by my grandfather's grandfather circa eighteen-fifty. Hand carved from black walnut, the MacClean family crest was carved on the knee of each leg. The squares scrimshawed with scenes of the Scottish Highlands. The chess pieces were works of art. Clansmen mounted on Clydesdale horses set to charge into battle. The MacClean crest was emblazoned on their shields. Laura marveled at the artistry, and had asked me to teach her how to play.

Mac ran his finger over the edge of the table again. I thought I noticed his eyes mist. "You have no idea how much I miss your grandparents." He moved over to the rose, but seemed concentrated more on the pawn. "I'll say one thing for the little creep. He has a set of balls. That will be the day I allow you to pawn my eighth square. How did he know you were playing white?"

I shrugged. "Don't know. That little fact hadn't occurred to me."

"Then start it occurring," he said. "Get Jim up here."

Chapter Fifty

I scowled at Mac. "I don't care if this is your turf. I'm telling you right now, Jim isn't part of the territory."

Mac placed a thumb and forefinger on the bridge of his nose, moving his fingers like he could straighten the broken parts. It was a habit he'd picked-up when people in his presence pissed him off. "You might think maybe so. But I'm telling you, your maybe is wrong. This is my turf. The things going on ain't right." He pointed a finger at my face. "Someone walked right into your apartment, messed with your chess set. Someone slipped a mannequin in your shower. How'd they do that? Why did they do that? I want answers, and I think Jim just might have some." He glared at me. "So get his ass up here!"

I phoned and caught Jim at home. He informed me he was about to enjoy lunch, and wouldn't be up until he'd finished—if then. Mac grabbed the phone and convinced him otherwise. As it was, he took his sweet time getting here.

"Where's the other key?' Mac asked.

"Taped under the desk drawer."

Mac laughed. "Taped. How clever. First place someone would look. You checked if it's there?"

I assured him it was. Mac wanted to check anyway.

Jim entered, helped himself to a beer and claimed a barstool. His eyes roamed from Mac to me. "I'se takes wanting my ass up here, has nuthin' to do with finishing the chess match I be winning."

"I hear Rik has confided all to you about his life-threatening situation," Mac said, concentrating on something other than Jim's presence. He turned his face toward me and glared. "And," Mac continued. "Rik says you don't believe him." Mac faced him with eyes penetrating into his soul.

Jim just snorted a laugh, and locked his eyes onto mine.

Mac tilted his head as he sized Jim. "Something funny? I don't see something funny. You have any idea why all of a sudden all kinds of strange things are going on in Rik's life?" Mac didn't wait for an answer. "How someone just walked in his place today and messed with his chessboard? And how come, as his friend, you don't care?" This time he waited for the expected response.

"If I'se shows any dis-appreciation over his so-called problems, it because he ain't give me much reason to believe he have any."

Mac took the cigar out of his mouth and turned it in his hand. "This one ain't near as good as the one this morning." He quit looking at the cigar and concentrated on Jim. "What if I tell you this isn't the first time someone broke into Rik's place? How does someone do that, Jim?"

Jim's eyes widened for a split second then narrowed as he focused on Mac. "What you trying to say? The phantom of the garage been up here? What he 'spose to do this time?"

Mac gave Jim a long study, and glanced at me. "We have a phantom? What he been doing to my boy, my boy ain't telling me?"

"What he do to the chessboard?" Jim grabbed a fresh beer, found some beer nuts and poured them into a bowl.

Mac sucked in a heavy dose of air. "You didn't notice the rose?"

Jim frosted Mac's face with a cold stare. Jim loves flowers. Give him an inch of dirt and flowers will sprout from it. But, his passion is roses. Touch one of his beauties, break it, and you'd better be fleet of foot. "It be my rose I'd grows. An American Beauty. Come from the pool area. Too good for someone give to shithead here."

Mac took in Jim's appraisal. "They available for picking by anybody?'"

Jim shook his head. "Only a tenant whose gots a key to pool. 'Cept for my buddy Rik here. He intruder don't need no key, mus' walk through things." He gave time for that to set in. "You 'member back when we have the ghost in the garage?" He didn't wait for Mac to answer. "Well, he done come back."

Mac motioned for a beer. I got him one. He took a long pull. "So," he said to Jim. "You telling me Rik here put the rose on the board?"

Jim sized up Mac. "No, I'm saying it be his ghost. So far, my buddy has me chasing rats don't exist." He waited for Mac to jump in; he didn't. "Tells me Baby gets scratched in garage by some ghost." Shook his head. "This ghost of his, also steals his garbage, and makes threatening phone calls, that never get recorded. And bests, shoots at Rick but can't hit him." Jim looked at Mac, smiled and shook his head in disbelief. He leveled a challenge at Mac. "Buts you don't wants to hear that." He rounded his shoulders, head down, shuffled toward the door. "You wants to think maybe 'ol Jim do all these ghost things."

He walked by the chess table and picked up the rose. "Rose too good to die here." He looked at Mac. "I go now, but you know wheres to find me. Does my janitoring job every day, Mr. Po-leezmens. Ise be here. Don't want no trouble with Mr. Po-leezmens." He was out the door.

"That went well," Mac said. "Guess I can forget Jim jumping in with any fresh insight. Time to get back to work anyway." He looked at me, shook his head. "Another ghost?" He left.

The phone rang.

I knew who it was on the other end and rushed out to the hall to grab Mac. The elevator was on its way down. The phone continued to ring.

I didn't need any more gay today. If it was somebody other than him, they could practice using a message machine. The day dragged. Still nothing from Tommy.

I worked on the book, quite successfully actually. My writing skills were tuning downright professional. I let my chest swell and almost missed the time to leave and pick-up Laura

Chapter Fifty-One

She freshened up. Mac called, his voice filled with excitement. I was to meet him tomorrow for breakfast at Gus's.

Modern day air-conditioning had chilled the apartment. A fire in the fire place warmed it. Homemade spaghetti with meat balls, garlic rolls, and an excellent Chianti temporarily satisfied her craving for food. Coffee, Tia Maria and Mozart passed the evening hours until she seductively told me it was time for bed. Morning came too early.

I turned and pressed myself against Laura. I blew on the back of her ear, and started a slow circular motion on the lower part of her stomach. She groaned as she awakened, purred as I lowered my hand.

"Stop it," she moaned. "It's work time."

"No, it's early, I set the clock ahead. We have hours yet," I answered.

"You're a liar," she purred. She grabbed my hand but didn't stop its motion.

We arrived late for work. She stopped short of entering. Lawrence paced the showroom, his back to us. His existence in the office didn't seem to please her. I was glad he was there. While I still felt he wouldn't be worth spit in a fight, his presence would act as a deterrent to Blue Boy.

Laura bit down on her lip. "He's back early, and I'm late for work." She fastened me with a not-too-friendly stare. "You're a bad boy."

"And here, earlier this morning," I whispered as I gently teased the back of her neck with my fingers, "I had the feeling you thought me rather good."

She blushed and pouted. She placed two fingers to her lips, kissed them, and then pressed them on my lips. "Now go."

Mac was sitting in his usual booth at Gus's. He motioned for me to join. He was eating the same breakfast he's eaten since I've known him. Ham, with eggs sunny-side, and runny, hash browns crisp. I ordered Gus's Greek toast and coffee.

He smiled. "Hope you brought money, cause you're buying. You definitely, positively owe me."

He left me wondering the where and why of the debt as he returned to eating and watching who came through the door. I ate my Greek toast and waited. He kept eating.

"Are we playing some kind of guessing game where I lose if I guess or not?"

He blended his tea until certain it was consistent with his favored Boston style. He took a sip, smiled, and then leaned back in the booth, focusing on nothing in particular. "Savoring the moment, my boy—savoring the moment."

I nodded as if I understood.

"Soon, I'll have the media and my superior up my ass." He let that settle in the space between us. "You and I have been traveling in circles. You, with your gay, me with my serial killer."

I didn't know about his serial killer, but I knew my gay would soon be mine for the asking. But I nodded agreement anyway.

His smile looked more shit-eating. "So, I get to figuring. All these guys my killer's left sliced up in garbage bins, are all young, clean-cut looking. Many with girlfriends. Not your normal cruising type, or wanting to be seen picked-up in gay bars." He pulled out a new cigar and began working on it. This was a signal Mac had a story to tell and would take his sweet time telling it. I ordered more coffee and settled back into the booth. "To make it short, when they decide to take a walk on the wild side, they don't want to be seen doing it."

He took another sip of tea, visibly enjoying it. "Then, I remember you telling me you spotted your gay in Washington Square Park, long, a place used by cruisers who didn't want to be noticed cruising." He smiled all big again. He had a captive audience and was enjoying abusing it. I didn't quite feel the same way.

"So, I decided to do some cruising on my own."

The image of Mac playing gay and available caught my coffee somewhere where it shouldn't be. It took some violent coughing, and a few tears to lodge it back in swallowing order.

My outburst didn't stop Mac from telling his story. "Last night I spot your boy hanging out in the park."

My interest in Mac's story picked-up considerably. "And?"

Mac laughed. "I park my car where he can't see it, but I can see him, and watch." He laughed again. "He's pretty pathetic really. Hit on only the young, clean-cut type, like the ones found in garbage bins. Never did get lucky. Tried like hell, but didn't even get a sniff." Mac moved his cigar with his tongue from one end of his mouth to the other. "So, he gives up and starts walking. I follow. We end up at the Oak Tree Restaurant."

"Jesus, Mac. You had him, why didn't you arrest him?"

Mac gave me a look of deep aggravation. "Arrest him on what? Loitering with intent?"

"On anything."

Mac shook his head in disgust. "And how long can I hold him before he's on the street and invisible again?"

I sighed and didn't answer.

"So, anyway, he sits down at the counter. I give him time to order and then stroll in and sit two stools down from him. I'll tell you one thing." He paused and let that hang for a minute or so. "This punk has had run-ins with the law before. He spots me as a cop right off."

I saw no reason to inform Mac a blind man would spot him right off as a cop.

"He gets real nervous," Mac continued. "Keeps playing with his water glass. By the time his food comes, he's a nervous wreck. He throws some bills on the counter and scoots his ass out of there." Mac leaned back and laughed.

I slammed my fist on the tabletop. "Christ! You had him and just let him go?"

"I had what I wanted. His fingerprints. I took his glass with me. If nothing shows up in our files, they will with the FBI's. Besides, I had nothing to hold him on."

"You let him walk? Let him walk! What if he's in nobody's files?"

Mac smiled and patted my arm. "He is. Nobody gets that nervous unless they're wanted somewhere."

I wasn't as confident as Mac that we had him at all. But, at least he was on the right track, and I was thankful for his time and effort, with the exception that the law can hinder a cop and move at a snail's pace. I didn't have that kind of grace period when it came to Laura. I decided not to tell Mac about my meeting with Tommy Dao, and that I intended to kill the gay when I found him.

Chapter Fifty-Two

The phone rang again. I'd expected it to. This time I answered it.

"Do you really think that old, fat, cop can help you?" He laughed. "Only you can help you, Rik. And so far you've done a really shitty job." He giggled. "Doesn't it just drive you crazy how I know your cop was in your apartment? Huh, huh? How do I know that? How do I know that? Huh, huh?" He laughed again. "I bet it makes you want to throw a tantrum, right, right? Jump up and down like a little boy. Scream and suck your thumb. Did you find the rose yet?"

I didn't answer, but was certain he could hear the thumping of my heart.

"Oh, yes. You did find it. Beautiful red, isn't it? The color of blood."

Nerves pinched behind my ears, centering pain in the middle of my forehead. "Who let you into my apartment?"

Another laugh, "Hee, Hee, Hee. "Oh, Rik, no one has to let me in. I can be anywhere in your life, your life belongs to me, at any time to my choosing." He paused. "Think of your life as a chessboard over which, as a master chess player, I have complete control." I heard him take a sip of something. "Ahhh,"

My head started pounding. He was getting to me today, and I couldn't control it.

"Ah, silence," he said. "Silence says so much about a person. It vividly speaks of fear." A sing-song hum. "But don't fear, I intend to give you knight's odds, although I'm not too sure what good that is in blind chess. What a bitch of a way to play the game."

"I know who you are," I said. "I will find you before you make your next move, and when I do, I'll kill you."

The words sounded hollow, languid. He picked–up on it and laughed. "You do? You do know me? Or, do you just think you do? Wouldn't it be melodramatic if you killed the wrong person?"

I didn't answer.

"By the by, you did see your pawn on my eighth square. Huh, huh?"

"If I did, why should I give a piss?"

"Oh, come now," he said. "You know why." A pause, nails on blackboard laugh. "Pretty girl." He slurped his drink. "I'm going to do her before I do you." He waited before speaking again. "Oh, relax, I can hear your nuts churning. I have no plans for anything as disgusting as sticking my dick in any part of her."

He stopped, a low-throat giggle. "But then, maybe I could conjure an erection if I did her in the ass." He waited. "Ah, the old silent treatment, huh? Honest to God, Rik, sometimes you're no fun at all. But, I am wondering. Will you be as infatuated with her when her face and breasts are all scarred?" He laughed. "Will you be able to look at her and not throw up?"

My temples pounded, blood on my lip welled from penetrating teeth, my chest so constricted I couldn't breathe. My hand shook violently, banging the phone against my ear. I wanted to scream at him that I was going to rip his dick off, shove it down his throat, and watch him choke to death. But, that was what he wanted, to show that he controlled my mind, my emotions. Suck it up. Breathe normally. Don't speak. Don't let him know you're all twisted up inside.

"Your silence screams."

My hand had a death grip on the phone. Anger dried my throat, parched my words. I yelled through gritted teeth "I'm–going–to rip–your fucking lungs out!" Christ! Shut-up, don't give him the pleasure he's waiting for.

"My turn again? Really, Rik, I expected more. But, by the by, you are familiar with the significance of your pawn being on my eighth square, are you not?"

I was, but figured I'd get his version.

"Come now," he said. "The eighth square. Of course you know. That's where your pawn becomes a queen." He laughed, all full of himself. "Well, I'm a queen, and I have your pawn. Before I torture you to death, I will make you my queen." He choked on his laughter. "My queen to sexually enjoy as I please."

His words burned in my chest. "Why wait? Let's meet. Now!"

"Ah, Rik, we don't want to spoil what makes our dreams wet, by rushing into it. We want to taste the anticipation of the sexual desire we so long to share with each other, dream of our bodies touching until ecstasy drives us insane."

"The only thing I desire is to hold your life in my hands." It was a pretty feeble response. He must have thought so, too.

His laughter crawled out of his stomach and left something vile in my mouth. "The foreplay will be exquisite, the lovemaking so erotic to rise above the poetic fantasies of the 'Bard'." He laughed again. "After you become my queen, we will get married. The wedding ceremony will be held in a cemetery of course." His laughter remained in the room as he hung up.

In all the years living here, that someone could break into my home had never been a probable reality to me until this asshole showed up. Who keeps letting the little prick in?

I went to the bar and slammed a shot of scotch whiskey down the pipes. Sometimes booze can clear the mind, or sometimes sharpen the thinking powers. At the moment, all I was asking of it was to keep me numb.

Aggravation, confusion, deep anger, but the perspective of the whole thing concerning the chessboard was too unbelievable to cause any breath-sucking, bone-chilling fear. Outside of hate, I had no specific feelings at the moment. Only the realization that until I killed him, never again would my life be my own.

I went to the bathroom and showered hot and then cold, letting the water cascade off my shoulders and down my back. I turned the water off, and didn't bother dressing. I leaned against the bathroom wall, my head resting on my forearm. I had to get a hold of myself. I can't let Laura see the sad-assed, beat-up wimp Blue Boy had left for her.

The doorbell rang. I cringed. I wasn't up to facing anyone until I could wash away the disgust I felt. The gay's perversion tainted me to the soul. I needed another shower. I'd just finished my second. It wasn't enough.

I opened the door. It wasn't the gay or Laura. I'd expected either. Margo. She pushed past me, something clutched to her chest. Panicked, frightened, she reached out to me. I wore only a towel. I felt a bit nervous.

"Rik," she hesitated. Tears started, then sobs. She reached for me, but not in a romantic way. More like a child reaching for a parent. I gripped her tight to my chest, stroking her hair. Her sobs became hiccups.

"What happened?" I looked down as she stepped out of my arms. She pushed the bundle she held toward me. I accepted.

"I don't know what to do or where to go. Renaldo killed Joe and he wants to kill me."

I turned her toward me. "What are you talking about? Renaldo would never let anything happen to you. He killed Joe?"

"It's in his journal. I didn't mean to read it. He rushed out earlier, angry. It was on his desk." Tears streamed down. "I saw my name and started flipping through it. He is going to sacrifice me to become some Aztec God King thingy. And he killed Joe because he was afraid I might not be a virgin. He planned on killing you, too." She twisted away and sat at the bar. "What are you going to do?"

I sat across, scanning the journal pages. Short entries, but everything was true. Renaldo hired someone to kill Joe after the attempted rape. He hired someone to kill me, too. Jesus, was that what started the gay? But why?

"Okay, honey. We'll need help. Jim can take care of you and Mac will deal with your brother."

"Will he be okay?"

"Reading this, he's snapped. Completely bonkers. I don't understand all this Aztec nation rising again crap, but he is a few fries short of a happy meal. I think Mac will put him in a safe place."

"He won't hurt my brother, will he?"

"No. We just want him to get better. That's all."

"What will happen to me?" she hiccupped. "Where will I go?"

"Until Renaldo is safe, Jim will look after you."

I picked up the phone. Jim would take Margo to the station and wait until her brother was picked up. Maybe Mac could check out Renaldo's assassin. It *had* to be the gay. No way two people were trying to kill me. No one is that unlucky.

Margo curled up on the couch. When Jim arrived, he took the journal and then helped Margo. She looked so fragile. Alone again, I headed back to the shower. Wash the gay out. Hoping it was forever. Hoping I never saw him again.

Could a simple bar of soap do all that? I doubt it. He'd made a complete freaking asshole out of me.

I went to the den and sat behind my desk and stared at the written manuscript I called my book. I might as well take a trip down the road to deep depression. My fingers rested on the keys and refused to move. I read the nonsense I'd written two days ago. It wasn't as bad as I thought it was. The characters were taking on a reality, talking to me, guiding me.

I typed. The words flowed, and found a home on the pages. I discovered myself really getting into the story, becoming part of it. Pages piled up. Morning turned into late afternoon. I could hardly wait to show my labors to Laura.

The phone rang. I hesitated, in no mood for the gay. I decided to answer the ring anyway.

"Tommy Dao, Rik." His voice like a whisper, his chest constricted, coughing and sucking out what little air remained in his lungs. "To weak to talk now. Maybe, we found your gay. Stop by tomorrow, noon–ish." He hung up.

Chapter Fifty-Three

Tommy lay on a hospital bed, propped-up in a semi-sitting position. Tubes, wires and electrodes protruded from all parts of his body. His face so pale he could be mistaken for being white. His skin was serving as only a thin covering on his bones, a shadow of the man he used to be. Eyes closed, no movement of his chest—I was too late. He was dead. I started to reach for his hand, a cough stopped me short.

He turned his head toward me, his eyes showing no recognition of who I was. He stared, then managed a slow smile, "Spider." He raised his hand and gripped my arm feebly. "So good to see you, my friend." A garbled cough filled with sputum. "But, you look worried. You are too young to be worried."

A short spasm of deep, uncontrolled coughing interrupted his concern. "Embarrassing, this cough. Please excuse," he said. He did not wait for me to excuse. "Your gay—my people were not familiar with him. They had to hunt him out, and were unable to come up with a residence or place of employment. He walks like a ghost, only as one who can cast a shadow where he walks." The wheezing grew stronger.

"What kind of talk is that, Tommy? Your people sampling your goods?" I asked with a laugh.

Tommy reached for my hand. His grasp weak—his voice weaker. "He is not to be laughed at, my son. His shadow veils an evil power, and he apparently terrifies those who have more than a passing acquaintance with him." He choked back a cough. "He seems to have no discernible pattern or habits to his life. No friends, nor, does he make the normal rounds of any gay bars."

I didn't like the way this was going, so far. "Then what do you have for me, Tommy?"

"A bar." Another coughing spasm, this one longer, deeper sounding. "One of my sources said he could be found there. A place called 'We Two', located on Belmont, off Clybourn. A real joint. It's avoided the Yuppie urbanization of the area, to this point."

This was not exactly what I'd been hoping for, but I felt a light surge of excitement. "When does he show up there?"

He started wheezing as his lungs fought for air, his voice close to inaudible. "That's a problem, Spider. My people cased the joint, found no preference on his part to any particular day. If he shows, it's normally around twelve at night."

"So, I go fish?"

"Sorry, best I could do for you. The man, like the wind, disappears and cannot be followed."

I held his hand in mine. His face was ashen, eyes sunken, and body becoming captive to physical strain. I started to ask if he was okay, but realized the idiocy of the question. "You did more than was asked for, Tommy. Can I do something for you in return?"

He laughed, it came out as a crackle. "If you have a chance for a new life in your pocket, I'll take it. If not, just think of me fondly when I'm gone."

"I've always thought of you fondly, Tommy."

"I know, Rik, I know." He was fading, his voice growing weak. "One more thing. The boys at 'We Two' are not exactly S and M, but they like their sex a little on the rougher side of leather, and, they're not exactly friendly to outsiders. So, take care."

"I always do," I said.

"Yes. At least you used to. Good-bye to you, my friend."

Tommy never said good-bye to anyone. In his line of business, he always expected to see you again. A shroud of sadness enveloped me. "You're not going anywhere, Tommy. We've been through too much together. I'll see you after I finish what he's forced me to do. We'll celebrate."

He tried a laugh, but a cough interfered with it. "Then make it soon my friend."

At home I went behind the bar and poured some single malt neatly into a rock glass. The booze had nothing to do with a weakness for drink. It was for Tommy. I took it in one swallow. I choked some, and felt my sadness deepen. I fought back something that felt like a tear with another whiskey. The phone rang.

"So pathetic you are. I'm so bored, Rik Burns. You are no challenge to me. That is why you have to die." He laughed. "After, of course, I grow tired of cutting up your bitch." His next laugh brought a chill slowly up my arm. He yawned. "So bored, so very bored, soon I will reach out for you." He hung up.

I walked to the chess board, moved my queen, knocked down the black knight—dead. Two black pawns—dead. Same for the bishop. Positioned my queen and checkmated his king. "Checkmate, hear, checkmate, tonight you're dead."

Laura was at a trade show in New York with Lawrence, a situation that made me less than happy. Lawrence didn't worry me, it was the slick, five-thousand-dollar suit guys that did, but it gave me the opportunity to go after Blue Boy without having to lie to her about what I was doing. I left to find 'We Two' at eleven thirty, deciding to ad-lib to whatever amounted to as good a game plan as any. The location of the freak's hang-out was not far from where I lived, a few miles north. It was not a bad neighborhood, but I felt it best to take a cab and leave Baby at home. I had the driver drop me off where Belmont and Clybourn crossed.

After some searching, I eventually found 'We Two' located between two abandoned, four story, brick and stone apartment buildings. A sign announced the plans of some realtor to turn the buildings into condos.

Pretty soon, this area, like others neighboring it, would be lined with BMW's on its streets. City stickers on car windows announcing a breed of people from the suburbs, with no ties or understanding of the once culturally proud ethnic background that made up the neighborhood. North Michigan Avenue fashions and foo-foo dogs, would replace the blue work clothes and junkyard hounds that claimed the area as home since time began. The future in-crowd of Cub baseball fans, who, occasionally remember that they're supposed to cheer for the home team while showing off their newest bonnet, or slathering ketchup on hot dogs, would also take up residence in the area.

'We Two' had a narrow front, twenty-five feet across with faded green paint, wood siding that stopped halfway down and gave way to aging brick. It supported no legend or address. The name, 'We Two' had been hand-painted in red above the door.

There was a small, circular window on my right, but, dirt and a neon Coor's beer sign blocked any view into the inside. Dark excitement coursed through me. The edge, I was walking on the edge again. It brought a feeling of being alive—of having purpose—as well as making me feel somewhat foolish. What was I trying to prove.

I took a deep breath and entered.

Chapter Fifty-Four

A small light over the door lit an approximately two-foot circumference on the floor. It seemed to serve no purpose in illuminating the rest of the place, just whoever entered. I felt like I was being exposed with my dick in my hand to whatever assemblage of specie gathered in this joint—a virgin at a trucker's convention. Nothing belonged here, and neither did I. Blue Boy or not.

Odors of spilled beer and sweat greeted me. The dark excitement of the edge began to be less exciting. I stepped out of the light and tried to adjust my eyes to the gloomy interior. I shouldn't have. The gloom served a purpose. The 'thing' that hides in kid's closets had copulated and deposited its offspring here.

In my cop days, I'd had my share of crashing leather bars, breaking up fights and the occasional S&M that went too far. But on the norm, those places were respectable looking. This joint was about fifty feet in length. The bar took up the middle and looped at both ends. All the walls and ceiling were painted black. Six neon signs advertising beer, provided the only light to the left side and rear of the room. A jukebox sat silent on the right side. Whoever owned this place hadn't put much thought into ambiance. Abandon hope all ye who enter here.

The bartender was the size of a small mountain. A dirty, twenty-watt light bulb, hung by an electric cord from the ceiling, lighting up liquor bottles and the beer cooler. Unlike the other gay bars I'd been in searching for Blue Boy, there was no overt mingling or sexual innuendos between the patrons. I headed for the bar as the bartender continued to watch me.

I picked up the sound of groans coming from the rear of the building. They sounded like a mixture of pain and pleasure. I could vaguely make out a figure of a man lying on top of a pool table. The cause of the groans, it appeared came from three men taking turns performing indescribable acts on him. Darkness and good sense stopped me from viewing them.

I reached the bar under the acute vigilance of the barkeep. His forearms were the size of my legs. His head was large, and his face was broad and flat, sporting snake eyes. The light over the bar reflected sweat off his bald head like the moon used to reflect the blood of dead soldiers off the sands of Iraq. I waited, so did he. He finally approached, resting a fist on top of the bar.

He eyed me up and down. "Don't think you belong here, and we don't like trouble. We get pissed-off something awful at people who are looking for trouble. What do you want?" He said in a threatening voice. His white tee shirt too small, though I doubted they came any larger.

"Beer."

He continued to eye me suspiciously, as did an assortment of patrons. "Don't think you do. Think you want to leave while you still can.

Everything that signaled good sense, told me coming here was not a good idea. I'd felt fairly certain I might need back-up, but I had no one I could ask. Captain Mac was out of the question, he'd make sure I never made it here. I couldn't ask Jim to chance getting in trouble with the police again. I'd rushed in here with no deep consideration of what I might find, or equipped with any game plan for the possible consequences that might face me. Just the burning adrenalin rush that said, 'finally Blue Boy is yours,' this is your day, exult in the glory of it.

I took one more look-see, saw nothing resembling a Blue Boy. I'd spent so many nights patrolling gay bars on Clark Street to no avail. Now I knew where Blue Boy played, and I ached severely with desire for my hands to break his body.

The mountain of a bartender was visibly agitated. I had yet to vacate my ass from the place. This bar belonged to Blue Boy and he could have it. I convinced myself I'd found his bar and I had many tomorrows to smash his body. I would have a plan next time that would at least make me look smarter, and finally, he would be mine.

I walked outside and took a deep breath to clear my lungs. From nowhere, two guys grabbed me, slamming my face into the outside wall of the bar. I felt blood. One of them gave me two sledgehammer blows to my kidneys, making my knees weak.

"Now just behave and do as you're told."

I had an instant need to piss, but knew it would be so painful doing so. I thought it best to try and hold it.

Chapter Fifty –Five

They pulled my hands behind my back and cuffed them, the cuffs biting into my wrists, no respect shown for my skin, or my feelings. Two guys, one on each arm, marched me to a tan, non-descript car and with no thought to the health of my body, roughly introduced me to the back floor of it. Unless you've had your hands cuffed behind your back, you have no idea how difficult it is to raise yourself off the floor of a car to a sitting position on the seat. Especially hard, when you're moving fast, the car weaving in and out of traffic, throwing you into the back of the front seats, or the front of the back seat.

We were moving fast, and hitting every bump in the road. I painfully forced myself to my knees, leaned against the front seat and used my legs as leverage to get to a sitting position on the seat. Two men sat in the front seat. The driver was black, with a clean-shaven, shiny head, the back of which had a tattoo of a Cobra snake coiled in position to strike. He had the neck and shoulders of a weightlifter. His thick neck disappeared into a black leather shirt. The guy sitting next to him looked about my height and build. He wore a Popeye hat. It looked completely stupid, but I doubted he was interested in receiving any fashion tips.

"What the hell is this all about?" I asked.

They didn't answer. I repeated the question. "Shut up," the black one answered. "Save your breath for the man. You gonna need it."

"What man? Where are you taking me?"

"Where you won't like it," Popeye answered.

Though I could find no landmarks I could recognize, from the amount of car traffic, we had to be on a main thoroughfare.

"Mind telling me…"

"I said, shut up asshole!" the black one said. Angry brown eyes peered at me from the rear view mirror.

I recognized the corners of Belmont and Western streets coming up, and relaxed.

"I wouldn't get too comfortable if I was you," Popeye said.

We came to a screeching halt, throwing me off the seat and into the back of the front seat. The black guy grabbed me, pulling me out of the car and shoved me toward the back door of Mac's police station. I was fast growing tired of this guy. We entered and he knocked on Mac's office door waiting for a response before pushing me into the room.

"Here's shithead," he told Mac.

Mac stared at me, his face red, voice brimming with volatile anger. "Sit," he ordered me.

I'd had more than enough of being told what to do today. "Am I supposed to wag my tail and wait for a good boy treat?"

"Sit, I said! And do it before I get up and sit you myself," he answered. The black cop smiled. I sat. Captain Mac looked over at my driver. "Right now, I'm sorry you had to interfere with his getting his ass kicked, but I guess I owe you thanks for bringing him in. Was our suspect there?"

He nodded. "Alex went back in after we secured dumb nuts here in the car to watch and follow, but he was gone."

Mac looked like he was going to explode. He stood, bringing his fists down so hard on the desk top, I thought it might break. My insensitive chauffeur left. Mac was in casual clothes. Tan slacks, light blue, short sleeved shirt, polished brown loafers. Wherever he'd been, it hadn't been here.

"That was Will Hutchinson. He and his partner Alex, are undercover cops. I assigned them to find Blue Boy, and stay close until we catch him doing something we can arrest him on. We finally find him, and what? Screw-up enters with dick in hand and blows weeks of police surveillance."

Mac glared at me with his silent 'Uncle' Mac reprimand stare. I didn't have the heart to tell him it had stopped working on me after I reached the age of twelve. He rose from his chair, stood, and silently stared at me. His anger caused veins to redden and pulsate on his face. He grabbed a paperweight and threw it across the room, putting a dent in the opposite wall. "God!" he screamed. "I can't believe what a fuck-up you are!"

He turned his back to me, audibly inhaling great gulps of air, and then turned back so he could face me. "So much work. So close. Then you!" His green eyes turned into ice. "What, Rik? You look at me and see some useless, old fart? A cop who no longer knows how to be a cop?"

"Of course not, Mac, it just seemed like you were taking so much time, and I don't have time…"

"Cram it!" He ordered. "We got a response on our fingerprints from the NYPD. Picture, name, and rap sheet." He left and got some coffee, forgetting to ask if I wanted some. "Our boy is a possible suspect in some gay serial killings over the last five years in and around New York City. Same M.O. as here. Apparently, he decided to skip out of the Big Apple and give our fair town a visit." He paused for his coffee.

I felt the need to put my two cents in. "Then it's over. Grab him and send him packing to New York."

Mac took in a deep sigh. His face reddened again. "A suspect, I said, Rik. The key word being 'possible.' That means our counterparts have no more on him than we do. Otherwise, they would have sent some cops down here to pick him up." He glared at me. "That is, if we had him." He sipped some more coffee, breathed in deeply and noisily expelled it. "I'm tired of this asshole. I want him in jail, or dead. I want this case closed, understand!"

I nodded I did.

Mac laughed, not a happy one. "His name is Robin Blue, if you can believe that." He didn't ask if I believed or not and motioned for me to retrieve his paperweight. I did, but put it on the wrong spot on the desk. He frowned at me and slid it to the right location.

"He grew a moustache just for us, dyed his hair from brown to black. He has quite a resume. Unfortunately, that's all it is. He's been in and out of jams since he was ten years old. The kid could pick a lock by the age of nine. He started out being arraigned on petty charges, which the local Catholic, do-gooder, priest got dismissed. At fifteen, he found assault and battery more fun." Mac shook his head. "Not your everyday shit kicking battery, but deep-seated masochistic—psycho shit stuff." He looked up at the ceiling and sighed heavily. "He's never been convicted on anything."

"How the hell is that?"

A cruel-looking smile parted his lips. "His victims had an uncommon penchant for suddenly dropping the charges or forgetting to show up in court." Mac reached for his coffee, drained it and pitched the paper cup at the waste basket, missing it. "He used to keep rats. Not the store-bought kind—the big, sewer loving kind. He walked the back alleys and captured them. "

He leaned back in his chair, rubbed his eyes and laughed to himself. "He would starve the suckers until they got real nasty, and then would present them as a present to the witnesses due to testify in court against him." Mac eyed the ceiling, as if studying it. "At night, in their beds, while they slept. People would wake to rats chewing on them. Nice, huh? Christ, what a sick-fuck!"

I nodded. "Guess I was lucky he chose my stairs."

The lines on Mac's face deepened, the whites of his eyes lined red. "New York brought him in for questioning. Kept it up until he cracked. Eventually he opened up, likes to brag, but gives nothing that leads to anything they can prove or convict him on." Mac leaned back in his chair, looked with weary eyes at nothing in particular. "Supposedly he can't handle rejection. Blames 'them', whoever the hell that is, for causing the rejections in his life, and for stealing his beloved boys from him. He claims he will find 'them,' and when he does, they will feel the wrath of his blade." He looked out at the streets. They were quiet. "He claims to be an artist with a blade; likes to carve people, especially their faces." He stared at me. "Anything sound familiar? We have no history of a Robin Blue living in Chicago--residence or job. That's why Alex and Will were in 'We Two', and had been for several nights. Our suspect finally comes in—AND SO DO YOU!"

He rose from his chair, and slammed his fists on the desk. The vase with the wilted flowers scooted over to the edge of the desk, fought for equilibrium, lost, and shattered onto the floor.

"JESUS!" Mac screamed. "You really piss me off!"

His breathing was extremely heavy and his face was bright red and for a moment, I feared for his heart.

"Okay, okay, Mac, I screwed up. Sorry. Calm down, okay?"

"Calm down! Calm down! You think that cuts it? This is not a John Wayne western. Keep your imaginary six guns and yourself out of this   Because of you, we're back at square one. NOWHERE!" He went to the water cooler and consumed two cups. "Don't you think I haven't been watching you? You think I didn't know you went to see Tommy Dao?"

I swallowed hard. "I had to do something, Mac."

He penetrated my insides with his stare. "If Tommy can find what bar this freak hangs out in, don't you think we can too? That I don't know you'll go off half-cocked and try to kill him? Don't you? Don't you?"

I tried to reply, give my side. He wouldn't let me.

"I can't believe what an asshole you are. No more gay bars. You stay home now, and take care of Laura, hear?" I hesitated too long. "I SAID HEAR?"

"Yes, Sir."

"Right now, the way I feel, I don't care if the freak demonstrates his skills with a blade on you, but, you better make sure he don't touch Miss Laura. Hear?"

I nodded.

"I mean it. He don't hurt, Laura. I like that gal." He stared until I let him know I understood. "I'll get you a ride," he said and dismissed me.

I waited outside his office. From somewhere, a bone chilling, sinister laugh, echoed through the station.

Chapter Fifty-Six

I picked Baby up from her beauty shop. They'd done a good job. If you hadn't known, you wouldn't know she'd been scarred. Still, my soul weighed heavy for her. She'd lost her virginity to a vicious, criminal attack, and while paint hid the crime, I could never look at her again and not know she was now second hand.

Laura was coming in from New York, but she and Lawrence were going to the office to clean up paper work. Lawrence would drop her off at my place when they were done. There was no color, no warmth in the apartment without Laura in it.

Mac called, said he wanted to meet Laura and me for lunch at Gus's. It was an order, no questions or objections accepted, just be there.

Laura icily informed me Captain Mac didn't plan her life, but dropped it at that.

Mac was seated at his usual booth. He motioned for us to join him. He was working on a blue plate special of lamb and browned potatoes. He didn't acknowledge us until finished. He fixed his tea to his taste and then gazed over at Laura.

"Rik introduced me to this joint. My cholesterol level has zoomed beyond repair ever since."

A definite sparkle to the eye. Mac looked rested, refreshed, younger, but his suit didn't. He continued to talk to Laura. "I knew you wouldn't want to hear this second hand. And I'm tired of baby-sitting you two."

He was full of himself and enjoying every minute making us wait for an explanation for this gathering. He shifted his eyes from one of us to the other until certain our focus contained only him.

Laura gave me a look asking for clarity—I could only shrug.

His face wasn't large enough to contain his smile. "We got him,"

"You got who, Mac?'

"My serial killer, your stalker." He waited for some reaction. "Did you hear me? You two are free. You have your lives back. Go, love—make babies—but smile, do something."

"After everything, it's so sudden." Laura said. "It doesn't want to soak in as a truth."

"When?—How? — Where?" I asked.

Mac stared at nothing in particular. "Last night." He concentrated on mixing his tea. "Clark and Oak." He sighed. "Unfortunately, not before he killed again. A good citizen saw him dumping a body and called us."

He took in a deep breath, sipped at his tea. "He wanted to be caught. He picked a spot where he would definitely be seen. He told me no one listens to his messages."

"Messages?" Laura inquired.

Mac absently drank his tea, lost somewhere other than Gus's. "I think he got off describing how he killed his victims. It disgusted me, yet there was something about his eyes. They held me. I couldn't turn away from them."

He returned to his tea. "As far as the mores of society, this guy doesn't belong to anything simulating the human species.

"He tell you why or how I entered into his life?" I asked.

Mac slowly leveled his eyes on mine. "Apparently, you weren't the only one he was stalking."

"Maybe, but he sure knew my name," I said.

Mac worked on a fresh cigar. "In his mind this Swain guy was still alive. He blames 'them' for taking him away."

Mac eyed his cigar and put it down. "To get Sam back, he had to kill, leave the victims as messages to those who had him. Return his Sam or die."

Mac looked at me and shook his head. "Somehow, you became one of 'them'. Whoever, or whatever they were to this guy. Don't ask me how, he never said."

He smiled at Laura, patted her hand. "But, it's all over now. I'm gonna leave, so you two can decide how to start realizing it."

Laura rose and kissed him, while fighting back tears. "Thank you."

Mac actually blushed, I laughed.

****

There's a small stretch of land and beach off Oakton Avenue designated for dogs so that they can romp in Lake Michigan leash-free. Laura and I sat on boulders, feet in the water and watched several dogs enjoy splashing in the waves. Neither one of us had yet to talk about our freedom from Blue Boy being a reality.

Laura looked over at me. "We should be dancing in the streets."

I nodded. "What now, Laura?"

She looked puzzled. "I'm not sure what you're asking me."

"We're free. Totally able to do with our lives as we please." The words stuck in my throat. "So what are we going to do?"

"I don't know. What do you think we should do?"

Jesus, somebody help me. It was so easy to say running it through my mind. I looked at her and smiled. It probably resembled something between Jimmy Carter and Mortimer Snerd.

"From the first time I saw you, I knew I didn't want you not in my life, so?" The words lodged in my throat again—she waited—the words remained captive. Jesus, somebody help me. PLEASE!

"That hasn't changed." No saliva, mouth so dry, I couldn't spit the words out. "Except maybe now, I think…maybe…maybe I can't imagine life without you."

She didn't say anything, just stared. I cupped her face in my hands.

Shit! "Sometimes…sometimes…" throat so dry, words stuck on the way up. "It hurts how much I want, need you." I took in some air.

She stared hard, tilted her head. "Is this a different way of asking me to bring some clothes to your place?"

"No —well yeah. Shit, Laura, you know what I want." She shook her head she didn't. "Rik?"

Breathing coming hard, I blurted it out. "Damn it, Laura—will you marry me?"

She stared at me, and then began softly laughing. That threw me. I didn't think girls were supposed to laugh when proposed to. Then the tears came, some sobbing, and suddenly she was in my arms.

"Ýes. Oh, yes, Rik." Her kiss weakened my knees. "I just hope I can make you understand how happy you've made me today. How so very, very happy."

We stopped at her place for some clothes. She walked out of her bedroom with a small canvas bag,

"The bag looks kind of small to carry much clothes-wise," I said

"For what I have in mind for this week-end, this is more than I need."

I never got her to my place faster.

Chapter Fifty- Eight

I was ready. She held my hands. "I'd like to freshen-up first, take a shower," her eyes teasing. "I want to make you anticipate me, and smell irresistible to you," she said through a smile.

"My major in college was erotic clothes removing."

She laughed. "Really? But I'm quite capable."

"My fingers are registered weapons in back-scrubbing."

She stood on tiptoe and brushed her lips with mine. "Life together is now ours. Give me a few minutes of solitude to savor my happiness."

I turned the air-conditioning down to make it chilly enough for a fire, and laughed as I could hear her singing over the sound of running water. The phone rang. I hesitated, then realized now, I could answer the thing without trepidation.

It was Jim.

"Having a party with friends tonight. You not invited. Case I run short can I grab some stuff at you place?'

"Yeah, but…"

"I'se know you have bicycle momma with you. Just don't do her on the couch, and you'll never know I'se was there."

I found a bottle of champagne, iced it and set two glasses around it. I didn't hear any running water coming from the shower. I turned, hoping to catch a scantily-dressed Laura walking down the stairs. On the walkway, looking down at me, stood Blue Boy. A .38 automatic pistol in one hand—a bright red rose in the other.

He held the rose up. "Beautiful isn't it? The color of your blood."

I knew my chin had dropped leaving my mouth open and my face a canvas painting of stupidity. I had no idea what other effects he'd caused. "You're in jail," I muttered.

He tilted his head as he looked at me, then the surroundings. He smiled. "I don't think so."

"You son-of- bitch. Laura! Where is she, what have you done to her?" I took two steps up to the walkway toward him.

I heard a loud pop, saw muzzle flash. Like a flesh wound, some leather on my right shoe disappeared. I could feel the heat from the bullet. "How about the pain you've caused me? Now stay where you are or I'll kill you on the spot."

Okay, would John Wayne just give in? "Where's Laura, you asshole?" All I got was a laugh.

Mac told me he was in jail. Why would Mac lie? At the moment, it didn't matter, whatever the why, the lie hurt more than the possibility of being shot. Who else had lied to me? Who was letting him into the building?

"Why?" I asked him. "Who are you? What do you want from me?"

"Who am I? Who am I? You should know by now. The game should have long been over. You had no right to make me spend this much time with you, I gave you clue after clue, but you are so stupid. You can't even play chess!"

He let out a scream. "My Sam, my beautiful Sam, I'm doing this for you." His face contorted, lower lip protruded, tongue coiled back and forth. As if possessed, his body started shaking violently. He raised a hand to his face, fingers tearing at it. Moustache, bushy eyebrows were torn from his face, thrown to the floor. He sailed the fedora, long hair settled on slender shoulders.

I looked into a set, rigid face of a woman filled with hate. My face must have mirrored my confusion. She answered it with a laugh of brimstone from hell.

"Yes, it's me, Rik. Do you feel your heart being slowly pulled out of your chest?" She did some soft shoe. "Oh God, I love it."

My heart beat rapidly, acid reflex filled my esophagus, I couldn't breathe. "What the hell? What is this? I don't understand. It isn't funny, Laura. God, what the hell are you doing?"

She stared at me like I was fresh excrement. "You don't understand! How can you not understand?" The violent shaking occurred again. "Oh, God, Sam, do you hear him?" She took in several deep breaths. "Of course it's not funny. Not funny at all." Her eyes mirrored how despicable she felt I was. "Serious. This is the most of the most serious. Time for you to pay."

Her eyes grew soft, but not for me, from a memory. "Did you ever wake at night, so you could watch me sleep? When my hand touched yours, did you lose your breath? Couldn't speak?" She choked back a sob. "When you gazed into my face, did you see your world and all the beauty it can hold?"

Hate overtook the softness of memories. "Did you? Did you? Tell me, tell me?"

I'd experienced some of what she spoke when she lay next to me, but I doubted at the moment it made any difference, "That was my life every minute of the day while I had my Sam. That's what you took from me."

I looked into her face. It held no answers to what was happening here, just the beauty that was my Laura. "What are you talking about? I don't even know a Sam."

I said something really wrong. Explosive anger choked back her words. The fierce flash of loathing in her eyes said more than words could anyway. "You don't know her name! God, Rik, you killed her and you don't know her name?" Shaking overtook her again.

"Her, her? What are you talking about? Who the hell is her?"

That was really the wrong thing to say. I thought she was going to instantly empty her gun into me.

"Yes, her, Rik. Connie, Rik. Do you even remember her?"

Things were coming too fast. "Connie, the waitress?"

"What was her last name, Rik?"

I had no idea.

"Samuels," she screamed. "Her last name was Samuels, you bastard. I called her Sam."

Everything was out of focus. I heard Laura, but her words rambled around in my head like she was speaking in tongues. "Stop, go back, Laura, you're not making any sense. You and Connie? How would you know someone like Connie?"

I could see the resurgence of anger. "Yes, Rik. Connie and me. We were lovers. She was my life." A sob escaped followed by uncontrollable tears. She inhaled, brought herself under control. "She'd drawn a bath for herself, slit her wrists, wrote a message on the wall with her blood. "Please come back." Laura's eyes flamed with hate. "I found the water in the tub, red from her blood. Found her dead. DEAD, RIK! She was the most beautiful person I've ever known. She filled my life with happiness and love, something you could never do."

"Dead? I didn't know."

"You didn't care. All you wanted to do was stick your dick in something. I didn't want any more days in my life. Only destroying you made my life bearable."

I became consumed with the need for alcohol. "I'm coming up to fix a drink. Shall I build one for you?"

"Don't, stay there," she ordered.

I didn't listen. The report from the gun filled the apartment. My left shoulder exploded with pain. The force of the bullet spun me around. I teetered on the arm of the couch then slid down to a sitting position.

"I said stay," she yelled. "One more time with a man, then I will know if I'm yours forever, Connie said. Let me prove to you I'm yours."

"I was vehemently against it, but she insisted." Tears started. "When I saw she'd picked you, I knew she'd picked wrong." She brushed some tears away. "I followed you until I knew your life better than you did. Knew where you hung out, your sex life, every disgusting thing about you. GOD, I HATE YOU! Get up."

It seemed like too much of an effort. I felt plugged like a watermelon. In the middle, where the reddest, tenderest meat is. "Try this," life seemed to be saying. "See how you like it." Only the plug was permanent. Even if they put the piece back, Laura had shot me. Actually shot me.

I looked at Laura's face. It still held the beauty and all the enticements that made me long for her. Her voice put ice on the longing.

"How do you like me now?"

I stared through my pain, scowled, then spit at her. "I don't know. Who are you? I would really like it if you gave me my Laura back."

"Give, give? Give to what? One little bullet and you're subdued, washed up. How pathetic. Laura would expect much more."

I wanted to tell her it wasn't the bullet sucking my life out of me, only I didn't. "If you hate me this much, why the masquerade that you loved me?" I asked her. "Why didn't you just kill me?"

Scorn dominated her words. "And kill what? You were already dead. You walked through life without seeing or feeling it. It held no color or emotion to you. Where would be the satisfaction or sense of revenge in killing you? So, I had to make you taste life, make you cherish it, want to live. Don't you see, before I could welcome you back to death again."

As hard as I tried to digest her words, make sense of them, I could do neither. "I don't believe you. Why all the trouble to make me love you?"

She looked at my face and laughed. "So you could feel my pain. The pain you caused when you killed my Sam and took her away from me."

"Damn it, Laura. I didn't kill her, she killed herself." That was the wrong thing to say, I thought for sure she was going to empty the gun—in my body.

She screamed. "Yea you did. You and all men like you. All you wanted was something to stick your dick in. Didn't you see how frail she was? Or, didn't you care?"

I didn't answer. Laura had already made her mind up.

"Lawrence bought the condo for us. It was our love nest." Anger consumed her eyes. "Do you have any idea the pain I felt when I saw you two together. For just four nights of lust, you destroyed the most beautiful, most sensitive person I've ever known."

Nothing she said spoke of reality, that it was Laura talking to me. "And you expect me to believe there were no feelings between us? That you felt nothing? I don't believe that, never will."

Her smile was so bitter it ate into me. "That's because the pain of discovering I don't love you is too excruciating to accept. You're beginning to feel my pain. But, yes, there were feelings. The feeling I was going to vomit every time you touched me. God, how I hated your body on mine."

She stopped, let her eyes speak the language of hate. "I hated, no, detested you every time you were inside me, every time you placed your lips on mine.! I washed and washed myself over and over until I rid myself of your scent."

I shook my head. "I can't make any of this real. None of what you say is true. Why the impersonation of being Blue Boy?"

Her laughter echoed through my apartment. "Oh, how glorious. That was no impersonation. I made you and everyone believe in Blue Boy." She laughed with glee. "What an outstanding actor I am. Blue Boy never wanted me, because there never was a Blue Boy, Rik. Because I'm Blue Boy—I'm your nemesis."

Confusion and anger hit me at the same time. Anger won. Although anything I was going to do with it would be feeble and pointless. So I stared at her, tried to get into her head, understand why my world was being crushed.

"Blue Boy, Blue Boy. How ingenious, how marvelous an idea, how marvelous the acting skills on my part." She looked at me for confirmation. I gave her none. She laughed. "Terror and torment. You had to feel my torment. Blue Boy provided the perfect messenger. Also, I had to feel some pleasure, a way to escape, while I suffered through being your lover. God, how I wanted to throw up each time you touched me."

Tired, I was so tired. My shoulder felt cold, stiff, the pain deadening. I found myself in the middle of a world spinning so fast I couldn't hang on, while my friends watched—laughing at me.   "That wasn't you at the school. Never, bullshit, Laura."

My face must have shown my disbelief.

She laughed hysterically. "Oh, Rik. My poor Rik. Believe, it was all me, everything was all me. I told you I studied dance at Northwestern. I had a high kick that would have been the envy of the Rockettes. I did fear I'd killed you. No big loss, except I wanted you alive so I could torture you more." She laughed, demonstrated the kick again. "I picked that school because of how disgusting it was—because of the rats. When you followed me in there, I knew I had you, that you believed in Blue Boy."

Her laughter almost bent her over. "God, what a good actor I am. I should be on Broadway, at least on film. Don't you agree Ricky…Dickey." She stared at me, disgust at what she saw covered her face. "God, the repulsion felt by my skin every time your skin touched it. How vomit tried to consume me when you lay on me, made love to me. But it was all so necessary."

More laughter. "The LSD on the letter." She paused "Wish I could have seen your reaction to it." She stopped for a laugh. "The rat in the car. That I saw, how enjoyable." Her eyes softened for a moment, then turned to ice. "Poor Baby. You will never know how much I enjoyed hurting her."

She looked at me with disgust. 'God, how pathetic. A grown man calling his car Baby." She smiled at me. "Did you hear her scream?" A laugh. "The only thing you could show any, could give any emotions to—a piece of metal. God, your whole life nothing but a piece of metal. What joy in destroying it. What joy causing you pain." She smiled, performed a little soft-shoe again. "Like me any better now?"

"I don't know. Maybe I feel for how pathetic you are, how pathetic your life is. I'll take my Laura now." I took the two stairs in one painful bound.

The bullet ripped into my right thigh bringing me down to my knees. I made it to the couch.

"The game's over, Rik. The black queen has made her final move. Checkmate!" She stared into my face. "Which hurts most? The bullets or the broken heart?"

I didn't answer. She probably knew anyway.

She looked at the coffee table. "Oh, how nice. Champagne. Pour us a glass. After all, it is celebration time." A warm smile, almost caring. "How you feeling, Rik?" Then a laugh. "And now you know, my dear Rik. When it comes to lost love there's no yes in yesterday. And now for you there is only no in tomorrow and forever."

"Why? Why make me propose? You had to know I'd fallen in love with you."

"If you had said the words,' I love you,' this celebration of ours would have ended sooner. But commitment is a very difficult thing for you. When you proposed, I knew I had won."

She aimed the gun at my chest, her eyes staring without anger, no look of termination in them. It was as if everything had been played out on a stage and my death another scene yet to be acted out.

"The pain from the bullets subsided. It was the twisting blade of Laura's words ripping my insides apart that became unbearable. "That's enough, I don't want to hear anymore."

"Good. Hurts too much? Then I'll continue. When I found Sam, all I wanted to do was kill you. Wanted you to know I wanted to. It was why I disguised my voice. I don't know. It made no difference to me at the time."

She walked behind the bar, made herself a drink. "It was later I found out my decision to sound like a gay must have been ordained. The little man dressed in blue at the funeral. Friday night after the movies when you chased the guy dressed in blue, I saw your intense reaction to him. He and I were close to the same size. That night, I became Blue Boy."

"I planned everything. Even how we would meet. The street around McCabe's is too busy. Gus's was perfect. All I had to do was make sure my top was loose enough so you could look down, see my breasts. Show lots of leg. The damsel in distress. And boy did you fall for it." It took a while before she stopped laughing.

"God, and to think how much I loved you."

"Poor Rik. Do you hurt really bad?"

"Answer one thing." I asked. "Someone had to be letting you into the building. Who?"

Laughter almost overcame her. "You did."

"What?"

"I had a duplicate set of your keys made after our first night of making love. You sleep very well after sex."

"I don't believe you."

"Do Rik. No one helped me, just as there was no Blue Boy. No Blue Boy chasing me in Lincoln Park. It never happened. It was all me threatening me, the ultimate in staged drama." Her smile was warm as she directed it at me. "The more you felt you had to protect me, the more you fell in love with me."

"You're not that good. Eventually I would have recognized your voice, seen through your drag routine."

"No. " She looked at me. "Never. My specialty was voice and dialect. I once performed backstage as the voice of a boy. Everyone thought it was really a boy." She paused, and seemed to reflect on a memory. "In New York, I once performed off-Broadway in a Lesbian theater." She laughed at my facial expression. "I wasn't gay then. I became very good at impersonating men." She paused, "It was at the theater that I discovered the joy of Lesbian love."

"That's enough," I yelled."

She looked at me and laughed.

"I said that's enough!"

"Not yet, Rik. Evelyn and Lawrence knew what I was up to, and helped in any way they could. Before Connie, Evelyn and I were lovers. It was okay with Lawrence as long as he could watch." She laughed at my expression again. "I know, Rik. Sometimes life can be so sick."

I'd heard enough. One way or another it was over. I rose. Pain racked my body, but I made it to the stairs. She watched, smiled.

"Margo will be so broken hearted at your death. I watched, finally saw her, saw her in a bikini." She ran her hand down her body, arched her back, as if experiencing an orgasm. "I plan on taking very good care of her."

"What a desirable body. How could you not want it, Rik? Never mind, I want it, and soon it will be mine. I will dry her tears, capture her love, and make her mine, all mine." She pointed her gun at my head. Her laughter filled the apartment.

I was concentrating on the gun, and didn't see him. Laura did. "No, I don't like you. You're not part of the game. Leave us alone."

The short, chopstyle punch buckled her knees and she crashed on her back.

"You all right?" he asked.

It was too deep a question to answer.

"Girl have funny way saying I love you."

Lying there, Laura's face looked like my Laura, like it did when I used to gaze at her asleep after we made love. This was all too surreal. "This has to be ... has to be—a mistake, not real," I said to Jim. "Too much love between us for it to be real." I reached for him to help me up.

Jim stared at me like I was something flies ate. "You head sick. Best you stay where you at."

I crawled to Laura, my body repulsing my movement. There was a slight mark were Jim had hit her. Otherwise her face was still perfect. My Laura's face. I couldn't stop from kissing her on the lips.

"Gee Christ. This bitch gonna kill you and you slobbering over her like she you first virgin." Jim continued to watch me, shook his head. "Wake up, Rik she ain't you Laura, cause you Laura never real, you Laura was only a dream."

He dialed the phone. "Tell him Rik Burns been shot. He'll find time to talk to me."

"His bike broad done it. Yeah, she gonna kill him."

"Yeah, he shot, twice. He look okay don't look like they hit anything serious. But who know what bouncing around in her head."

"Don't know why she shoot him. But she all dressed up in a blue suit, if that mean something."

"I'se gots people at my place, a party. Okay— you hurry, guess I can stay with the sorry piece of shit."

I looked in the mirror behind the bar. Saw a strange-looking face staring back. It didn't belong to any one I knew, and I swear it was fighting back tears.

So, this is what makes the world go round, love? Yeah? Then it can go fuck itself. I stared at the reflection again. Who invited you to the party? Are those tears? Really? What an asshole—get the hell out of here, asshole.

EPILOGUE

The bullet traveled clean through my shoulder, somehow not hitting anything important. Outside of the occasional complaint that it had been shot, it was fine. The leg was a different story. They had to dig the bullet out, causing some minor complications that extended my stay in the hospital for the wound and observation—Jim and Margo volunteered to observe me, as long as that was all they had to do.

I think Mac made sure I stayed there—sort of a term of imprisonment for my actions, or lack thereof. Her sentence, if any, would be light, unless I pressed charges. At the moment, I refused to do so, mainly because at first I kept telling myself her shooting me wasn't real, a mistake, she didn't really want to kill me. Perhaps more now, because I didn't care if she had.

Either way, Mac had gone ballistic. She was back on the street, he informed me. Her boss posted her bail, and he hoped she paid me a visit and finished what she'd started in my apartment. I let him know I didn't care where Laura's pretty ass was located.

Jim and Margo kept visiting me. I didn't ask them to, and informed Jim I didn't want them. He kept bringing Margo as if that would change my mind. She would walk to my bed all smiles, I didn't return them. I would have gladly walked out of the hospital and out of their lives, except I had no place to walk to. Jim told me Tommy Dao had died, leaving me feeling entirely empty and friendless.

Jim was here now, leaning against the door frame. His irreverent, irksome smile plastered on his face. "I'se just here for Captain Mac," he said. "He wants me make sure you don't die 'fore you gets some sense and press charges against you bitch."

I gave him the courtesy of a grunt, which was more than I had given to any of his idle chitchat from previous visits.

"Margo now, there be a different story. That girl be here night and day fussin' and worryin' bout you. Make me hurt deep inside seein' her wasting her time carin' 'bout shit like you. She deserve much more better than you."

I'd been aware of Margo's visits. I just pretended to be under drug-induced sleep each time she came. "That's her problem, not mine. Nobody asked her to care," I said.

Jim didn't say anything, not for a long time—just stared at me so hard I wanted to look away.

"Sometimes I'se hates myself big time being in you place that night and getting there fo' she kill you."

Margo entered the room. She smiled at Jim. He gave both of us a knowing nod and left the room. There was no way I could fake being asleep. She walked over to me. I didn't acknowledge her presence. She fluffed the pillow, stared down at me, finger combed the hair off my forehead. I'd had enough of women fussing over me. I turned my face away from her.

She remained at my bedside. Margo, the high school beauty who walked into my life and filled my days with sunshine when no one else could. Margo, excited for womanhood, to fulfill all her dreams. Margo, whose only transgression in life was falling in love with me.

Jim was right, she deserved better from me better than what I was giving her. But my betters were gone, I had nothing left to give her.

I'd taken Bobby McCabe's advice and given life and love a chance. He'd been wrong on both counts. Neither one seemed worth the effort. It was time for me to crawl back to where it was safe—behind my wall. So, the last thing I needed was some female standing in my way.

"When you get home, I'll take care of you," she said "You'll see, things will be all right."

All right? What the hell does she know about all right?

She fussed with the bedsheet. I turned and looked at her. "Margo, stop it!"

She pulled her hands back like a child caught reaching for the candy bowl.

"Just leave me alone!" Her eyes widened in disbelief. "Just do it. Just get the fuck away from me."

Her hands went to her mouth. She made short, unintelligible sounds. Tears started. No sobs, just tears.

Christ, what was with women and tears?

She spun on her heels, and ran from me. Uncontrollable sobs, rapid, and highly audible. Shit! Margo, who'd never done anything but brighten my day. And I'd just crushed her.

"Margo, wait!"

She kept going.

"Please, Margo, come back."

She'd reached the door and was headed down the hall. I vaulted out of bed, though not very gracefully, getting tangled up in things the hospital had stuck in me and ending up doing a head over heels tumble. Gadgets, gidgets, tubes and other hospital stuff followed me, spewing a little of my blood. My gown opened wide providing a shot of my ass for anyone interested in seeing it.

I removed the things still connected to my body and stumbled after Margo. She was not too far away. Using the wall as a brace as her body convulsed with sobs, she saw me.

"Get away from me. I never want to see you again." Her face drawn up in a mixture of hurt and anger, though she didn't reject my hand on her shoulder.

"Margo, please, forgive me. I'm so sorry." She turned and faced me. "Don't walk out of my life."

"Why?" she asked.

"I don't deserve you. I don't know why I said those things. I'm so sorry, I didn't mean any of it. "

I turned her so she had to face me. "Maybe it's because at the moment I have so little to offer you, and you deserve better than that."

She stopped crying and I wiped away her tears. "Today, I have nothing of myself to give you." I took her hand. "But, maybe tomorrow I will. Can you live with that? I really want you to say yes."

She looked down at the hand I was holding, and leaned against my chest. "I…I don't know. If you promise to try and love me, I'll give it a shot. I'll wait for at least a while."

A woman walked down the hall, glanced over at us. "Nice ass."

"Thank you."

Margo reached up, and caressed my face.

"You need a shave."

"Then let's go home and you can shave me."

She smiled through joyful tears. It was that special one, meant only for me.

The End

~ ~ ~

Author Bio:

G.R. Akin grew up in the farmlands and foothills of the Ozark Mountains in Southern Illinois and developed a deep love of nature while walking many a mile through woods and creeks.

He moved to Myakka City, Florida and resided deep in the woods and wetlands surrounded by nature's flora and fauna. His love of nature led him to become an environmental advocate.

Surrounded by his boxers, goats, and other animals, wild and domesticated, he lived with his niece on a small ranch doing what he enjoyed most.

Made in the USA
Lexington, KY
19 June 2016